RAW WOUNDS

RAW WOUNDS

A Tess Grey Thriller

Matt Hilton

This first world edition published 2017
in Great Britain and the USA by
SEVERN HOUSE PUBLISHERS LTD of
19 Cedar Road, Sutton, Surrey, England, SM2 5DA.
Trade paperback edition first published
in Great Britain and the USA 2017 by
SEVERN HOUSE PUBLISHERS LTD

British Library Cataloguing in Publication Data
A CIP catalogue record for this title is available from the British Library.

ISBN-13: 978-0-7278-8705-4 (cased)
ISBN-13: 978-1-84751-811-8 (trade paper)
ISBN-13: 978-1-78010-875-9 (e-book)

All Severn House titles are printed on acid-free paper.

Severn House Publishers support the Forest Stewardship Council™ [FSC™],
the leading international forest certification organisation.
All our titles that are printed on FSC certified paper carry the FSC logo.

Typeset by Palimpsest Book Production Ltd.,
Falkirk, Stirlingshire, Scotland.
Printed and bound in Great Britain by
TJ International, Padstow, Cornwall.

This one is for my lost girls Megan and Izzy.

ONE

'This place gives me the creeps.' Emilia peered out of the insect-dotted windshield at the swamp. It was after sundown and the Ford's headlights only added to the eeriness as mist swallowed their lights. The mist coiled and writhed on a breeze that swirled between the trees, forming wraith-like shadows that melted away in one instant, only to twirl up elsewhere the next. 'It feels as if we're being watched by unseen eyes. It's horrible, Jace. Like we're only a few seconds away from being grabbed.'

Jason glanced at her, his mouth turning up wryly. 'You don't believe all that superstitious bullshit people are talking about?'

'I'm more worried about the cops catching us.'

'The cops ain't interested in staking out a few guys selling weed. They have bigger fish to fry.'

'Yeah . . .' Emilia's tone dropped with foreboding. She tugged distractedly at her strappy top. 'The sooner they catch that crazy son of a bitch the better. I really don't think we should be out here with a rougarou on the loose.'

'Rougarou my ass! I thought you said you didn't have any truck with that BS. Next you'll be telling me you believe in the Skunk Ape, and the damn Tooth Fairy.'

'You can laugh all you want. But whether or not it's a rougarou, something's responsible for all those animal attacks.'

Jason snorted. 'Probably coyotes. Or one of them hybrid coy-wolves I've heard about.'

'Coy-wolves? You're making that up. What, are they shy or something?'

Jason snorted again, but this time in humour. 'No. They're a cross between a coyote and a wolf. Bigger and badder than the usual coyotes we get around here.'

'Now who's talking BS?'

'It's true . . . I saw it on the Discovery Channel.'

'Oh, yeah? Well, I saw something about the rougarou on TV too. So who's to say it doesn't exist?'

'Jeez, and that's before you get started on the good weed.'

Branches strung with Spanish moss scraped the cab of Jason's truck. The sound was reminiscent of nails on a washboard, but so familiar to the truck's passengers that it passed without notice. They'd often driven similar routes, though they weren't intimate with every dip and rise in this track. Subconsciously they adjusted their body weight in the seats, riding out each sway or pitch as they were jostled uncomfortably. Alongside her boyfriend, Emilia clung to the handle above the door. She felt nauseous, and fought it by clenching her abdominal muscles. They'd come off the levee road into the wetlands surrounding Bayou Chene, west of the Atchafalaya River, just about as far as Jason's 4x4 could carry them before they'd be forced to switch to a boat to go deeper into the swamp. Emilia had no intention of getting her feet wet though, not for all the cannabis in Iberia Parish. Thankfully the Thibodaux brothers hadn't set up their trapping camp too far into the bog.

'Don't see why you can't just buy off one of the dealers in town,' Emilia griped for the tenth time since Jason had picked her up from home, 'instead of hauling our asses all the way out here.'

'I told you.' Jason winked at her. 'Only the best for my girl. Why have schwag when we can have headies?'

'It's all just weed to me.'

'You'll know the difference when you smoke the good stuff. Trust me.'

'Trust you? If I had any sense I wouldn't be here at all. Maybe we should go back, Jace . . .'

'We're almost there. Stick it out. You'll thank me in a few minutes.' Jason wiggled one eyebrow.

'So how's it a couple of retards like the Thibodauxs have the best weed in Louisiana, anyway?'

'They ain't retards. Well, not really. Being uneducated doesn't necessarily make them stupid.' Jason took his foot off the gas and the truck coasted to a halt at the entrance of a small clearing in the woods. 'They have contacts in N'awleans who supply them. Comes in straight off the ships, I heard.'

'So they're not growing their own crop?'

'No. They just keep the stuff out here. Any closer to town and they'd be beating every stoner in New Iberia off with a stick.'

Jason hadn't moved the truck further.

'So what are you waiting for?' Emilia prompted.

'I don't like this.'

She followed his gaze across the clearing. There was a ramshackle hut, barely picked out in the headlights. There were no lamps burning behind the window shutters. The hut was strung with netting and surrounded by various wooden trestles and other equipment particular to a trapping outfit. She had little idea of what any of it was used for. A truck, not dissimilar to the one Jason drove, but with more wear and tear showing on its paintwork, sat abandoned in front of the shack. One door hung open.

'So where are they?' Emilia asked. 'I thought you said the Thibodauxs were expecting us.'

Jason didn't reply. He stared harder at the shack, before his gaze slid towards the vacant cab of the truck. He visibly jerked. 'I *really* don't like this.'

'What's up?' Emilia tried hard to make out what had concerned Jason. She saw it a moment later. An amorphous heap lying ten feet from the truck. In the glow of their headlights the shape steamed. One clawed hand was all that was immediately recognizable, it jutted up from the eviscerated corpse as if its final act had been in trying to ward off an attacker. 'Oh my God! Is that . . .'

'I think it's Hal Thibodaux!' Jason croaked.

'He . . . he's dead!' Emilia's stricken gaze alighted on another shapeless form, on the porch. Jamie Thibodaux sat with his legs splayed, hands in his lap as though he'd died attempting to push his intestines back into the gaping wound in his abdomen. Emilia had struggled to contain her sickness. Now it bubbled up her throat. She coughed, gagged, then swallowed bile before she could speak. 'Jesus Christ! What happened to them, Jace?'

Without clarifying, Jason rammed the truck into reverse. He hit the gas and the Ford raced backwards, the engine whining. But he had no hope of steering the truck all the way up the tortuous trail like that. Cursing under his breath, he halted, the tires skidding on the wet earth. Then the truck shot forward again. Emilia stared at him as if he was insane.

'I need to turn us around,' he said.

'Shouldn't we help them?' Emilia's question was pointless. The Thibodaux brothers were beyond any help.

'No. We have to get the cops out here.'

'Are you mad, Jason? We came here to buy drugs! We'll be locked up!'

Jason snapped a frown of dismay on her, as he spun the truck in the glade. Emilia blinked rapidly, as if realizing the inanity of her words. 'Yes. You're right. Let's just get the hell out of here. We can call the cops anonymously when we get back to town.'

Jason hit the gas.

Then he stepped on the brake and they were both thrown forward against their seatbelts.

'What the hell?' Emilia demanded, but it wasn't at his reckless driving.

A figure had stepped from the woods and barred the entrance to the trail.

It was painted by the glow of their headlights. Emilia's horrified gaze swept upwards. He was shaggy with hair, and huge. Blood glistened wetly on his broad chest and up his thickly knotted forearms, but her eyes travelled higher, held on the face and glaring eyes. Behind the windshield Emilia and Jason would be indistinct, but it was as if the piercing eyes of the figure zoned in on Emilia, and his mouth opened wide, showing bloody teeth.

'I . . . I don't believe it,' Jason croaked, even as Emilia moaned in recognition.

The figure lurched towards them, and in that moment Emilia knew exactly who the killer of the Thibodaux brothers was, and that they would not be allowed to leave that place alive.

She screeched in terror.

TWO

'Strangled?'

'F'sure.'

'By ligature?'

'Nuh-uh. By hand, I guess.'

In a house west of Portland, Maine, Tess Grey crouched for a closer view of Ron Bowen. She held her breath so she didn't smell him.

Standing at the other side of the unkempt room Nicolas 'Po' Villere appeared untroubled by the sweet stench of decomposition, but then he wasn't the type who was ruffled by violent death. He'd seen enough in the past to haunt most people, and his hand had dealt some of it. But that didn't make him a bad guy, not when Tess understood the circumstances behind those killings.

'How can you tell from way over there, Po?'

'There's no obvious bruising to the throat.' Po nodded at the corpse without advancing. 'Take a closer look. I bet you won't even find thumb prints.'

Pulling a sleeve over her fingers, Tess worked down Bowen's collar to inspect his neck. Po was right about the lack of bruising. She looked instead at Bowen's face. The capillaries in his eyes had ruptured, little threads like bloodworms star-bursting outward from the tear ducts. His mouth was wide, the palate was ridged and pale, the colour of a fish's underbelly, but the tongue was distended and swollen. The force of his dying had dislodged a row of dentures in front, and now two snaggle teeth were all that framed the fattened tongue. It sure looked as if he'd been strangled.

'How exactly was he killed, Sherlock?' she asked.

'From behind, I bet,' said Po. 'Someone looped an elbow around his neck, pressured the life outta him. One of those jiu-jitsu holds, f'sure. Want me to demonstrate?'

'No thanks. I'll take your word for it.' Standing up, Tess

again looked down at the body before casting her gaze in an ever-widening sweep. The living room was untidy, but even through the squalor it was apparent that some of the furniture was off-kilter, and some unopened mail had been scattered, swept possibly off one of the tables near the entrance. 'The place is a mess. There was quite a struggle before Bowen went down.'

'Yup. His killer wasn't an expert,' Po said. 'Applied correctly, a hold like that can render the victim unconscious in seconds. Looks as if there was a bit of a ruckus before the killer got an arm around Bowen's neck.'

'So we aren't looking for a rogue black belt, then?'

'Black belts aren't infallible. The fight coulda started, Bowen coulda got his licks in, then the killer managed to apply a finishing hold. It'd explain why the furniture has been shoved about. But that wasn't what I meant. When I say expert, I mean a professional with a capital "P". As in "someone who kills for a living".'

'Professionals aren't infallible either,' Tess cautioned. 'Bowen could have fought with a pro killer, too.'

'Maybe. But I doubt it. What are the chances of a hitman coming after him with their bare hands? Smacks more of a personal killing to me.'

'Spur of the moment?'

'Maybe. Maybe not. There are no signs of forced entry, so Bowen must have let his killer in. That says the killer is known to him, or he was somebody he was expecting at least.'

'Maybe Bowen was a trusting guy. Could've been a random stranger for all we know.'

'Coulda been. Maybe a neighbour who called round for a cup of sugar and got pissed when Bowen only had Sweetex.'

'There's no need for sarcasm. Or was that what you call a saccharine wit?'

'Sorry. I was only kidding.'

'So was I. You seriously need to check your irony button, Po. I think it's got stuck in neutral.'

Po raised an eyebrow, and Tess caught a twinkle of humour in his turquoise gaze. He loved it when he got a rise out of her. She turned from him with a grunt and crouched again at Bowen's side. As she often did when in contemplation she clucked her tongue, and rubbed distractedly at a scar on her right wrist. The injury was old now, but severe enough that it periodically troubled her. Frequently she suffered pins and needles when her damaged nerves misfired. Right then her hand was numb.

'You want me to call the cops?' Po asked.

'Yeah, but give me a minute or two. I want to take a look around first.'

'Leave it to the cops,' Po said. 'We came here to serve notice on the guy, not find his murderer.'

Her partner was right. They'd visited Ron Bowen with the intention of serving a court summons on behalf of his estranged wife. She was chasing him for alimony, and previous attempts at getting him in front of a judge had failed. Through Tess's employer, Emma Clancy, whose firm contracted to the local District Attorney's Office, Tess had been tasked with locating Bowen on behalf of the Office of Child Support Enforcement. She'd accessed the Federal Parent Locator Service, an initiative to assist state and local child-support agencies in locating case participants, and had discovered his current address easily enough. He wasn't exactly hiding, but serving papers on the deadbeat father had always proven tricky before. Now it was impossible.

'You don't suppose this had anything to do with Mrs Bowen?' she wondered.

'She's after his cash, ain't she? What purpose would it serve having him strangled to death before he paid up?'

'Life insurance?'

Po shrugged.

'Remind me to check if he had a policy, will you?' said Tess.

'Leave it to the cops,' Po warned again.

Tess grimaced. Sometimes she forgot she was no longer a sergeant with the Cumberland County Sheriff's Office, other times she was just being stubborn. Po was right. Investigating Ron Bowen's death wasn't her responsibility. Still, how could she not be intrigued by the man's sudden death and want to discover the truth behind it? It wasn't as if Bowen had walked into speeding traffic; he'd been choked to death in his own home, and that made for a mystery Tess wished to solve.

Po took out his cell. 'I'm ringing the police now.'

'For an ex-con you're quick to summon the cops,' Tess muttered. 'I thought you guys usually avoided them at all costs.'

'There's a clue in the name. "Ex". As in I no longer have any beef with the law.'

Tess squeezed him a grimace. 'Remember that irony button I mentioned?'

He shook his head. 'And some people think I got my name through being po-faced.'

'I don't even know what that means,' Tess muttered.

'I heard it from some Brit guy once; who said it was the distasteful expression you adopt when presented with the contents of a chamber pot. Over there some Brits call a baby's potty a po.'

Tess stared at him. 'As much as I find this all very fascinating . . .'

'You asked,' said Po.

'So the guy intimated you had a face like the contents of a potty? Yeah, I can see that.' She chuckled.

'Weren't you listening?'

'Not really. Anyway, I was lying. I know what po-faced means, just wanted to hear your take on it.'

'I'm confused,' said Po. 'D'you want to hear or don't you?'

'How to distract a dim-wit . . .' Tess grinned. She licked her forefinger and swiped it in the air in front of her. 'One–nil to me.'

'Son of a bitch,' Po said, and turned away, pulling up the saved number for the local police office in his cellphone.

Her humour dissipated as she again studied Bowen. Behind her Po called in their discovery, but his words were a murmur and she paid no attention. She concentrated on the dead man's features, wondering at Po's conclusion on the manner of death. Her partner was probably right. When it came to the mechanics of rendering someone unconscious, he understood his subject well. To suggest who was behind the killing was a different matter, and one they'd probably never know until a full patho-logical and forensic investigation was concluded. Nevertheless, it didn't stop her wanting to know who the killer was now.

She remained in a crouch alongside the corpse, taking care

not to disturb anything on the floor that might prove evidential, and stared into the bloodshot eyes. More than the identity of his slayer she wanted to figure out the motive behind Bowen's murder, but there was nothing in the cataract stare to enlighten her.

Finally she stood, distractedly rubbing her wrist as she watched Po slip away his cellphone.

'Cops are on their way,' he said.

'We should get our stories straight,' Tess said.

'And I'm supposed to be the lawless one.'

Ignoring his snarky comeback, she indicated the door. 'Take a step outside and pull the door to where it was when we arrived. Tell me if you can see anything of Bowen from there.'

'Not possible.' Po wasn't being insubordinate; he was stating fact. The direction the door swung on its hinges, there was no possible way they could have spotted Bowen through the narrow gap before they'd entered. Tess didn't want to admit to trespassing in the house without good reason. They were there to serve a summons but with no legal right to enter the premises uninvited. 'Take a deep breath, Tess.'

She nodded, getting his point.

'OK. So when we arrived we found the door partially open. When we knocked it opened a bit more and we got a waft of decomposition. Concerned for Mr Bowen's welfare, I called out, took a quick look inside and spotted him lying here. We entered hoping we might be able to help him.'

'I didn't enter further than stepping through the door,' said Po.

Tess nodded. 'Only I entered. Right. But I didn't touch him because it was obvious he was dead.'

'You touched his collar,' Po said.

She'd used her sleeve to cover her fingers when rolling down Bowen's collar to inspect his neck, but she could have transferred trace evidence when the two fabrics touched. She was going to have to come clean, admit to touching Bowen, which wouldn't go down well with the investigating officers. It was a case of admitting her curiosity had gotten the better of her, rather than becoming a possible suspect in Bowen's killing if any trace evidence was matched to her. As a retired sheriff's deputy samples of her DNA were still on record – taken supposedly for the process of elimination when she was still a law-enforcement officer, and she doubted her records had been deleted now she was a civilian once again.

'OK. So I leaned over him to check for signs of life,' she decided, 'so if there was any transference it must've happened then.'

'Don't know what you're concerned about,' said Po. 'By the smell of him Bowen's been dead for days. Nobody in their right mind would suggest we had anything to do with his death.'

'Just covering our bases.' Tess knew how these things worked. As and when a suspect was found, she didn't want a case against him clouded by conflicting evidence: a defence team would question the validity of any forensic evidence against their client if a conflicting DNA match had corrupted it. 'I'm going to admit to checking him out, and have myself eliminated from the get go. I'll probably get my knuckles rapped for this.'

'Now you know why I didn't join you over there.'

'Po,' she said cagily, 'sometimes I worry that you know too much about police work. Are you sure you've left your old ways behind?'

'I'm one of the good guys these days,' he reassured her. There was no necessity. Tess knew exactly what Po was, and it was because there was something dangerous about him that she couldn't resist. She wondered what things would have been like between them if she'd never left her law-enforcement career behind: but it was moot, because then they would probably never have met.

'Your hand troubling you?' Po asked.

'I'm good. Can't say as much for ol' Ron over there. You're as intrigued about his death as I am, right?'

'Gotta admit, it's got me wondering. But . . .' He held up his palms. 'The cops are coming. It's their case now. Let's just back off from this before we get in too deep again.'

As much as it irked her, Tess exhaled in defeat.

Po's cellphone chimed.

He glanced at the screen, and she watched his mouth draw a tight line, a match for those in his frown.

'Is that the cops?' Tess asked, though she knew it wasn't normal protocol for cops to send texts in response to a call.

'Nope. It's Pinky."

He held out the phone and Tess read the message.

CALL ME. URGENT!

Their friend Pinky Leclerc was flamboyant, even when composing his text messages.

Those three short clipped words meant something was seriously wrong.

THREE

'So he was dead when you arrived?' The cop was thin-necked, his hair shaved high and tight, and his uniform appeared to have come direct from its packaging, bypassing the steam iron en route. He looked to Tess to be about fifteen years old. Had she ever looked as fresh-faced when first she'd donned a similar uniform?

'I got here about a half hour ago,' Tess said, making no attempt at disguising her frustration. 'I didn't hang around for days before calling it in. So what do you reckon?'

'Ma'am, I know you're a little rattled, but it'd help us both if you answered my questions simply.'

Ma'am. The title rankled her. Made her feel old.

The cop tapped his pen alongside his chin, waiting for Tess to continue. She frowned in response. The guy had a job to do and the sooner she helped him get it done, the sooner she could address what had grabbed her attention.

'He was dead when I arrived.' She pursed her lips. Decided to come clean and get her faux pas out of the way. 'When I knocked on the door it swung open and I smelled him. I used to be a cop . . .'

She caught the soft nod of professional courtesy from the young man, but his expression remained nonplussed.

'I recognized the smell as decomposition. So I took a step inside and spotted Bowen lying there.'

'Did you touch him?'

'Only to check his vitals.'

'Oh? When he already stank so badly?'

'For all I knew the smell could've been from a pet that had died. I checked to make sure I couldn't help him. You would have done the same.'

He nodded again, scribbled notes. 'You said you were here to serve a court summons? Can you corroborate that?'

'You can call the DA if you want.' Tess waved a short stack

of papers at him. 'Or take a look at these. I didn't get to serve the summons after all.'

The cop accepted the official papers from her, and studied them acutely. She doubted he was familiar with a court summons, being so young in service. Tess moved from foot to foot, glancing out the open door to where Po stood.

Discovering the circumstances of Ron Bowen's murder had taken second place in Tess's thoughts the instant she'd watched a cold mask descend over Po's features. While she initially spoke with the responding police officers, explaining how and why she was at the scene of a murder, Po had gone to stand beside his black Ford Mustang car while calling Pinky Leclerc down in Baton Rouge. Normally Po wasn't the most emotive of men, but now the lack of any outward manifestation of his feelings told her more than if he were running back and forward tearing out clumps of his hair. His usual demeanor was languid; he had visibly tensed up, his spine rigid. Whatever Pinky had told him was bad. She just wanted to finish up with the cop and go to him. Preferably, she would attend the local police office later and give a full and concise statement, but the young patrolman was determined to get every last detail from her written into his notebook. He was ticking boxes, as he'd been taught to do, so there'd be no complaints about him from the Homicide detectives when they arrived.

'These seem to be in order,' the cop said, handing back the summons. 'Now, if you could tell me . . .'

Tess wasn't paying him attention any longer. Po had just kicked angrily at the ground.

She held up a hand to the cop, forestalling him. 'Look. You have my details and my first account. That'll have to do for now. Excuse me.' Before he could answer she was out of the door and down the front steps. Po spotted her coming, and grimaced at her.

'What's wrong?' She approached close enough that she could touch him, laying a hand on his right wrist. He clenched his phone as if it were a hot rock he was trying to squeeze the heat out of.

'Something has come up.'

'Is Pinky OK?'

'Pinky's fine. It's not him, Tess, it's . . . somebody else.'

He turned from her, but didn't walk away. 'I can't talk about this. Not here. Not now.'

'Then let's get out of here.' Tess aimed a nod at his Mustang.

Po glanced back at the house. 'What about Bowen's murder?'

'Not important now.'

'The cops finished with you?'

'They know how to find us if they need anything else.'

'I might be unavailable for a few days,' Po said.

'What? How? Po, what's going on?'

'I gotta go to Louisiana.'

'When?'

'Right now.'

He headed for the driver's door of his car and pulled it open. Tess only looked at him, open-mouthed.

'You coming with me?' He stood, peering back at her over the open door.

'You're going to drive there?' Po had a deep and intense aversion to flying that went beyond the norm. So his response surprised her.

'Can you book me a flight online? I need to get moving.'

Tess climbed inside the Mustang alongside Po, without giving much thought to anything else. He hit the ignition and the muscle car started with a growl as she buckled up. 'You going to tell me what's going on now? What's so urgent that you have to leave this minute?'

'My mother's dying.' He looked across at her. His turquoise gaze had dimmed. 'She wants to see me before she goes.'

Tess again found her mouth hanging open.

'But . . . I thought you hated her?'

'I do. Almost as much as she hates me. But who am I to ignore the last wish of a dying woman?'

'Even if it means . . .' She didn't finish her thought because Po nodded sharply.

'Even if it means burying the hatchet with the Chatards,' he said. 'It's unavoidable, I guess. My mom has held out the olive branch, I'm not going to be the asshole to refuse it. If the Chatards have other ideas, then I'll deal with it: a hatchet can be buried in more ways than one.'

FOUR

Tess didn't know what to say. She was sitting in the kitchen of Po's ranch-style house near Presumpscot Falls, having returned there with him to throw together a couple of travel bags for their journey down south.

'Now you know all about me,' Po said. 'Might explain why I don't like to talk about my past, and why going home isn't usually the first thing on my mind.'

Puffing out her cheeks, Tess still had no words. Po turned away, poured coffee from the pot he had going. He placed a steaming mug before her. 'I know it's a lot to take in, Tess. Believe me, I'm not looking forward to this, not one bit. But I have to go.'

She nodded, though there was no conscious process to her response. She was still mulling over the bombshell he had just related to her, fitting it onto the sequence of his life events she'd already grown aware of since they met a few months ago.

Po had spent a dozen years incarcerated at the Farm – otherwise known as Angola or the Louisiana State Penitentiary – after killing a man as an act of revenge. While he was serving his time, a brother of Po's victim tried to avenge his sibling, coming at Po with a shiv, intending to take out his eyes. Po still wore the scars on his forearms that saved both his vision and his life. The brother wasn't as lucky. After taking the shiv off him, Po returned the makeshift weapon, seating it in his would-be killer's neck. Both dead men belonged to the Chatard family. She knew all that.

Also, Tess had learned that Po's father Jacques had died during a heated confrontation, and that her partner had subsequently killed the man that murdered him. She also knew that the confrontation had come as a result of bubbling hatred between the Villere and Chatard families, and had something to do with the behaviour of his estranged mother. But she'd never gotten the full story from Po before. Po was guarded when it came to talking about his mother, though he made no attempt to conceal his disliking of her or her actions. He'd once intimated, in a roundabout manner, that his mother was the perpetrator of domestic abuse, directed mainly at his father, but she'd formed the impression that perhaps as a boy Po had also experienced her wrath. She had never pushed him for details, because she knew it was difficult to open up about a difficult past. When first they met and she was yet to trust him, she'd tried to look into his history but came to a dead end. She could have done some more digging, used her skills as an investigator to get to the story without teasing it from him, but she'd come to respect his privacy too much. Sooner rather than later Po would have opened up to her in his own time, and she'd been prepared to wait. Discovering the truth after a brief text message from their friend down in Baton Rouge was a huge surprise.

Clara had been an unfaithful wife to Po's father. Not once but on a number of occasions, and with different lovers. His parents had split up more times than Po was willing to recount, but Clara had always come crawling back to their family home when she realized that the grass wasn't greener in any other relationship. Whenever she returned to the fold Clara would weep, make promises about her faithfulness, but they never lasted: they were crocodile tears and false pledges. Soon she'd twist things, and when his dad wouldn't admit to being the one to blame for her infidelity, the tears would come again, but this time driven by a fury that transformed her into a screaming banshee that enforced her argument with a vicious tongue and swinging fists.

The final straw was when Po's father learned Clara had been sneaking around again. One man's tolerance could last only so long. This time it was him who sent her packing, and she'd rushed directly into the arms of her latest lover, Darius Chatard, a supposed friend of his. Shortly afterwards their neighbours were whispering about how Clara had conceived a child with her latest beau. Stinging with ignominy, Jacques couldn't endure the shame for long. He was a quiet man, but he couldn't take the whispers behind his back, the ridicule or the suggestion that Clara had left him because he was unable to father another child with her. He'd gone to set the record straight. But he hadn't found his old friend waiting, but one of his adult sons, and what happened next had set the tone of Po's life for the following quarter-century.

'The man you killed was your stepbrother?' Tess finally said.

'We weren't related at the time. My mother didn't marry Darius Chatard until after I was locked up at the Farm.'

'What about the brother that tried to stab you to death?'

'He didn't make it to the wedding. Besides, I'll never think of any of those a-holes as family. My mother might've joined them, but the Chatards mean nothing to me.'

'But those who've sworn this blood feud with you are your stepbrothers now,' she went on.

There were two living brothers, not to mention a bunch of cousins who had sworn to avenge their dead kin. During a trip to Louisiana a few months ago, Tess had witnessed first-hand the kind of trouble their pledge meant for Po when two armed thugs tried to claim the bounty on his head. Thankfully she'd been there to even the odds in Po's favour. Things could have ended very differently otherwise.

'You do understand no good will come of this?' she said.

'You don't want me to go?'

'You *must* go, and I'm coming with you. But for some reason, I'm not sure it's the best decision I've ever made. Not after everything that's happened. I mean . . . I thought my relation-ship with my mom was prickly, but this goes way beyond any disagreement I've ever had with her.'

'Your mom is an angel compared to mine.'

'I think that's a matter of perspective.' Tess reached tentatively for her coffee, but never touched the mug. Instead her fingers went through her hair. 'Then again maybe not. My mom can be a disapproving bitch at times, but she's never sicked a bunch of killers on me before.'

Po's eyebrows made a slow dance as he mulled things over. 'My mother isn't behind the bounty on me. That's on her husband and stepsons. But then again, she hasn't done much to play mediator either. Who knows, maybe this is all a ploy to get me where her menfolk can get their hands on me.'

'You can't be serious?'

'Nope. I'm talking BS.' He flicked a hand at the laptop she'd set aside on the kitchen counter. 'How'd you get on with booking us seats?'

'I've got us on a six a.m. flight out of Portland that gets us to Baton Rouge for midday.' She watched Po's face fold at the prospect of being trapped within an airplane for hours. 'We have a stopover in Atlanta, so you'll be able to stretch your legs, grab a cigarette or whatever. Best I could do at short notice. Flying to New Orleans shaves half an hour off the time, but then you won't be able to collect Pinky on the way.'

He shrugged. 'I'll have to endure it: Pinky's worth the extra half hour. I'll have him meet us at Baton Rouge. We can drive to the hospital from there, should make it there by late afternoon.' He laughed without humour. 'That's if Mom doesn't decide to slight me again. Wouldn't put it past her to die before I can get there.'

Tess turned her face aside, burning at her guilty thoughts. Maybe Clara dying before he reached the hospital would be best for them all. According to Pinky, Clara wanted to impart something important to her son, but it was as she'd already attested, nothing good could come from hearing the woman's last words. She hoped it was to tell Po how sorry she was and ask for his forgiveness, but in her gut, Tess knew that wasn't it.

FIVE

'I expected it to be warmer than this.' Tess glared up at a sky dense with clouds the colour of burnished brass. During their last trip to Baton Rouge, the city had been baking under a hot spell, and her northern blood had struggled with the humidity. She hadn't expected a chilly wind to greet her as she stepped through the arrivals exit at Baton Rouge Metropolitan Airport.

'What? It's February, you thought it was always hot down this way?' Po asked as he pulled out a pack of Marlboros and lit up. His smoke was snatched away on the breeze. He squeezed her a grin. 'What you complaining about, anyway? It's still warmer than it was in Maine.'

'Back home I was dressed for the weather, not in this . . .' She tugged at the thin cotton jacket she'd pulled on before their connecting flight out of Atlanta. 'All my previous misconceptions of moving to the balmy south have been dispelled, and not in a good way.'

'You can say whatever you want about the south, Tess, but you don't hear of many folks retiring to the north.'

'What does that say about you then, Po?'

'I haven't retired yet.'

'No, you're just over the hill.'

He offered one of his lazy smiles, smoke curling from one side of his mouth. 'Didn't hear you complaining last night.'

'For an old guy with a gut wound, you didn't do too badly,' she reassured him.

'Old guy,' he whispered under his breath, eliciting another chuckle from Tess.

In truth, he was older than her, being in his forties, but if you disregarded the lines around his eyes and mouth, Po could pass for a man much younger. She occasionally wondered if the twelve years he'd spent incarcerated at Angola had anything to do with it: with nothing better to do with their time many

inmates spent a good portion of it working out. But that wasn't
it, because Po had been out of prison for an equally long time,
and yet he hadn't grown soft. Much of his rangy frame and sinewy
strength was down to genetics. He could eat like a horse and
barely put an ounce on his lean frame, and Tess wished she could
bottle whatever made his metabolism work like that. She too was
a product of genetics and if she didn't watch her calorie intake
and work out regularly, she'd soon have a butt as wide as her
mom's.

'How are you feeling?' she asked as he ground out his
cigarette on the edge of a concrete bin.

'A bit stiff from being cooped up on the plane, but I'm holding
up fine.' He touched his abdomen, and winced slightly. Not
long ago he'd been almost gutted by a demented killer, and
getting into another fight with an equally demented rapist a few
months later hadn't helped his recovery. Tess assumed he was
in more discomfort than he was letting on, but that wasn't what
she'd meant. She was referring to his mental well-being now
that they were only hours away from attending his mother's
bedside. He nodded at the parking lot. 'We should get moving.
Pinky's waiting.'

Pinky had grabbed a slot in a 'no-stopping' zone. He was
engaged in a heated argument with an old Latino guy marshalling taxis and minibuses as Tess and Po approached. Immediately
his demeanor changed when he spotted them, and he flipped
off the taxi supervisor with a curt remark, to turn a beaming
grin on them.

Jerome 'Pinky' Leclerc was an unusual man in many respects.
He suffered from a medical condition that caused him to bloat
from the waist down, so his legs looked swollen and tubular,
while his arms appeared skinny twigs by comparison. His pointy
head, hair shaved almost to the roots, sat perched on sloping
shoulders, a football threatening to roll either direction with
every nod. He was a similar age to Po, but his brown skin was
smooth and seamless, making him look much younger. He was
gay, or he was bisexual, or he might even be uninterested in
sex: Tess hadn't fully made up her mind yet. His speech patterns
were odd to say the least. But all those quirks weren't what
made him unusual. It was the contradiction in his character that

threw her most. He was a criminal, a man who made his living in the shady world of illegal firearms and God knew what else, but he was also one of the nicest, most loyal friends she could wish for. Recently Pinky had almost given his life to save hers. Back when she was a Sheriff's deputy it would have been her mission to arrest men like Pinky Leclerc, now all she wanted to do was hug him.

She trotted ahead of Po and into Pinky's arms. As was his way, he lifted her off her feet, swinging her around as he planted kisses on her cheeks and forehead.

'Pretty Tess, I'm so glad to see you, me!' he said as he set her on her feet once more.

'Me too,' she told him, then made way so Po could greet his old friend. Their hug was more manly, a slap on each other's shoulder, but with no less affection.

'As usual, though, it saddens me that we only meet under awkward circumstances.' Pinky's features had grown sombre. He clamped a hand on Po's shoulder. 'I know you're here because I called for you, but I think you are making a mistake, you.'

'That remains to be seen,' Po said. 'Maybe it's time I made my peace with my mom. Doesn't mean I have to have anything to do with her other kin.'

'The Chatards might not see things that way.'

'Fuck the Chatards.' Po didn't frequently swear, so the curse was all the more grating because of it.

'She made her bed, I'd let her lie in it, me.'

'Yeah. Except this is her death bed.' Po's lips pinched. 'Man, as callous as it sounds, my mother dying might not be a bad thing. At least I'll be free of any connection to those a-holes after this. There'll be nothing to stop me from sorting things with them once my mom's out of the firing line.' He glimpsed at Tess, maybe expecting reproof, but she said nothing. She always knew that his feud with the Chatards would come to a head sooner or later. And that she'd be there to support her man.

The taxi supervisor came storming back, waving an officious notice at Pinky, and jabbing at the 'no-stopping' signs on the nearby concrete posts.

'OK, better pile in gang,' said Pinky, indicating a large black panel van parked at curbside. He turned his gaze on the Latino. 'Hey, I told you I'd only be a few minutes. So chill out, before you take an embolism, you . . . when I give you a slap upside yo head.'

The supervisor backed off muttering under his breath. Pinky hauled his bulk into the driving seat, while Tess and Po settled in alongside him after dropping their travel bags behind the seat.

'Maybe I shouldn't have said that, me,' said Pinky with a nod at the Latino, who still glared at him.

'He probably hears worse a thousand times a day,' said Po.

'I was meaning the crack about the embolism, considering what's going on with your mother. It was insensitive of me, I'm sorry, Nicolas.'

Po's mother didn't have an embolism to her brain. But she had suffered a blockage to her pulmonary artery that had brought on a severe cardiac arrest, and the requirement of open-heart surgery to fit a by-pass. Unfortunately, pre-existing conditions made her unsuitable for the life-saving operation and she was failing, her life expectancy only days. For all they knew she'd already died, because there had been no further contact from anyone in New Iberia. The initial call had come to Pinky via an old acquaintance that Clara had reached out to for help in contacting her wayward son. Tess had suggested to Po to contact Clara's husband directly, but Po didn't want to give the Chatards forewarning of his arrival. He'd also put off phoning the hospital in case a well-meaning nurse informed the wrong person that Clara's son had been in touch.

Why did family disputes have to be so damn complicated? Though, Tess had to admit, there were few families she knew of with the kind of problems the Villeres shared with the Chatards.

SIX

'Where's Zeke?'

Alistair Keane stared directly at the huge man towering over him. The man stared back, but it was as if his gaze rested on a point somewhere beyond Keane's shoulder, maybe not even in the same room or even on the same planet. His pale green eyes were slightly unfocused, and his mouth moved silently, conversing with someone equally beyond Keane's reality.

'Cleary! Cleary, snap out of it! Are you listening to me, goddamnit?' Keane jabbed a finger into the giant's denim-clad gut, and slowly Cleary's head tilted down, and his green gaze settled on Keane's face. 'I asked you where your brother is.'

'Zeke.'

'How many damn brothers have you got?'

'Only Zeke.'

'So where is he?'

Cleary's head went up and he looked at the single exit from the trailer. If Keane didn't know otherwise he'd believe that Cleary's ability for divining a person's location by pinpointing them with some kind of innate – and infinitely weird – built-in radar was real. But Cleary didn't possess a magical power; he was simply being literal. 'Outside,' he said.

'I know he's outside, but where?'

A hand the size of a grizzly bear's paw jabbed at the door.

Frustrated by Cleary's stupidity, Keane shook his head. 'Well, go tell him I want him in here.'

Cleary sniffed, then wiped the back of his thick, hirsute wrist across his top lip.

'Now would be a good time,' Keane said, his head forced forward for emphasis.

Cleary clumped across the floor, the entire structure quaking under his weight. He opened the door, and had to duck to exit. Keane listened to his slow progress down the steps. It could still be heard over the roar of heavy machinery. Diesel fumes wafted inside the trailer, and Keane cursed the big idiot for neglecting to close the door behind him. Maybe Cleary had purposefully left it ajar: he didn't like taking commands from Keane and decided a rebellious act was in order. It wasn't. Keane needed to have a word with Zeke about his brother's behaviour. If it weren't sorted, Cleary, for all he was a handy man to have around, would have to go. But he didn't want to speak with Zeke about the big idiot just now; there was something more important. He scurried over and pulled the door to, and returned to his desk, looking again at the screen of his cellphone, and the message that had urged him into sending for Ezekiel Menon.

He cursed under his breath. What the hell was he paying the morons for if they couldn't do the goddamn job right? The question was rhetorical. But it was most likely being asked of him by his own boss. In any organization the shit rolled downhill, well he was determined it wasn't going to end up heaped on his shoulders.

It was minutes before he heard boots on the steps. He spun around his desk chair but didn't rise. Zeke Menon didn't knock, he came straight in. He wasn't as huge as his freakish brother, but he was still tall, and had to duck to gain clear headroom. He was wearing a stained ball cap. The broken peak was frayed along its edges, the cotton dark with grease from his fingers. The remainder of his clothing was in better condition, neat almost, and the cap was an aberration. Keane had once asked why he didn't get a new cap, and Zeke had called it his lucky hat, and pointed at what appeared to be a scorch mark along one side. He swore it had saved his skull when it deflected a bullet during a shootout with some bikers over in Morgan City a few years ago. Pointing out that the meagre cloth had little to do with saving his skull, but that he was lucky to have been fired at by a poor shot was a waste of Keane's breath, because he seriously suspected that the cap had been in place so long it would have to be surgically removed and Zeke wasn't for changing it now.

'You were looking for me, Al?' Zeke was smoking a cigarette, and looked at the glowing embers instead of Keane.

'Where were you?'

Zeke swung the peak of his cap at the door, then took another drag on his cigarette.

Keane grimaced. Cleary was a moron, so he had an excuse for being stupid. 'There an extra ingredient in that?'

'Executive perks,' said Zeke and offered a lazy smile.

Keane eyed him a moment longer, then returned his attention to his cellphone. He held it up so Zeke could read the screen. The man only nodded, and had another toke of his joint.

'Well?' Keane prompted.

'I've got everything in hand.'

'That isn't the way Corbin sees things. It isn't the way I see things.'

Zeke exhaled and Keane winced at the sickly sweet smoke that engulfed him. He wafted a hand. 'Put that fucking thing out, will ya.'

Zeke smoked on. But at least this time he sent the plumes of smoke out the side of his mouth so that Keane was spared. 'Don't know what all the fuss is about. The Thibodauxs are outta the picture, like I promised. They're in a hole in the ground and will never be found.'

'It isn't the damn Thibodauxs Corbin's asking about. What's the deal with the stoners who disturbed you at the site?'

'We got one of them, the other's in the wind, but we'll find her.' Zeke used his joint as a pointer at the phone. 'You can let Mr Corbin know he has nothing to worry about.'

'There's a witness who can tie both you and Cleary to the murders. I don't have to remind you that you're both distinctive dudes, and any cop in New Iberia will know exactly who she's describing the second she opens her mouth.'

Zeke shrugged. 'Bitch knows my name.' He forestalled Keane's lurch of alarm with an upraised finger. 'She also knows what will happen if she mentions it to anyone. She ran from us, but she was in earshot and I made it clear what would happen to everyone she holds dear if she even whispers my name in her sleep.'

Keane made a sound in the back of his throat.

Zeke smiled at his disdain. 'My reputation precedes me.'

'Your reputation will mean shit if the cops come for us.

If she knows you, then she probably knows you work for me, and that I work for Nate Corbin. I'm warning you, Zeke, and with best intentions, if your identity does come out and it leads back to Corbin, your name won't mean a damn thing. You and Cleary aren't the only muscle he has on his payroll.'

'I ain't afraid of any man.'

'I know. But another word of caution . . . you should be.'

Zeke ground the stub of his cigarette under a heel, ignoring the indignation on Keane's face. 'Like I said, let Corbin know I've got everything in hand. I've my eyes and ears reporting back to me: it's handy having an army of stoners beholding to you, right? Sooner rather than later, one of them is going to come across her and let me know where she can be found.' He mimed slicing his throat, made a little whistle for emphasis. 'Then she'll get it.'

'Would be better if I can report back to Corbin that you're actively looking for her.'

'So tell him that.'

'Those eyes and ears you mentioned, you don't think they're reporting to Corbin too?'

'Fair point. I'll go get Cleary. I think he's bored hanging around this dump anyways. Do him good to join me for a drive before he gets into mischief.'

'You have somewhere in mind or are you just spinning me a line?'

Zeke smiled sarcastically. 'Actually, I do have somewhere in mind. I heard Emilia's mother has had a bad turn and is in hospital. If she's any kind of daughter, I'm betting she won't stay away from the old hag's bedside.'

SEVEN

Tess was familiar with hospitals, but she never felt at home in one. After her hand was almost severed by a crazed knifeman attempting to escape a bungled robbery, she had spent a lot of time in hospital and at a specialist rehabilitation unit to help regain mobility of her reconstructed wrist. She still attended private physiotherapy sessions, but on the whole her hospital appointments had ended, for which she was thankful. Yet it felt like only yesterday since she'd last sat in an overcrowded waiting room for what seemed an age before being called in to see her doctor, and there she was again. Pinky was keeping her company, but he wasn't being his usual ebullient self, his face pinched as he checked out those seated nearby or coming and going down the adjacent corridor. He was on the lookout, tense, and prepared for the worst.

Strolling into Iberia General Hospital and Medical Center was akin to shoving their hands into a wasps' nest and expecting to come away unscathed. Through association with Po they were courting danger.

She sensed Pinky stiffen, before he tapped the back of his hand against her thigh.

Tess remained as nonchalant as possible as she followed the directions of his wiggling fingers and spotted the man at the end of the hall. He was as tall as Po, and as rangy, but his face was leaner, sterner, and partly obscured beneath the peak of a battered old ball cap. He wore denims – jeans and shirt – and cowboy boots. His gaze swept the hall, alighted momentarily on Tess, and she felt a trickle of unease go through her at his brief scrutiny that weighed and discarded her as below his contempt. As he walked out of view, his head turning to and fro as he searched for something, Tess looked at Pinky.

'Was that one of the Chatards?'

'Not that I know of. But I didn't like the look of him, me.'

Tess hadn't liked the look of the stranger either, but that

wasn't saying much. She had an ex-cop's talent for spotting scumballs. The man in the grimy hat wasn't the first undesirable she'd laid eyes on since entering the hospital, and surely wouldn't be the last. If he wasn't a member of the Chatard family, then he wasn't worth paying further attention to. She returned to her silent vigil, waiting for Po's return.

After a few more interminable minutes Po appeared from the opposite end of the hall.

Before he reached them he nodded back the way he'd just come. Tess and Pinky stood, and Po waited for them to join him. Other visitors to the hospital gamely ignored them.

'She's this way,' he announced.

'You want us to come with you?' Tess asked.

'Yeah. Not sure they'll let us all in to see her—' he looked pointedly at Pinky – 'there's a restriction on family visitors only. I can probably get Tess by the nurses . . .'

'That's OK by me,' Pinky announced. 'She don't need to see my ugly mug, will only set her back in her recovery.'

Po smiled at the lame joke, but he was also saddened by it. 'There's no chance of recovery. I need you to stay outside and watch for any of those a-holes turning up unannounced. Don't want to cause a scene at my mother's bedside.'

'I'm there for you, Nicolas.'

Po clapped his friend on the shoulder.

Trepidation flooded through Tess as she followed Po along the spartan corridors. She was curious about Clara Chatard: she wanted to look at the face of the woman who'd picked a new family over her first, to a point where she had chosen sides in the battle between the Villeres and the Chatards. She'd already decided she didn't like the woman – for what she was and what she'd done, but really she had no right to make such a judgement. Po had answered the dying woman's summons, and it seemed with an open mind if not an open heart yet, so she should reserve her own opinion. In fact, Tess had been dreading this moment. She hoped that Clara would greet her son fondly, that she was looking for closure, and perhaps forgiveness, but doubt burned in the back of her mind. This brief visit to his mother's deathbed might be Po's mental undoing, but, like Pinky had just pledged, Tess would be there to help pick him up. She reached for his hand and gave it a gentle squeeze of reassurance.

The hospital offered acute care, and Clara was certainly in need of it. She was in a private room, hooked up to all manner of equipment and drips. She had the look of a skeleton wired to hold all her flimsy constituent parts together. She was aged beyond her sixty-five years, her skin loose and translucent, dotted with darker pigmentation on her hands and cheeks. In contrast her hair was thick and lustrous, though it was ice-white. If it weren't for the steady bleeping of a nearby ECG monitor, Tess would have sworn the woman had already given up the ghost.

Po didn't proceed beyond the door. He simply stared at the patient lying in the bed as if she was a stranger. Perhaps she was to him: the last time he had set eyes on her was almost a quarter of a century ago. Back then she'd have been young, still in her full bloom, vital. This woman was an empty husk by comparison.

Tess had to give him a nudge to prompt him over the threshold, and he almost tripped into the room. He steadied himself, and leaned backwards into Tess. She gently pressed him forward. She could understand his reluctance, but he was there now: no going back. 'Go on, Po. Go see your mom.'

He tilted his eyes to her, and she didn't recognize the look. He was normally fearless, meeting danger head on, but in the face of greeting his mother for the first time in decades he was afraid.

'It'll be fine,' Tess said.

He exhaled, but nodded and moved alongside the bed.

Over the sounds of bleeping machinery, and the ambient noises of the hospital Clara shouldn't have heard his approach. Yet she stirred, and her eyelids flickered open. Her eyes were a similar shade of turquoise as Po's, but dulled. As she looked up at him it took a moment for recognition to filter through her mind, and suddenly her gaze sparked into clarity. Her lips opened but she made no sound. Her right hand lifted, trailing tubes from a cannula, and her fingers twitched.

Tess waited. Po had stopped, looking down at the frail woman but his hands hung loosely at his sides.

'Take her hand,' Tess whispered.

But he didn't. If anything he moved back a few inches.

'He . . . llo, Nicolas.' Clara's voice was whisper-thin.

Still Po remained silent.

'Thank you for coming . . . son,' Clara went on, and again her fingers fluttered.

'I got your message. I came as you asked.'

Clara's eyelids slid shut. Her lips twitched, and Tess thought she was fighting uncommon emotions. But when she looked up at her son again it was with dry eyes. 'I knew you would.'

Po shrugged. Stirred awkwardly, stuck for words. Clara glanced at Tess, and they both squeezed out the tiniest of smiles.

'Who . . . are you?' Clara asked.

'I'm Tess. I'm a friend of Nicolas.'

Clara returned her attention to her son. Her voice was a tad stronger. 'You aren't married yet?'

Po didn't answer.

'Haven't given me any grandchildren yet?' When Clara's gaze settled on Tess again it held disappointment. Now it was Tess that stirred uncomfortably.

'You didn't want to know me,' Po said, 'if I had kids would there be any difference?'

Clara shuffled herself up the bed a few inches. It was an unnecessary effort, and Tess was first to reach for her, trying to stop her. But Clara had something to say, and didn't want it to be delivered while flat on her back. The heart-rate monitor picked up pace. 'If things could have been different . . .'

'They couldn't. You chose your side, and it wasn't mine.' Now Po stepped forward, but it wasn't to comfort the old woman.

Clara's jaw firmed.

'I was placed in the worst situation imaginable. Whose side could I take when everything was out of my control?'

'You put yourself in that situation,' Po said, and Tess was surprised at his snarky tone. Usually he reserved sarcasm for when he was poking fun at her; but this was different than when he was cajoling her. He was bitter, but it was hardly unexpected.

'You don't know what kind of life I had with your father,' Clara said, but Po's palm shot out, stalling her.

'You don't get to insult my dad,' he warned. 'He wasn't the one in the wrong. It was all on you, Ma.' It was the first time he'd referred to her by the title he must have used as a child. 'You were the one to have an affair with his friend. You chose Darius Chatard over him, even after his son kicked my dad to death. You stuck by that sumbitch and his family when I needed you most.'

'What could I do when you took everything outta my hands going after Lucas like that?'

Lucas was the first of the Chatard brothers to die at Po's hands, and it had been swift retaliation. He hadn't hidden from the law, turning himself in within minutes of beating the life out of his father's killer. Tess had heard from him that Clara had never shown at his court appearances and hadn't once visited him while he was locked up in Angola. She had certainly taken the side of his enemies, but Tess could understand how difficult it must have been for her. Maybe she had no option but stand by Darius, because what was the alternative when her husband was in his grave and her only son imprisoned?

Po of course wouldn't see things Clara's way. And he was growing angrier by the second. Tess touched his forearm. This wasn't the time or place for recrimination. 'Take it easy,' she whispered.

He snorted, but relented. He rubbed a hand over his face.

'You wanted to tell me something, Ma. I came all this way, so what is it?'

'Maybe I only wanted to see you one last time,' Clara said.

'Nope. You didn't have me come here just to lay eyes on me. If you've something to say, do it now. Otherwise I'm leaving.'

'You always were a stubborn child.'

'I'm not a child anymore.'

For the first time there was crinkle of fondness around Clara's eyes. 'You always were Jacques's boy, and you haven't changed one bit. I'm so glad.'

Po only stared at her, and even Tess wondered what the hell she meant. Throughout his childhood she'd only ever shown Po's father disrespect and disloyalty: how could she claim to have any fondness for her son if he reminded her so much of his dad? Perhaps she was casting her mind further back to a time when she did still love Jacques Villere, before her inherent selfishness had taken its unrelenting hold on her and their stormy relationship.

'There is something I gotta tell you, Nicolas.' Clara again tried to shuffle up the bed, but didn't have the required strength. Tess was tempted to help her, but Po didn't move. She took her example from him. Clara sank back into the sheets, exhaling wearily. 'Don't know how you're gonna take this, but I'm gonna say it.'

'Just say it and have done,' Po said, his voice barely above a whisper.

Clara worked her mouth. White froth had collected at the corners of her lips. There was a jug of water, a plastic beaker and drinking straw on a bedside cabinet. Po finally reached for the beaker and fed the straw to his mother's mouth. She sipped. Then nodded gratefully.

'I'm dying,' she said. 'No two ways about it. The doctors want to do an angi-somethin'-or-other, but they're only wasting their time and mine. Want to put stents into my veins and blow them up with little balloons. But they already told me that there's too much damage to my heart and lungs, and that the angi-thing will only alleviate the problem for a short while. Me . . . well, I've had enough. I don't want to prolong things. If I'm going, I'd rather do it now before things get much worse.'

Tess glanced at Po and saw his eyes narrow. She couldn't read him, wasn't sure if he was happy with Clara's decision to forgo treatment or not.

'But I didn't bring you all the way here to tell you my time is up. You already know that, and I'm betting you don't much care.' She fluttered a hand towards him. 'I can't blame you, son: can't say as I've been the best of mothers to you.'

When Po didn't challenge the point, Clara again exhaled. Her next inhalation was a struggle. Phlegm crackled in her throat and her chest heaved beneath the sheets. Tess again glimpsed at Po, but this time he didn't need any urging. He offered the water again and Clara sipped gratefully. As her look of mild panic subsided, Clara again shuffled further up the bed. 'My damn lungs are giving out on me,' she said. 'You still smoking, Nicolas? If I can do one good thing in my life for you it's to advise you to throw them away. Lookit what they've done to me.'

Po didn't reply. He wasn't there for a lecture on his bad habits, or hers.

'I shouldn't put it off any longer,' said Clara, and now she wasn't preaching. 'After me and your dad split, you know I had another child.'

'Yeah.' His mother had given birth to a girl after she'd switched her affections to the Chatard family.

'She wasn't Darius's child.' Clara peered up at Po, her eyes surprisingly brighter than they had been earlier; they shone with tears. 'Despite what you might have heard, and what even my husband Darius might believe, that baby girl wasn't his.'

'What are you saying, Ma?'

'I think you're wise enough to figure things out for yourself, Nicolas.'

'I've got a sister?'

'She was Jacques's baby, and full blood kin to you.'

Tess felt the admission like a punch to her gut. God only knew how Po had taken the news because he showed no hint of surprise beyond a brief pinching of his mouth. Perhaps he'd suspected all along, because he knew about the girl, and it wouldn't have taken much figuring out if anyone had taken the time to tally the dates between Clara leaving Jacques and the birth of the girl. But then, Tess was under the impression that Clara had been having an affair with Darius Chatard beforehand, and so everyone had assumed that the girl was his.

'You've never met her,' Clara went on. 'But she's your spitting double, son. There's no denying who her father is.' She reached for the bedside cabinet. Po followed her gaze and noted a couple of 'Get well soon'-type greetings cards collapsed on top of it. 'Could you pass me those?'

Po reached for the cards and picked them up. He opened and discarded the first, then opened the next. Inside it was a photograph. Po made a sound in his chest as he peered intently at the face smiling back at him.

'That's Emilia, your sister,' Clara confirmed.

Intrigued, Tess wanted to take a look, but the door opened behind her.

Pinky made a brief perusal of Clara Chatard, and his brow puckered. Then he snapped his gaze from the still, silent form of Po onto Tess. 'Maybe you should see this, pretty Tess,' he announced *sotto voce*, as if by speaking aloud he'd shatter whatever scene he'd just stumbled into.

'What is it?' she asked, equally as quiet.

'Not so much what as *who*,' Pinky said.

Tess nodded briefly at Clara, who was too intent on gauging Po's reaction to give them any notice.

Pinky again frowned at Clara. 'No, it ain't one of her brood. It's that creep again; the one strutting roun' like he's Chuck Norris's tougher brother.'

EIGHT

Visiting a hospital with the intention of strong-arming a patient into offering up the location of her wayward daughter probably wasn't the best idea that Zeke Menon had ever come up with. He had drawn the curiosity of too many people – nurses, doctors, patients, and visitors alike – for him to get down and ugly on the old Chatard bitch now. He wondered if any of those whose attention had lingered on him for longer than a fraction of a beat, and who'd formed an impression of him based on their base instincts, had already tipped off the hospital security personnel. For all he knew his movements were being tracked via CCTV: for one he'd appear on plenty of footage should anyone care to check the recordings later. He'd originally intended slipping into Clara Chatard's private room, asking her about Emilia, and if she wasn't forthcoming with the information he needed, pushing her into telling him. Such action was unadvisable now. Particularly since he'd stared down that fat-assed black guy who had barred his way as he'd approached her room.

'You is in the wrong place, bra,' the black man had told him.

'I choose my own path, nigger,' Zeke had replied.

The black man had flapped a skinny hand back the way Zeke had come from. 'Then choose it that way, you.'

Zeke had hooked a thumb in his belt, enough to tug down the top of his jeans to show the handle of a knife beneath the tail of his shirt. 'Prefer to blaze my own trails.'

The black man slipped aside the front of his jacket and showed the butt of a semi-automatic pistol nestled under his left armpit. 'I'm also in the blazing business, me.'

Zeke had eyed the black man, and the guy had stood his ground, wearing the faintest of smiles on his wide mouth. To look at the weirdly shaped guy appeared soft: but his expression said otherwise. Zeke thought he could gut the fat man before he got a hand on his gun, but he'd have to cut him deep and long to cause any lasting impression on all that blubber. Any other time Zeke would have welcomed the challenge, because for one he had no liking of niggers, but a busy location like a hospital ward probably wasn't the best place to butcher him. But neither was he about to back down without regaining face.

'I'll be seeing you again, negra.'

'You got a date, cracker.'

Zeke snorted, but allowed his gaze to slip. There were slats on the blinds of Clara's room, but they were tilted to allow in some light from the hall. Through the gaps Zeke made out two figures inside. A good-looking fair-haired woman was nearest the door. But it was the other person who caught and held his attention. It was fifteen years since last he'd seen that aquiline visage, and it had aged a little, the lines about his eyes and mouth deeper, but Zeke was under no illusion. What the fuck was Nicolas Villere doing standing over the bed of Clara Chatard?

The black man moved a few inches, effectively blocking any view that Zeke had of the man he'd once known, but Zeke had seen enough anyway. He spat between his boots in a show of disdain and then turned slowly on his heel to walk away. It was a struggle not to pick up his pace, but he didn't want the nigger to know he was in a hurry to leave. His recent conversation with Al Keane was dancing in his mind as he turned around a corner in the corridor, where Zeke had told him he wasn't afraid of any man.

Keane had replied with his words of caution: '. . . you should be.'

Now, he was full certain that his employer hadn't been talking about Nicolas Villere in person, for how could he know that Villere was back in town? But his warning was apt. If ever there was a man who'd placed something approaching fear into Zeke Menon's heart then it was the bad ass currently standing guard over Emilia's mother. Villere's attendance in New Iberia couldn't be a coincidence either.

But what was he doing there, and what was his interest in Clara Chatard?

It took him a moment to remember the details, because it had been many years since he'd thought about any of the gossip that swirled around the exercise yard at the Farm. Villere was jailed for killing a Chatard, and had later stuck a shiv into another who tried to blind him. That was the connection. But why visit the mother of the men he'd just slain? There was a part of that story he wasn't familiar with, and now he wanted to know it. He came to a halt, turned, and looked back the way he'd just come. Clara's room and the man standing guard before it were out of sight, but he still peered back that way as if it would help him recall something else. That goddamn nigger. He recognized him too. Porky, or Pricky, or some other damn stupid name he'd gone by in Angola. He was a skinny kid back then with a tight butt; a sweet ass on which Zeke and some other good ol' boys had taken their turn before Villere had appeared like the damn queer's knight in shining armour and laid about them with the business end of a lug wrench smuggled out of the tractor maintenance shop. Zeke still wore a scar on his left shoulder, from where Villere had broken his collarbone with a smack from that wrench. He'd gotten off lightly on that occasion, because Villere had concentrated his cold rage on some of the older guys, almost ignoring Zeke for a misguided kid carried along by the dirty tide he'd got caught up in. Villere had sent two more of them to hospital, one with a broken arm, the other with a shattered jaw. The other two were bloodied, knocked cold, but all right after a few days of nursing their aching heads. After that nobody fucked with Villere, or by virtue of his protection with . . . Pinky! That was the nigger's name. Fucking Pinky Leclerc. Although Zeke had seethed for vengeance, as had the others Villere had beaten to within an inch of their lives, none of them moved on him, and they'd all been punished for it. Villere had become known as 'the Man' and only those with suicidal tendencies would have gone at him. Even Zeke, who had never understood the concept of fear before, was suddenly cautious of trying anything against the most fearsome animal in the zoo: if only Cleary was inside with him things would have been different. But Cleary was locked up in another institute back then, one with rubber walls.

That was then, Zeke supposed.

Things are different now.

He strode off in search of his brother, all thoughts of hunting a frightened girl now taking second place to a reunion with Villere.

NINE

Tess watched the tall man in the grungy hat climb into a pickup truck he'd left illegally parked in an ambulance bay. His simple act of disregard for the acceptable decorum – let alone the official rules and regulations – in such a location pissed her almost as much as how he'd acted towards Pinky minutes ago. She'd heard a brief summation of the man's inherent racism and bad attitude in a few curt words from Pinky before trailing him through the hospital. Now she stood in the weak sunlight filtering through the overcast sky, surrounded by the loamy smell of nearby Bayou Teche brought to her on a fluttering breeze. She felt colder than she had when leaving the airport terminal earlier, and again pulled her thin jacket tightly around her. Her chill had nothing to do with the weather, but what the tall man's interest in Clara Chatard might signify.

He was trouble. No second thought about it. But it begged a question: what kind of trouble followed that man?

He drove the pickup as if he was in a hurry to get away, and she edged out to log the licence number in her memory. On the tailgate was a company name and she ensured she had that firmly lodged in her mind too.

Pinky stepped up behind her. He'd held back in pursuit because he was too obvious a figure to conduct close surveillance.

'There's something about that dude . . .'

'Trouble.' Tess looked at him, and watched Pinky's eyes widen.

'He's that, f'sure, him. But I meant there's some*thing* about him I recognize. Can't place from where, but I've seen that face before, me.'

'And you're absolutely sure he isn't one of Clara's family?'

Pinky shrugged. 'If he were he'd have said so. He would've had more right to see her than I had to stop him.'

'And the first thing he did was make threats?'

'Showed me the hilt of a knife. Was an unspoken threat if ever there was one.'

'What else did he say?'

'Nothing of importance. Just your typical racist bullshit. Has a liking for the word "nigger", you ax me.' Again Pinky shrugged. 'Water off a duck's back. Trust me, pretty Tess, I've been called much worse, me. Someday I'd like to meet one of those racist buttheads who has more imagination when it comes to insults. Being called a fat-ugly-nigger-faggot grows a bit boring when you've heard it a million times.'

The pickup was out of sight. Tess wondered when she'd see its driver again. Probably sooner than she'd like, even if it were years from then. 'We should get back to Po.'

Pinky had never gotten used to Nicolas's new name. He'd only been nicknamed Po after moving north and those who learned he hailed from the bayous had named him after a southern delicacy. Po was quick to put them straight, and the 'boy' had firmly been dropped from 'po'boy'. Even she thought his nickname a little whimsical when the three of them got together. Pinky, Po and Tess: they sounded like characters in a children's cartoon.

'Nicolas was shocked when I looked in on you,' Pinky prompted.

'Yeah. You could say that. He just heard he's got a baby sister.'

Pinky's head cocked to one side. 'Oh?'

'Apparently Clara's youngest isn't a Chatard at all. She's Jacques Villere's daughter. Nicolas's full sister.'

'He-he! Talk about confusing an already complicated matter.' He ran a palm over his scalp. 'You think maybe we should get them all together on the *Jerry Springer Show* to work out their differences?'

'I'm not sure that show is still current,' Tess said.

'I was only joking, pretty Tess.'

'Yeah,' she said, thinking back to a similar ridiculous conversation she'd had with Po while standing over the corpse of Ron Bowen. 'I was too. Who needs Jerry Springer when people air all their dirty washing on the social networks these days?'

Po came out of the exit behind them, and immediately fed

a cigarette to his lips. He didn't light up, but it was inevitable. His eyebrows made a literal 'V' as he walked towards them. 'Wondered where you'd got to,' he said by way of greeting. Both Tess and Pinky waited for him to say more. But he simply strode by, looking for a place to smoke.

'Thought you might need a few minutes' privacy with your mom,' Tess told him. Now really wasn't the best time to trouble him with news about the stranger's unhealthy interest in Clara.

'There wasn't much to say.' Po continued walking, heading in the general direction of the parking lot where they'd left Pinky's van. Once he was a respectable distance from the hospital he lit his cigarette from a Zippo. His mother's advice on giving up smoking had fallen on deaf ears, but Tess didn't begrudge him the nicotine: hearing such a revelation as he had many other people might turn to alcohol for their emotional crutch.

She waited until he'd expelled half a dozen plumes of smoke overhead. 'That was quite a revelation back there.'

Po's eyebrows rose, then knit into a 'V' again. 'And then some.'

'You never suspected you had a sister?'

'I heard about Emilia's birth, but that was about as far as my interest went. Far as I knew she was Darius Chatard's kid, and if anything I held only contempt for her.' He shrugged apologetically. 'That was then. I was young, hot-headed, and had just gone to war with her family. Haven't given her much thought over the years.'

'And now?'

Po ground his cigarette under his boot. Lit up another.

'She's still a stranger to me.'

'You mean she's still a Chatard as far as you're concerned?'

'I've only my mother's word that Emilia's my sister. And her word ain't worth spit.'

'You never counted up the dates?' Tess wondered. Po squinted at her. He was a guy; what did he know of such things?

'I counted. If Emilia is my full sister, my mom must've conceived a day or two before she ran off to her new beau. Far as I could recall my parents weren't in a happy place before she lit out. Last thing I imagined was them sleeping together,

'specially if she was already running behind my dad's back.'
He looked over at Pinky, who'd positioned himself near enough
to be supportive if necessary, but wasn't crowding them during
their private moment. Po nodded him over. Pinky was the
nearest thing to real family that Po had here in the south. 'You
should hear this too, bra.'

Pinky joined them.

'You want to meet the girl, you?' he asked.

'That's beside the point,' Po said.

Tess took his words the wrong way. Her first thought was
that nurture might trump nature in this case. 'You don't think
she'll want to meet you? Considering all that's happened
between you and her family, it could be a difficult decision for
her. I can only imagine that you're the bad guy in her eyes.'

'That ain't it.' Po took a long draw on his cigarette and flicked
a column of ash. 'She's just not in any position to meet me.'

'What do you mean?'

'Apparently Emilia has gone off the grid.'

'She's missing?'

'Not so much missing as out of contact. But my mom says
it's not unusual for her. Emilia's a free spirit, and not exactly
a child any longer. She comes and goes as she pleases, but it's
troubling that she hasn't answered any calls from her family to
get her to her mom's bedside. They've even gone as far as
checking out some of her known haunts, but no luck.'

'When you say it's troubling you,' said Pinky, 'does that
mean you're troubled by her no-show?'

'Don't know what I think,' Po admitted. 'My mom asked me
to go look for her, though. She wants Emilia by her side before
she goes. She wants Emilia to learn she's my sister from no
other lips than hers.'

Tess stared at Po. Waiting. But she knew there was only one
thing he could do. He took another drag on his cigarette and
looked back at her.

'Your mother give you a home address for Emilia?' she finally
prompted.

'So you think I should go look for her?'

Tess snorted. It was a damn stupid question: he'd only waited
for her to make the suggestion so it sounded like her idea.

'I've got an address, but it has already been checked. You know where that means we must go next?'

Pinky flickered a grin. 'Been looking forward to this for years,' he said and surreptitiously scratched under his armpit where Tess knew he had a holstered weapon.

She shook her head.

'We start at the beginning and go from there. Not directly into a needless confrontation.'

'Not needless,' Po corrected her. 'Inevitable.'

'Nothing's inevitable. You've seen your mom now . . . we could just go home.'

Neither man answered her, but as they clambered into the van she knew they weren't returning to the airport. But that hadn't been her intention.

TEN

Emilia had no idea what had become of Jason Lombard. Some boyfriend he'd turned out to be. She should have known he was unreliable, particularly when the most effort he'd put into their burgeoning relationship was scoring them some of the finest weed in Iberia Parish. When that blood-splashed maniac had barred their escape from the Thibodaux trapper camp, Jason had shown his alacrity, but not in her defence. He jumped out of his truck and ran into the swamp. There was nothing heroic about his dash; he wasn't trying to lure the bad guy away so that Emilia could escape. He hadn't even given her a heads up before he'd sprinted for the trees. To be fair, she probably wouldn't have heard him, because she was screaming so loudly. Her screech did more to win her some time than anything. The big shaggy-haired brute watched her – gleeful at her terror – and by then Jason was gone. Spotting his fleeing quarry, predatory instincts pulled at the giant and he struck out after Jason like a hound on a rabbit's trail.

Emilia leapt from the truck and ran for the swamp on the other side of the clearing. Her only thought was to put as much distance between her and the crazed thing that had slaughtered Hal and Jamie Thibodaux, and who she believed would do the same to her next.

'Emilia Chatard!' She heard a voice call to her, and stumbled for a moment, thinking it was a rescuer. But then its crowing quality struck her, and she knew she wasn't being hailed to safety. No, the second figure to have appeared from the front door of the Thibodauxs' cabin was letting her know that he'd recognized her. She knew who it was clumping down the wooden steps in pursuit without having to look, but instinctive terror forced her to check and Zeke Menon showed her the bloody knife he gripped.

Emilia fled then, her voice caught in her throat as Zeke chased her to the edge of the clearing. He was being vocal enough for both of them.

'You can run, gal, but there's no escape from this. I know you, and you know I know you! I know all you Chatards and here's the thing. If you don't come back here, I can go cut them up instead. That what you want, bitch? You want your brothers slaughtered, your daddy cut to ribbons? What about your dear ol' mamma? Come on back here . . . I can be a reasonable man. We can come to another arrangement. You don't have to die; things can be made more pleasant for you. For both of us. Y'hear me?'

Emilia kept running, ducking and swiping wildly, forcing a path through the low hanging branches. Spanish moss swiped her face and caught in her hair. The sharp ends of twigs dug painfully into her flesh. She didn't reply to Zeke's hollers. She barely understood his words beyond that they were malicious threats whatever action she chose next.

'I know you can hear me, Emilia. Emilia Chatard, you'd better listen up. One word, bitch . . . one word about what you saw here and everyone you care for dies. You hear me? *Do you* fucking *hear me?*'

She heard, not exactly the words, but definitely their meaning, but she kept running.

Then she was forging through soft muck that threatened to pull her down. Roots tangled her feet, and jagged stumps reared up around her. She had almost floundered into a tributary of the bayou. The stench of rotting vegetation hung around her, but she smelled nothing. Her senses had closed down to sight and sound only, and neither of those made much sense. She turned left, and ran again, her feet churning through stinking mud, her hands grabbing at tree trunks to help her flight. Fingernails were broken and torn off. She lost a sneaker. But she kept going, her breath burning in her throat, until she collapsed onto drier land. She crawled then, getting deeper into the evening shadows, and scrunched into a hollow between the great exposed roots of a spreading oak tree.

She hid, quaking, shivering as much from the adrenalin surging through her body as the clammy dampness from wading through the mire. Occasional creaks of the overhead branches or the soft crackle of breaking twigs set her heart racing again, her imagination telling her that Zeke Menon or his demented brother was closing in on her hiding place. But she knew it wasn't so, because she could hear them much further away to the west. They were howling like damn wolves, catcalling to each other as they chased Jason to ground. She only heard one hint of her fleeing boyfriend when a third voice joined the cacophony, but this one higher pitched, screaming in terror and agony. Emilia wept into her hands as the mist rose from the swamp to add further concealment.

She had a cellphone in her pocket, but who could she call? She didn't doubt that Zeke Menon was capable of carrying out his threat to slaughter her family: the evidence of what had happened to the Thibodaux brothers had been plain to see. Alerting the police would only bring a swift and brutal end to another person dear to her, before Zeke or Cleary were caught. Perhaps she was giving their abilities too much credit, but fear tended to magnify the capabilities of those terrorizing you. She could call her brothers, or her father, warn them about the Menons, but by doing so she knew they wouldn't rest until they'd taken the fight back to them. Her family was connected to the criminal underworld, but not in the way the Menons were: go after them and they would be taking on Nathaniel Corbin and all the resources he could bring to a fight, and that would end in one way: very badly for the Chatards.

She didn't take out her phone. Deep in the bog it would be highly unlikely she'd get a signal anyway. Best action, she decided, was to stay hidden, wait for the Menons to finish what they were doing to Jason, and then leave the swamp. She could go into hiding, keep silent about all she'd witnessed there, and hopefully things would blow over. Once the Menons were convinced she could be relied upon to keep their secret, they might allow her to live. They would leave her folks alone. She'd only stumbled into their midst by chance, and they must see that. Stay hidden, stay silent, and protect her family. 'Stay hidden. Stay alive.'

That was her mantra for the next four days.

Once she walked out of the swamp she kept to the back roads, fearful that if she tried to return to town via the highway, the Menons would find her and drag her back. Her ex-boyfriend, she now understood, because Jason Lombard wasn't coming out of the swamp alive. His death troubled her, but not in the way it should have. She didn't really have deep feelings for him; he was only one of a number of young men who'd chased her these past few years. She didn't love him, wasn't even sure she was even fond of him: he was just a friend with whom she'd shared intimacy, and a penchant for a wild time. She'd never expected their hell-raising lifestyle to bring them face-on with actual demons in the flesh. When she'd mentioned being frightened of the rougarou earlier, she had not really been serious: now she understood there were worse things to fear in the swamp than a mythological wolfman. Then again, grinning at her with blood on his teeth, what else had Cleary Menon resembled?

She headed north on the levee road, trudging along through the darkest hours of the night on one shoe, which she later discarded. She heard the distant sounds of heavy machinery, off to the west in the woods where a pipeline was under construction, but she stayed well clear. As dawn broke she finally walked into a tiny cluster of houses called Catahoula, where she finally took out her phone, called a friend, Rachel Boreas, and asked her to come fetch her. Rachel arrived an hour later, to find Emilia streaked with dried mud, barefoot with torn clothing, and with twigs in her hair. She fired questions in rapid sequence, but Emilia refused to answer, only asking that Rachel take her back to Lafayette, from where Rachel hailed these days. Thirty miles, Emilia suspected, wasn't enough distance to place between her and the Menons, but it was a start and in the right direction . . . away.

On the drive back Rachel tried to coax from Emilia what had happened. Emilia assured her she didn't want to know, and when Rachel persisted, Emilia begged her not to ask again. 'Please, trust me, Rachel. If I tell you, then you will be in danger too.'

Unlike Emilia, Rachel didn't enjoy a wild lifestyle; she didn't run around with stoners like Jason Lombard anymore; she had responsibilities. She was a married woman with two small children. She didn't ask again, and Emilia remained silent. On arrival at Rachel's home, Emilia thanked her friend for picking her up, but immediately tried to walk away. If by some chance the Menons were on her trail she didn't want to lead them to a house with two small children inside. When she wouldn't enter the house, Rachel pressed some cash into her hand, gave her the sneakers off her own feet, and told her to find a motel someplace and clean herself up. She then asked about Emilia's family.

'You can't tell them, Rachel, you can't tell them a thing.'

'Are you hiding from them?' In the past Emilia had suffered a rocky relationship with her older siblings, and more than once had been on the receiving end of a disciplinary slap or two. Rachel quite understandably thought she was running from a similar beating again.

'Yes.' Emilia's face was stricken. 'But only to save their lives.'

'What? Oh, Emilia, what have you gotten yourself into this time?'

'The worst thing imaginable,' Emilia said, and tears sprung fresh down her cheeks. 'Promise me, Rachel: don't contact them. Don't tell them a thing. Don't tell anyone you saw me, for their sake. For *your* sake, and for the sake of your babies too. Oh God! I shouldn't have come here . . .'

She'd hurried away then, leaving Rachel staring in horror after her, and over again she repeated the same words she had as she emerged from the swamp. 'Stay hidden, stay alive.'

By contacting her old school friend she'd already jeopardized the first rule. She couldn't allow a similar mistake again. Instead of seeking a room in a hotel, she headed directly to the bus station and paid for a ticket out.

ELEVEN

'Looks deserted,' Tess said.

'No kidding.'

The address Clara had supplied for Emilia led to a decrepit apartment over a convenience store that looked as if it had closed its doors many years ago. From the front seat of Pinky's van, Po cast a glance over the grimy shop front, and an equally dissatisfied sweep of the surrounding streets. Emilia had moved out of the Chatard family home to live in a rundown section of town, and though he'd never met his sister, and had no idea of her character, he was angered – perhaps disappointed – by her living conditions. Then again, he had been bottling up his emotions since meeting with his mother, so the foul string of curses he emitted under his breath was hardly unexpected.

Tess patted him on his thigh. 'We should still check she isn't home.'

Po left the vehicle, and Tess joined him on the sidewalk. Pinky stayed with the van. To leave it unattended in a blighted neighbourhood like this would be inviting trouble.

Tess glanced up at the apartment. Hers was of a similar design back home in Portland, also set above a shop. But there the similarity ended. Tess's building was well maintained, painted brightly, not a crumbling, faded husk like this one. Her access to her upper floor was via steps at the side of the building, but there was no immediately apparent way up to Emilia's apartment from the front.

Po led the way along a track worn into the hard-packed dirt alongside the store and into a rear yard. Somebody had built a fire, and singed wood and cardboard had been strewn around by the wind, or kids with nothing better to do. The air stank. Other people had used the yard as a latrine, and not only to take a leak. Po growled a curse again.

The steps up were rickety. The only attempt at security was a linked chain strung between the handrails, padlocked in place, but anyone could step over, or bend under it. Po chose the former, then yanked up the chain so Tess could duck beneath.

As they approached the door, it looked shut, but the lock was busted and the handle hanging off by its screws. The imprint of a dirty boot sole was vivid against the faded blue paint.

They shared a glance.

'You know what we found last time we walked uninvited through an unsecured door,' said Po.

'Don't even suggest it,' Tess said. Finding the corpse of Ron Bowen had been horrible enough, but discovering the body of someone related to Po would be terrible.

Po pressed the door inward with the back of a hand, but didn't proceed. He was testing the air that seeped from within. Tess could almost taste the rancidity, but it was the stink of spoiled food and dirty ashtrays, not of decomposition. Nevertheless, it didn't mean they weren't in for a nasty surprise.

'Emilia?' Po called. 'You in there?'

There was no answer. The place felt deserted, about which Tess had mixed feelings.

She followed Po inside. A search wouldn't take long. The upper floor of the building was one original room, with drywall partitions forming a tiny bathroom in one corner. There was an equally small kitchenette taking up the opposite corner. Dirty dishes in the sink, pans on the hob, and an overflowing refuse sack that looked as if it had made an ill-fated break for freedom from the trashcan hinted at the source of the rank smell. Tess immediately recognized another tang in the room: a sweet smell that at once reminded her of some of the drug dens she'd raided when she was a cop. She again glanced at Po and noted that he'd recognized the aroma too.

He walked to the centre of the living space. Emilia apparently slept on the settee, testament of which was a tangle of bedding crumpled up at one end. He ignored his sister's sleeping arrangements, and instead peered into an ashtray defying gravity as it teetered on the arm of the settee. It was stacked high with the filtered ends of cigarettes, but in among them were a number of hand-rolled reefers. His search swept wider, and Tess knew he was checking for paraphernalia that would hint at Emilia having a stronger drug habit. There was nothing evident.

'Don't judge her for smoking a little weed,' Tess said. 'Even I tried it when I was in college.'

'I ain't. I'm judging her on the state of this place: it was a damn shit hole before whoever kicked their way inside trashed the room. Has the girl got no goddamn standards?' He made a grumble in his chest. 'Then again, knowing who raised her, I'd be surprised if she wasn't a complete skank.'

Tess clucked her tongue at him. 'Take it easy, Po. Don't forget that's your sister you're talking about.'

'That remains to be seen,' he said. 'My mother never was the most truthful, always could twist things to suit her, or to cause trouble for others. I've known snakes that spit less venom than she does.'

'You think she's lying about Emilia's parentage?'

Po shook his head. He was venting. He'd seen a photograph of Emilia, and already told her she had his father's eyes and jawline. As had Po. Tess had imagined Emilia as looking like a younger Po in drag: the poor thing.

'I just think she tugged on my heartstrings so's I'd go look for Emilia for her. Don't think it has anything to do with wanting to introduce us as siblings before she shuffles off. She'll have her own selfish reasons.'

Tess didn't reply. Po was bitter, but it was unsurprising. But she also knew her man, and try as he might to bury things behind an angry mask he was hurting. He wanted to find Emilia too, but not in these kinds of surroundings. Did he think he'd betrayed the young woman all these years, by not being there to support her? Not knowing about her before this didn't help, but ignorance wasn't always bliss.

'None of this is down to you, Po,' she reminded him, as she indicated their scruffy surroundings. 'Let's just put Emilia's plight down to circumstances out of your hands, and concentrate on making things better in future.'

'I only hope that's a possibility.' Po again cast his gaze over the room. Drawers had been emptied out, their contents scattered on the floor. The cushions on an easy chair were upended. Somebody had searched the place, and neither of them thought the invader was seeking Emilia's secret stash of marijuana.

'You see a tablet or laptop anywhere?' Tess prompted.

'Nope. Think she can afford one living in a dump like this?'

'She's a young woman, she'll have one or the other.'

'Don't the young ones do everythin' on their smart phones these days?'

His comment earned him a smile from Tess: he was such an analogue dinosaur.

'Most of them have more than one of those new-fangled gadgets,' she said, deliberately hokey. 'If she left, she'd take them with her. But if you ask me, Emilia had no intention of running away when she last got out of bed. You see the food on the hob?'

Po nodded. It was food that Emilia had prepared for later: peeled, but raw potatoes in one pan had gone brown and a creamy sauce in another was scummy, and had separated – some of the foul smell came from it. An uncooked chicken could be seen in the oven. The dishes in her sink were probably from breakfast, but she'd intended returning home for dinner.

'Any clue on how long she's been gone?' Po asked.

'Days only. I wouldn't taste that food on the stove for a million bucks, but it doesn't look as if it has started to rot yet.' Tess waved away her estimate. 'I'm only guessing. But look.'

Po glanced down at the trash on the floor. Tess poked at an opened envelope but Po couldn't see what she was referring to. 'The postmark's only a week old. Now supposing it was Emilia who opened it, I'm guessing it was within the past six days.'

'Unless it was opened by the a-hole who turned the room over.'

Tess let her silence speak for agreement. But she didn't think it was the case. Whoever had searched Emilia's apartment had done so with the finesse of the proverbial bull in a china shop. The envelope had been neatly peeled open, not torn apart.

'So we go with a five-day window,' said Po, and Tess nodded.

Knowing when she disappeared would help find Emilia: it would give them a starting point. Tess had hoped to find a computer she could interrogate. There would have been plenty of breadcrumbs to follow simply by checking the young woman's social networks activity and other web-browsing history. It would be something she'd do in due course. For now she was seeking something more immediate and tangible. Often

when people made plans they left clues in the form of hand-
written notes or print-offs of travel and accommodation tickets
or routes they'd planned online. If there had been anything as
obvious as those, then whoever had beaten them to the
apartment had already taken them.

'You think one of her brothers did this?'

Po bristled slightly at mention of Emilia's Chatard siblings,
but he shook his head. 'They surely wouldn't show this level
of disrespect to their own sister's place.'

'That was my thought too. This was someone else.'

'F'sure; a junky looking for a fix or something portable to
steal? Maybe there was a tablet or computer and he took it.'

Until they found Emilia they'd never know. But Tess
believed otherwise. She thought that the one who'd kicked in
the door and turned the place over had done so with the same
reason in mind as them; they were searching for Emilia too.
In itself it was a clue; it meant that Emilia knew she was being
sought and had gone into hiding. She didn't share her next
thought with Po for fear that suggesting it would make the
worst possible scenario come true. Had Emilia's hunter already
caught up with her, and her disappearance was now permanent
because she was dead?

'Look for anything with an address or name on it,' she
suggested.

'You want to know who her friends and acquaintances are?'
said Po. 'Then let's go speak to somebody who'll be able to
tell us, not waste our time here.'

He meant Emilia's family. It was the obvious thing to do,
but Tess suspected it would only provoke a conflict she'd rather
they avoid.

She eyed the teetering ashtray.

'You smoke Marlboros, right?' she said. 'Usually stick to the
one brand.'

'Uh-huh.' Now Po peered at the stumps ground into the thick
mound of ashes. As well as the remnants of various hand-rolled
cigarettes there were two branded cigarette types. 'I see what
you mean. Looks as if Emilia had company before she left.'

He glanced at the settee, and it didn't take a detective to
figure out why the cumbersome bedding had been kicked into

an untidy pile at one end. A line deepened between his eyebrows.

'Emilia has a beau,' he said needlessly. 'We find him, I bet we find her too.'

Tess nodded over at the prepared food. 'She wasn't cooking for one. Looks like she made enough food for when they got home with a serious case of the munchies. Whoever it is she's seeing, he didn't come back either.'

Po sniffed. The boyfriend was of no concern to him, other than that he might be the one responsible for Emilia's disappearing act.

'I need to get online,' Tess said. 'You seen all you want to see here, Po?'

'About two seconds after we came in,' he said. 'Let's get outta here.'

'Just give me a moment.' Tess trawled through the papers scattered on the floor and found some old credit-card statements. They probably wouldn't hint at where Emilia was now, but Tess had another use for them. She also found an invoice for her cellphone usage. She placed the papers in her purse. Po secured the door behind them as best he could. Not that there was much to steal but he didn't wish to leave an open invitation to any local sneak thief.

Pinky was standing on the sidewalk alongside his van as they came around the side of the building.

His usually jovial expression had tightened, and he held himself more rigid than normal. He had one hand strategically placed inside his jacket. 'Was about to call you, me,' he announced. 'We got company.'

TWELVE

Two men stared at them from behind the bird-crap-dotted windshield of a Dodge pickup parked about twenty yards away. The driver gunned the engine a few times, as if in warning, but then laid off the gas and allowed the engine to grumble. Blue smoke puffed from the tailpipe. The late-afternoon sunlight made their faces indistinguishable behind the glass, but they stirred and the passenger hung a hairy elbow out the side window. His forearm was as thick as a ham.

'How long have they just sat there like that?' Po asked.

Pinky said, 'Only minutes. Cruised past first, all eyes on Emilia's place, but then they spotted me. They swung around, parked there, and been giving me the stink-eye since.'

'You think it's the Chatards?' Tess asked. Po only shrugged. There was no way of telling. Even if he could get a good look at their faces, how could he be sure they were men he'd last seen almost a quarter of a century ago? Tess glanced again at the truck, but didn't need to check the licence tag to know it wasn't the one driven away by the stranger at the hospital. This one looked less like a work vehicle than a souped-up redneck toy, plus it bore the decal of a local scrap-metal dealership.

'They're as interested in us as we are in them,' Po announced. 'I'm gonna go ask them why.'

'Sounds like a plan,' said Pinky, and again his hand crept under his jacket.

'You're inviting trouble,' Tess warned.

'Why? I'm going to ask them nicely,' Po said.

Tess shook her head, but she fell into step behind him.

As they strode across the street towards the pickup, the driver backed it away. Halted again after a few seconds. He gunned the engine. The pickup jumped forward a few feet.

'What's his game?' Pinky said out the corner of his mouth.

'Playing at intimidation. Or he's a clumsy driver.' Po was

unperturbed by the driver's antics. He held up the flat of his palm: the universal sign for peace.

'Be careful,' Tess said to his back.

'Don't worry, I'm not going to start anything.'

Tess grimaced. She knew exactly what Po meant.

'Hey, bra,' Po called out as he approached the driver's window. 'There something you want from us?'

The driver returned Po's question with a malicious grin. He was a slim-faced man with a wispy beard and a spray of acne scars across his nose and cheeks.

'Wouldn't mind a piece of that sweet ass you towing behind you,' the man finally said, with a nod at Tess.

It came as a surprise to Tess when Po didn't punch the guy's face through the open window. Instead Po hung his head and laughed into his chest. Slowly his head rose and he moved alongside the door and rested his right arm on the roof. His left hand flicked at Tess. 'You couldn't handle her. That's suggesting that I'd stand aside for you, of course. Which I won't. You want to say that again, bra?'

The man was forced to look up at Po, and Tess spotted a gold incisor glinting as he again grinned. 'You her pimp?'

Again Po surprised Tess. He turned and nodded up at Emilia's apartment. 'You seen another pimp around here?'

The driver shrugged, and glanced across at his buddy. The second man was huge, almost filling the cab with his bulk. His beard was thicker, but then his entire body – or as much of it that wasn't concealed behind plaid and denim – was heavily furred. Apart from the top of his dome of a skull, that was bald, blotched with strawberry-coloured pigmentation. 'Whaddabout you, Rory? You seen any pimps aroun' here, bra?'

Rory laughed, his voice deep and gravely. 'Do I look like d'kinda guy has to pay for a piece of ass?'

Inadvertently they'd just answered Po's unspoken question. He'd been wondering if his sister was turning tricks for rednecks up in her apartment, and if somebody else, perhaps in exchange for drugs, was pushing her into it. Evidently the answer was no, because the two guys in the truck were the type who'd have said so.

'D'you know the girl who lives up there?' Po continued.

'Who are you, her social worker?' answered the driver.

'You know her, you don't know her, doesn't much matter to me.'

'I don't know her,' said the driver, and his grin was even wider.

'Then why are you watching her place?'

'Why are you watching her place?' the driver countered.

Po leaned down again. He stared at the younger man for a long beat. 'Are you the one she's avoiding?'

He got no reply, only a steady, fixed grin. The man wasn't clever enough to formulate a convincing lie.

The driver's right hand crept down the side of his thigh, but the surreptitious move wasn't missed by Po, though he didn't let on. He only winked at Pinky over the top of the cab, who edged around the hood. Tess watched the drama unfolding as if a timer ticked down to detonation. Suddenly her mouth was very dry. She took a slow step backwards, making room.

As the driver began to bring up a revolver from between the seats, Po grabbed him by his bottom lip, twisting and pinching it with such sudden ferocity that the gun fell from the driver's fingers and clattered in the footwell. Po yanked the man out of his seat, got his other hand in the younger man's hair and dragged him bodily through the open window. Rory, bear-like in appearance, roared, and grabbed at his friend's legs, but only assisted in upending the driver who went down head first to the asphalt. Po never relinquished his grip on the man's lip, twitching him into submission as if he was wrangling a recalcitrant horse. The driver screeched in agony, and flopped around.

Rory threw open the door, and met Pinky coming at him. The pistol aimed at his gut didn't faze the giant redneck. He made the stupid move of swiping it aside with one hairy forearm, and launched a punch at Pinky's jaw. Except Pinky didn't hang around for the lumbering fool to land either move. He stepped aside, and struck the barrel of the pistol dead centre on the giant's blotchy pate. The skin split, and the blood that poured down his features was redder than the check in his tartan shirt. Rory's hands went to his head as he attempted to stem the blood flow, and Pinky drove a shoulder into him, shoving him back against the hood of the pickup. A quick trip of his ankle and Rory went down on his back at Pinky's feet.

Tess watched it all unfold in a few shocking seconds, open-mouthed. Then she quickly glanced around, checking for witnesses, but the street was as deserted as Emilia's home had been. Her attention returned to her friends' exploits.

'Now you stay down, you,' Pinky warned as he leaned in and placed the muzzle of his pistol to the side of Rory's neck, 'an' we can stay on friendly terms, us.'

Po used the fulcrum of the driver's tortured lip to flip the man flat on his back. He kneeled on the driver's chest as his free hand went into the top of his boot and came out with a knife. Pinky, Tess assumed, must have supplied Po with the blade, because he certainly hadn't flown here with it concealed on his person. Po released the lip, but only so there was room for him to insert the tip of his dagger in the driver's flaring left nostril. 'Don't move,' Po warned. 'If you want to keep your looks you'd better be a good boy. Now I can promise you I've a steady hand, and I won't cut you on purpose. But shake your head an inch and you lose your nose. Try to get up; it's your own brain you'll be spearing. You get me?'

Before he was hauled out the pickup, the driver had been a picture of facetiousness, now he was simply terrified. His mouth was blanched of colour from the savage twisting Po had given it, now the remainder of his features had paled equally. 'I . . . I . . . get you, bra.'

'You going to be civil now and answer my questions? Nah-ah. Don't nod,' Po reminded him.

'Wh . . . Whaddaya wanna know?'

Po looked over at Emilia's place.

'You do know the woman who lives there. Was it you that kicked down her door and ransacked the place?'

'No. I mean, yeah. I know her, but it wasn' us who broke in.'

'You've been inside though, right?'

'We took a look, yeah. But that was all. Saw the place was trashed, Emilia wasn't home, so we left again.'

'And now you're back. You and that ape over there.'

The driver rolled his eyes, and could see his buddy Rory in

a similar uncomfortable position through the gap beneath the pickup.

Po turned the blade a fraction of an inch, and the driver's attention switched back on him.

'Why'd you come back?'

'We were told to keep an eye on her place.'

'I figured,' said Po. 'On whose order?'

'Zeke Menon's.'

'Zeke Menon?' Po's eyelids pinched, and even from where she stood slightly disassociated from reality, like an observer of players on a stage, Tess saw recognition of the name in the tightening of his features. 'What's his interest in Emilia?'

'I don't know. Seriously, bra, I haven't a clue. Zeke Menon isn't the kinda guy you quiz. You get me?'

'Seriously, bra, I'm not either. He must've told you why to watch for her.'

'He didn't. Swear to God, man. Just told me to take Rory and keep a watch on this place, an' if the bitch come home, we'd to call him.'

'So call him.'

'Emilia ain't back yet,' the driver objected.

'So tell Zeke I want to see him. See—' Po leaned in a fraction and the man's face almost collapsed in anticipation of the blade driving through his skull – 'he's looking for the same person I am, but I don't believe his intentions are as good as mine. I'd like to know why, so you get him here for me.'

'You might as well stab me in the face now,' the driver whined. 'If I help set Zeke up, Cleary will eat me alive, bra.'

'Who is Cleary?'

'A fuckin' retard,' said the driver, with a sudden flash of terror through his eyes. 'Zeke's brother, man. He's not right, you get me? He's *scary* wrong. You don't believe me, ask Rory. Rory ain't afraid of no man, but even he hides when Cleary's around.'

Po pursed his lips, unimpressed by Cleary Menon's legend. 'What was the deal with the gun? The one you were about to pull on me.'

'I don't know who you are, man. This is a bad neighbourhood . . .'

'Made worse by a-holes like you pulling weapons on folks,' Po told him. 'You're lucky I'm a reasonable man.'

'I'm lying on my ass with a knife up my nose.'

'Consider the alternative,' Po said.

Tess laid a hand softly on Po's shoulder. He glanced at her, nodded softly. Withdrew the blade and stood. Neither man was a genuine threat to them. Torturing further information from them was only going to attract unwanted attention.

'You OK over there, Pinky?'

'Fatty knows his place,' said Pinky, and he stepped away and his gun went back into its holster. To Rory, he said, 'Get your butt back inside that truck, you, and no funny business.'

The driver stayed on his back, but put tentative fingers to his face, checking for missing portions of his features. His bottom lip had swollen to twice its normal size, and he'd lost a few wispy hairs off his chin, but Po hadn't seriously harmed him. His nostrils were still whole, despite a shallow nick in the one abused by Po's blade.

'You can get up,' Po told him.

'I'm not calling Zeke.'

'Fair enough, I don't want you to become dinner for his brother. But gimme his number.'

'No way, bra. He's gonna know who you got it from.'

'Buddy, I can soon find his number by other methods, so you may as well give me it before your usefulness runs out.'

Po wasn't hinting at finding Zeke Menon's number by way of Tess's superlative detective skills. Feeling like a third wheel on a bicycle, Tess moved aside and left him to it. She was intensely uncomfortable at the way Po and Pinky had played things, but wasn't about to complain. Being an ex-cop it some-times felt alien taking off the gloves like that, but she couldn't deny that her friends' methods got results. They were nowhere nearer to finding Emilia, but in a few short minutes they'd determined why she was missing, and more importantly that she was still alive. Otherwise, why would her enemies – the Menon brothers – still be hunting her?

Rory was back in the pickup, stemming the blood from his scalp with some wadded paper, still under the watchful gaze of Pinky. The driver was leaning against the cab as he plucked at his abused lip with one hand, the other digging in a pocket for his cellphone. Po stood nearby, nonchalant. The scene looked calm; an observer coming across them would have no idea of how desperate it had been only moments earlier.

Po took the cellphone. Its owner complained, but Po simply flattened a palm against the man's chest and pressed him back against the pickup. Perhaps he was afraid that Po was going to ring Zeke Menon directly from his personal phone, but Po only noted the number, committing it to memory. Po handed back the phone and the man looked at it as if it was a stick of dynamite with a lit fuse. Tess couldn't help feeling it was a decent metaphor for her own sense of the impending. The call that Po was sure to make would determine the future, for good or bad. Probably bad.

She could overhear Po quizzing the man further. He'd claimed to know Emilia. Po asked how.

'Just from around, bra.'

'Around where?'

'The scene. Y'know?'

Po didn't push him on 'what' scene; it didn't take too much imagination to figure it out.

'Who does she usually hang with?'

The guy was regaining some of his sneer now that the knife was no longer in his nostril. 'She's a popular gal, if you get my drift?'

'She have a regular friend?'

'The fuck would I know, man?'

'So you're only casting unfounded aspersions?'

The man blinked at Po with a total lack of understanding.

'You're just talking shit,' Po clarified for him.

The facetious grin flickered back in place, light winking off the gold tooth.

'Give me a name, then get the hell outta here,' Po said.

'I don't know names of any of those limp dicks,' said the young man, 'but the chicks is another matter. Emilia hung out with a coupla girls we knew from when we was all back in high school. Jenna Cornell and Tracey Redding, but she was always besties with Rachel Paterno.'

'I take it you've already been around and spoken to these girls about Emilia's whereabouts?'

'Not me, bra. Like I said, all I was told to do was keep an eye on her place, and let Zeke know if she showed up. Rest of it: nothing to do with me.'

'So what happens now?'

The man only grinned, but his smile was uncertain, wondering how he should play things.

Po told him. 'Here's what happens now. You and your buddy get the fuck outta here. You don't come back. If Zeke isn't happy with that, tell him I'll be in touch and we can come to acceptable terms then.'

'You can't tell us what to do,' the guy said, but he had no confidence in his proclamation.

'There's a big swamp just outside of town,' Po reminded him. 'A large number of people get lost in it all the time. How'd you and Rory like to become statistics?'

'Fuck that, bra. I'm only being paid pocket change . . .'

'Is that all your life's worth to you?'

The guy turned to get in the pickup.

'Hold it.' Po pushed him aside and delved in the footwell. He found the dropped revolver wedged against the gas pedal. As he weathered the driver's baleful stare, he fed the revolver into his belt at the small of his back. 'We don't want any more stupidity from you, do we?'

'Buddy,' the driver said as he shoved the stick to drive. 'I ain't the stupid one. You bait those Menons, it's you who needs to visit a shrink.'

As the pickup roared off, billowing smoke, Tess looked up at Po. 'That parting shot he made . . . first bit of sense I heard out of him.'

'Maybe,' Po said. 'But it doesn't make a difference. Zeke Menon is chasing Emilia, and I want to know why. And if I halt him in his tracks, she might stop running.'

THIRTEEN

'Where the hell have you got to now, Cleary?'

Zeke Menon scanned the construction site. The working day was coming to an end, but there were still a number of guys in hard hats and fluorescent jackets clumping around, and a couple of large dumper trucks still sent up clouds of dust and diesel smoke as they added to the mounds of excavated dirt. Zeke squinted against the fume-filled clouds billowing around him, pulled down the peak of his ball cap, and tried to pinpoint the familiar – and very distinct – shape of his brother. Cleary was nowhere to be seen.

It would have been better if he had taken Cleary with him when he'd visited the hospital earlier, even if it meant ordering him to stay in the pickup while he went inside alone. Cleary would have happily sat and read one of his books while Zeke saw to business. But he'd decided against it after leaving Al Keane's trailer office and now Cleary was AWOL. Knowing his habits, Cleary had likely wandered off alone into the swamp. Searching for Cleary would have taken time and effort he could do without, but now it just meant he was looking for Cleary with no idea of where he could be. Cleary carried a cellphone, but he didn't answer the damn thing when Zeke called: he had a unique take on reality, and often the *actual* world didn't impinge upon his. Zeke left a voicemail message, though he was doubtful his brother would listen to it or respond unless he became so inclined. Dealing with Cleary could be frustrating. There were times when Zeke was tempted to take his brother by the throat and shake some sense into him, but he dared not. As much as he'd assumed control of their partnership, the alpha of their two-wolves pack, if Cleary ever challenged him for leadership then he knew his ass was grass. When he turned violent, Cleary had no off switch.

If ever Cleary's condition was diagnosed, Zeke believed it'd be somewhere high up the autistic spectrum. His brother was endowed with above-average intelligence. But it rarely manifested in a way acceptable in civilized society. As with other forms of autism Cleary exhibited a delay in motor skills, and through his lack of understanding when it came to the abstract use of language he was perfunctory and literal in his responses: the concepts of humour, irony and give-and-take were lost on him. He showed unhealthy levels of interest in specific items, and his reactions to a gamut of differing stimuli could set him off in different ways. Spotting the brightly coloured plumage of a bird could take him into the woods in pursuit, with a view to either petting it or ripping it limb from limb. But his brother hadn't been diagnosed, and therefore he was simply known for being batshit crazy, and Zeke wasn't medically qualified enough to disagree. Perhaps his condition had nothing to do with autism, and more to do with being in 'the world according to Cleary Menon' and that's all there was to it. Their father used to apologize for Cleary when they were kids, usually stating, 'Cleary has his own ways,' as if that made him immune to acceptable behaviour, while Zeke had simply been 'a nasty piece of shit'. Growing up with a father like theirs, the way they turned out was hardly surprising. Then again, maybe dear ol' dad had a point: Zeke was under no illusion, he was a nasty piece of shit, and he worked hard to maintain the image. Nice guys didn't get on in his business.

Then again, neither did getting sidetracked on a personal vendetta. Al Keane was paying him to clear up a problem, and he should concentrate on finding Emilia Chatard, and shutting her up for good. Keane's business arrangement with Nathaniel Corbin was jeopardized by Zeke's failure to do that one simple task. Keane's ire he could take with a pinch of salt, but he knew he was jabbing a hornets' nest in pissing off Nate Corbin. He'd earlier boasted to Keane that he feared no man, but his words had been typical macho bullshit. You didn't cross someone like Corbin, as much as it irked to admit it.

Corbin wasn't your typical tough guy, no crazy man who'd stick a gun in your face at his first displeasure, but he had plenty people on his payroll who would. Zeke could pretend he didn't give a hoot for any of Corbin's hired guns and – taken singly – he didn't, but it was a different story entirely when Corbin was wealthy enough to send an army. For all Zeke and Cleary made a formidable pairing it didn't mean a damn thing when hitters could be brought against them from all angles. To keep Corbin happy, he needed to keep Al Keane onside too. Keane he gave less regard to, but Keane was the one passing down the boss's orders. In Zeke's opinion, Keane was a dick, and a limp one at that: Corbin would be better off dealing directly with the Menons and do away with Keane. Except that wasn't going to happen. Keane could offer equipment, premises, and a workforce required for Corbin's operation here in New Iberia: what could Zeke offer by comparison? Jeez, right now he couldn't even offer a crazy motherfucker that was guaranteed to terrify the opposition into surrender. Where the hell had Cleary gotten to?

Zeke stood at the edge of the construction site, staring into the deep shadows beneath the nearest overhanging boughs. There wasn't a hint of his brother forging a path through the undergrowth, any sound drowned beneath the thrum of the excavation equipment behind him. Tracking Cleary through the swamp was becoming unavoidable. Without him there was no way he was going up against Nicolas Villere and Pinky Leclerc, but it was his desire to do so that was causing the distraction to finding Emilia Chatard. Fate, he thought, was a fickle beast. What had brought his old enemies to his notice but for a chance meeting in the hospital? If Emilia hadn't stumbled upon the scene at the Thibodaux camp, she wouldn't have gone into hiding and there would never have been a reason for Zeke to be in the hospital seeking her whereabouts from her sick mom. Villere and Leclerc could have come and gone again without him ever laying eyes on either. He would believe that the planets were aligning or some other such bullshit, if not for the fact his damned brother had gone and thwarted fate's grand design with this no-show.

He checked his phone again. There'd been no reply. He rang Cleary's number but received an automated response stating the recipient was unavailable.

'Son of a bitch.' He glanced down at his new cowboy boots.

Damnit if he wasn't going to have to purchase new footwear.

Muttering at the clinging muck, he went down the side of a heap of sticky dirt and immediately into the fringe of the swamp.

'Cleary? Cleary? If you're off chasing toads again, I'll make you eat the damn things raw!'

'Why you shouting, Zeke? I hear you fine.'

Spinning around, he glared up at the mound of dirt he'd just clambered down. The broad-shouldered silhouette of his brother was vivid against the setting sun.

'Goddamnit, Cleary! Where you been all this time?'

'All this time.'

'Yeah, all this goddamn time! I've been looking for you all over.'

'No. You walked from Keane's trailer to there.' Cleary pointed at Zeke's current position. 'You haven't been all over.'

'You were watching me?'

'Uh-huh. Watching you.'

'Then why the hell didn't you say?' Zeke started climbing the dirt pile, his feet sinking deep in the loose muck.

Cleary shrugged. 'Say what?'

'That you were there.'

'I wasn't here. I was back there.' He gestured back towards the hub of the construction site, and earned a headshake of disbelief from Zeke.

'I've been calling your cell,' Zeke said.

'I turned it off. I was reading. I don't like to be disturbed when I'm reading.'

'Well, thank fuck you called me back when you did. I was about to go traipsing through the damn swamp looking for you.'

'I finished my book,' said Cleary.

Zeke had finally scrambled to the top. He stood before his brother, but words failed him.

'I need another book, Zeke,' Cleary announced.

'I'll get you another book, but there's something we have to do first. There's some people I want to introduce you to.'

'I don't want to meet nobody.' The big man's face crumpled, as if he was about to weep.

'It's OK,' Zeke said, and he laid a calming hand on his brother's shoulder. 'These people, you don't have to be polite to them. In fact, you can tell 'em how much you don't like 'em . . . or you can show them if you like.'

Zeke waited a beat, and then his mouth turned up in a smile. 'Will that turn that frown upside down?' he cajoled in a singsong tone.

Cleary's tusk-like teeth flashed an eager grin.

FOURTEEN

'I don't believe it! Zeke Menon, him!' Pinky shook his head, then looked at Po for further proof.

Po shrugged. His friend hadn't been in earshot, and was too engaged with controlling Rory to take any notice of what was going on at the other side of the pickup truck. 'According to that guy, it's Menon who paid him to keep an eye on Emilia's place.'

'Yeah. I hear you, Nicolas.' Now Pinky looked at Tess and nodded encouragement.

Tess pinched her lips, then exhaled noisily as she understood where Pinky was leading. 'There was a guy at the hospital, Po. It's why I left you and went outside. Pinky stopped him from going in Clara's room.'

'He wasn't going to take no for an answer 'til I showed him I was serious, me.' Pinky flicked back his jacket to display the holstered pistol for emphasis. 'There was something familiar 'bout that a-hole, but I couldn't put my finger on it. Zeke Menon grew big, Nicolas.'

'Neither of you thought to mention this sooner?' Po asked.

'Things kind of overtook us,' Tess argued. 'You'd just learned you had a sister, and couldn't wait to start looking for her. To be honest, I pretty much forgot about the guy the second you joined us outside the hospital.'

'So Menon wanted to speak with Clara?' Po went on.

'If you ax me, he wasn't there for a civil conversation, him.' Pinky briefly went over the sequence of events in the corridor outside Clara's room. 'If'n I'd recognized him, I'd have sent him on his way with more than a subtle warning. My shoe would've been in his ass.'

Tess wanted to know the history between her friends and this Menon guy. It wasn't good, judging by the anger manifesting around Pinky's eyes in twitches and tics. Po was sombre, but that was often his way. Instead of pushing them for the story, she stuck to the facts pertinent to the present. 'Who is he?'

'White trash,' Pinky stated.

'He ran with a branch of the Aryan Nation when we were inside,' Po explained. 'A pissant follower back then, doing what was ordered of him so he'd fit in.'

Tess glanced at Pinky, but for once he didn't return her scrutiny with a wide smile. His thoughts were locked on something that had happened decades ago. His ethnicity, let alone his sexual confusion, would have made him a target of the kind of people Zeke Menon ran with back then. She'd learned how Po and Pinky grew to be firm friends after they had stood together against the animals at the Farm.

'You said he's grown big,' Po said.

Pinky nodded. 'Too big for his boots.'

They weren't talking about his physical size per se, but about his attitude. Zeke had apparently grown a pair of *cojones* since last they'd had any interaction with him.

'Did he recognize you, Pinky?'

'If he did, he didn't show it. Too busy being a racist cracker, him.' Pinky shrugged. 'Zeke Menon doesn't sweat me, Nicolas. It's what he has to do with Emilia's disappearance that's more worrying.'

'F'sure.' After a final glance up at his sister's deserted home, Po indicated they get back in the van. 'Let's get outta here. I want to contact the a-hole and ask him why, but not while we're out in the open like this.'

'Zeke doesn't know where Emilia is,' Tess said after they'd clambered back into the van, and Pinky had got it rolling. 'Involving him directly is only going to slow down our search for her.'

Po's head rocked slightly on his neck. 'Like I said: if she's running from him, he needs stopping. You're the detective, Tess.'

He meant her skills were best served in locating his missing sister, while his could be put to a different use. He told her the names of the old school friends Emilia was supposed to be closest to, and Tess scribbled them in a notebook she took from her purse. 'I'll get on it as soon as I'm online,' she promised. 'But if you think I'm staying cooped up in a hotel room while

you two go running around town like a pair of gun-toting
vigilantes, think again.'

The men shared a conspiratorial glimpse, but she didn't miss
it. How could she when she was wedged between two testosterone-
laden bookends? 'I mean it, guys, you aren't going off on a
personal vendetta and leaving me to pick up the pieces.'

'Things might turn nasty,' Po warned.

'Since when has that ever stopped me?'

She wasn't bragging. The three of them each owed the others
their lives, and Tess had proven she was no slouch when the
proverbial shit hit the fan. But she'd prefer if they could get
resolution in the case without resorting to violence. Engaging
in a battle with Zeke Menon would achieve as little to help
finding Emilia as confronting the Chatards. Sadly, she suspected
that both were on the cards though. She'd known that coming
to Louisiana again, particularly to this locality, would guarantee
confrontation, but she hadn't expected the odds to be stacked
against them so rapidly. Po had promised to find Emilia. It
wasn't a promise he'd made only to Clara, but to himself. And
by virtue, by accompanying him, both Pinky and especially
Tess had made a similar promise. Perhaps knowing why Zeke
was looking for Emilia might explain why she was missing,
and it could lead them to her quicker. 'All I'm saying,' Tess
added, 'is I'll do what I can, when I can to help locate her, but
you aren't leaving me behind. No sneaking off on me when my
back is turned.'

'Wouldn't think of it, pretty Tess.' Now Pinky smiled at her,
but his gaze went back to the road when he caught a brief frown
from Po.

Earlier, they'd booked rooms at a Best Western near Bayou
Teche, only a short journey from the hospital. Pinky drove there
without any bidding. They all went into the double reserved for
Tess and Po, before Pinky nipped out on an errand to fetch
some food and drinks. Tess hit the bathroom and when she
came out Po was peering from the front window across the
parking lot to where the trees alongside the bayou were now a
uniform black as evening descended. She could sense his need
to get moving again, though there was no outward manifestation
of his anxiety.

'C'mon over here,' she said, an invitation as opposed to an instruction. He walked over and peered down at her. Tess laid her head against his chest and wrapped her arms around his lower back. She shouldn't forget that Po had received some shocking news in the last couple of days, and that his emotions would be all over the place. She hugged him, and after a moment he hugged her in return. 'We'll find her,' she said.

'I know.'

She patted him on his backside, and turned for where she'd laid her laptop on the bed. 'Let's get started, then.'

FIFTEEN

There were basics to be covered in any investigation prior to moving on to exotic theories and extrapolation. Searching Emilia's apartment had turned up no obvious clues that would lead them directly to her location, but it had hinted at her lifestyle and that she was probably sharing it with another. A top-to-bottom fingertip search in all the usual places underwear drawers, under the cushions of the settee/bed, in closets, and in the pockets of clothing, even in the icebox and the washer/dryer where some people hid their most important possessions, might have turned up more, but trashing the place had obliterated any opportunity of putting together a better timeline than that she'd been gone for less than a week.

Emilia didn't appear to have a full-time job. When she hadn't shown up at her workplace questions would have been asked and her disappearance brought to the attention of local law-enforcement. Clara, though concerned about her daughter's disappearing trick, wasn't overly concerned – yet – so Emilia was probably the free spirit that Clara had claimed, and her bout of non-communication with her family probably wasn't out of the norm. Tess wondered if the Chatards were seeking their wayward kin, because she hadn't confirmed it with Po. But Emilia was being sought, for reasons as yet unknown, by Zeke Menon.

Approaching the Chatards directly was out of the question, and Tess hadn't yet located Emilia's friends, so she moved on to other methods of tracking her. Because she subcontracted to Emma Clancy's firm, who worked hand-in-hand with the District Attorney's Office in Portland, Maine, she had access to various web resources unavailable to others in her line of work. She set searches in motion to alert her if Emilia's name cropped up in any police reports or communications, and also set a watch alert on her credit-card and bank-account usage. She identified Emilia's cellphone number and set up an alert on it too, but only after the GPS tracking system came back as a dead end. Perhaps Emilia had changed phones, or switched hers off. Nevertheless, initiating an alert on a missing girl's phone had recently led Tess and her friends to the lair of the brute that had snatched her and various other women, so she saw the value in allowing the program to run. Hopefully Emilia would deem it safe to use her phone soon, switch it on and they'd get an exact location.

After that Tess turned to less conventional methods, and hacked into Emilia's Facebook, Twitter, Snapchat, and Instagram accounts. Emilia hadn't been active on any of them in five days. But again Tess set up alerts to inform her of any new status updates. Then she began delving deeper. She concentrated on Facebook, and soon found photographs of Emilia and a young man referred to as 'Jace'. It was the work of minutes to cross-reference Jace with Emilia's friends and find that a number were mutual friends with a guy called Jason Henry Lombard. A quick check on his profile picture confirmed Jace and Lombard were one and the same. She didn't know how she felt when she checked Lombard's Facebook account and found that it too had been inert since the same day Emilia cut all communication.

'They've run off together?' Po asked.

'It's a fair assumption,' Tess replied, without lifting her head from her computer.

Po leaned in and gazed at the picture of Jason Lombard. 'Looks like a creep,' he said, but it was with the judgement of a disapproving older sibling looking out for his sister. 'What's he into?'

Tess checked his feed. Lombard was your typical young man, she supposed. His posts reflected an unhealthy sexual fixation on large-breasted blondes, drinking too much alcohol during binge sessions, and extolling his allegiance to the Church of Marijuana. 'I guess those were his joints in Emilia's ashtray.'

'It's a fair assumption,' Po echoed. 'Can you find his address?'

'Give me a moment.' She tapped and cross-referenced, and brought up a Google map pinpointing Jason Lombard's last known address.

'Soon as Pinky gets back we'll head on over there,' he announced.

'Except he isn't home.'

'No. But there might be someone there who knows where he is.'

Tess nodded agreement. Then she wondered about Pinky. He should have returned with their supplies by now. She'd heard nothing to indicate he'd entered his adjoining room, nor heard any familiar engine noise from his van. She looked up at Po, and his mouth formed a tight line.

'What are you guys up to?' she challenged.

He didn't insult her intelligence by countering her question. 'We need weapons. Pinky knows people.'

'Jesus Christ! I should've known.' She shook her head. 'Are you determined to turn this into an all-out war?'

'It's about resolution, Tess. I thought you understood that.'

'Resolution doesn't mean killing anyone.'

'That's not my intention. But I'm not going to stand around and let anyone kill me either. And then there's you to consider. You demanded you come with us; I'm not going to let anyone hurt you either.'

'Don't use me as an excuse for a fight, not when it's a fight you're pushing for.'

'I'm looking for my sister. Her *other* brothers might not want me looking for her.'

'And you think their hatred of you will be more important to them than finding their sister?'

Po shrugged marginally. 'I asked Clara if they were looking for Emilia, she said beyond calling her, no.'

'Are they even aware the girl's missing?'

'Clara said yes, but they aren't actively looking. Emilia cut ties with her siblings a couple of years ago. They aren't the closest of families. Darius apparently tried to get in touch with Emilia when Clara took ill, but as far as she's concerned he hasn't done much to find her since. I get the impression that Darius isn't close to Emilia, I don't think he's too close to Clara these days either.' He didn't gloat with his announcement. 'When Clara contacted Pinky, to summon me here, it wasn't with any of the Chatards' knowledge. Clara hoped to keep things that way, but if we're in town asking around about the girl, word will soon filter back. Don't forget, the Chatards have allies in

New Iberia, and plenty buttheads keen to claim the bounty they placed on my head.'

'What about this Zeke Menon character? Is he allied to the Chatards in some way?'

'Only if they're aware she's missing and they asked him to find Emilia, but I doubt it.' He thought hard, and his turquoise eyes grew as hard as flint. 'I should call him and have done; find out why he's looking for her. But you're right, maybe encouraging a fight isn't my best ever plan.' He nodded at the screen. 'Let's check out this Jace dude first, then if he proves a dead end . . . well, we'll have to start shaking a few branches and see what falls outta the ugly tree.'

Pinky returned minutes later. He entered the room, his face instantly averting from Tess's when he spotted her glaring at him. 'Uh, so you figured I was up to no good, you? I'm sorry, pretty Tess, I don't enjoy lying to you.'

Tess snorted, but she had no real scorn for Pinky, not when he and Po were just doing what came naturally to them. 'I don't care about the weapons, Pinky, where's my food? I'm starving and you're hogging all the good stuff.'

He handed over a grocery bag bulging with food and drinks, but it was the holdall slung over one shoulder that held Po's interest.

'Your friend came through?'

Pinky's grin flickered to life as Tess delved in the bag and pulled out burgers wrapped in greasy paper. She looked happy now. He winked at Po. 'Let me show you the delights in my sack. You'll swear I'm Jolly Saint Nick, me.'

SIXTEEN

There were things you didn't do when you wanted to disappear, and in the modern era Emilia believed that the paramount rule was to avoid leaving a digital trail. It was difficult for a young woman who'd grown up in an age where a cellphone was an almost symbiotic attachment, and where most of her socializing was done online, and she was suffering mild withdrawal symptoms having not only switched off her phone, but later disassembled it and scattered the parts in various trash bins. She'd taken the SIM card out of her iPad too, though she'd kept the tablet itself. She avoided using ATMs, though she must do something to replenish her dwindling finances soon because the little money Rachel had spared wouldn't stretch much further. The cold snap was killing her: the majority of cash had gone to renting a room. She'd made do with an ask-no-questions dive, where the desk clerk had more interest in her breasts than in the ID she'd flashed or the fake name she'd entered in the register. She'd paid cash in advance for one week. Now, as she stared around the stinking hovel she doubted she'd last that long before she had to flee simply to catch a breath of fresh air.

Her room was the last on the uppermost story of a duplex apartment/hotel complex on the outskirts of a seedy neighbourhood of 'Upper' Lafayette. Outside there was a balcony-style walkway, with corroded iron railings in dire need of maintenance, from which she'd learned a suicide had recently hung themselves. It was that kind of hotel. She shared the complex with crackheads and five-dollar whores. Not that she was being judgmental: scornfully, she asked herself if she were any better than her neighbours, when she had taken drugs, and might even be forced to turn tricks to pay her way. She was cold, hungry, afraid, and thoroughly miserable.

As she lay on the thin, lumpy mattress of a bed she hadn't yet slept a full night in, she went over the events that had brought her there. Tears flowed down her cheeks as she thought about Jason. Not because she had any longing for him, but because she'd allowed him to influence the worst decision of her life. It had been pure chance that they'd travelled out to the Thibodaux brothers' place, on the promise of scoring some quality weed, when they did. She'd tried to convince Jace that she was happy with a few puffs of a joint from his regular dealer, but he wanted to impress her by flaunting his underworld connections. Jace wasn't connected; he was a joke playing at being the big man. He was good-looking, decent in the sack, but there his attractive qualities ended, and no amount of high-quality dope would have elevated him in her affections. Hell, if the truth was told, she didn't even enjoy smoking weed, she only did it to fit in with the crowd she'd fallen into, many of whom she didn't care for either. If she hadn't allowed Jace to talk her into taking the drive out into the boonies, throwing them into the midst of a gangland hit, dangerous people wouldn't now be hunting her. It was bad timing and worse luck. She was a victim of circumstance, that was all, and one she should try to change for the better.

So what was her best state of play?

She should contact Zeke Menon and appeal to what little good sense he might possess. If she convinced him that she could be trusted to stay quiet about what she had witnessed – which didn't amount to much, she'd assure him – then would he allow her to return home unmolested? No. He would not. She didn't know Zeke well, but had heard enough stories around town, and knew he was a violent and unpredictable man. How he wasn't permanently behind bars astounded her, but it didn't take too much figuring out: his victims' fear of retribution against their loved ones.

Her brothers were not the kind to be intimidated, and if the shoe were on the other foot she knew they'd take the fight back to Zeke. But they would die or go to jail, and she didn't want that. She had never been particularly close to either of her brothers, both of whom were a generation older than her, and her dad had proven an uncaring, aloof man who had never shown her any love, but she wished no harm would come to them. And then there was her mom. Clara had enough on her plate with her fading health and the last Emilia wanted was to bring her any more stress. She had watched her mother fading in the last few months, and trouble with the Menons might just be the last straw.

She wondered how her mother was faring now. Was she worried about Emilia's sudden disappearance, or had she even noticed she'd gone? Sadly, because it would mean spending more time around her father, Emilia had been neglectful of her mother's care so had rarely visited or made contact since leaving home. The realization shamed her. Brought forth fresh tears, these hotter and fed by different emotions than before.

She thought long and hard about calling her mom, but only to tell her that she was going to be out of town for a few days and not to worry, and with the caveat that she told nobody they'd spoken. She kept putting the call off. But finally, she reached for her cellphone. And recalled that it was in several composite parts spread around town.

Outside her room a woman shrieked.

Emilia bolted upright. Had Zeke found her, and murdered a witness to his impending crime?

Further down the walkway another woman laughed. And then the first's scream turned into a sputter of laughter and bawdy, but friendly insults. Together the two women retreated, still laughing in the exaggerated way of drunken people. Emilia relaxed marginally, but she still slipped from the bed and went tentatively to her window. She teased aside curtains the colour of cow dung and peeked through the narrow gap. She couldn't see the women but could hear them descending the rickety stairs at the far end of the walkway, their high heels clacking on the metal. She guessed they were heading out to their favourite street corners to ply their trade to passing motorists.

Nearby a TV roared at full volume, machineguns and explosions competing. Some guys argued angrily beyond the parking lot. Traffic groaned by on the congested highway behind the motel. Next door, she heard voices and the clatter of an item thrown haphazardly into the kitchenette sink. One of the room's inhabitants swore at the other and seconds later a door slammed below her. The neighbourhood was taking on a different atmosphere as night descended: and it had been bad enough in daylight.

Emilia retreated from the window. She took another look around at the shabby carpet, the stained bedclothes, and the doors hanging off the sunken cupboards in her kitchenette. There was a small TV, an ancient thing formed of cream-colored plastic with ungainly black knobs and dials. The curtains were horrible and stank of cigarette smoke. She couldn't abide to be in the place any longer.

She'd fetched little by way of belongings with her. She had the one set of clothes she stood up in, and her purse, into which she'd shoved her tablet. She was of a mind to request a refund from the desk clerk, but knew she would be on the losing side of the argument. Besides, she had no intention of bringing notice to her. If she asked for her rent back, the man's eyes would be forced from her chest to meet her gaze. It wasn't a risk she was about to take, despite being down to her last few dollars.

She pulled the door shut behind her, then paused, checking along the walkway for any familiar faces. A man squatted in an open doorway, a stringy guy with greasy, unkempt hair lying on the shoulders of a dingy grey undershirt, and denims with holes at the knees. His feet were bare, filthy, and his toenails long and yellow. He didn't hide the fact he was shooting heroin into his arm as she edged past him. She kept to the railing, fearful that he might try to snag her ankle and drag her back inside his reeking hovel with him, but the creaking metal railings warned her not to place too much security in them. She picked up speed and made it to the steps down. She didn't look back.

As she fled from her hotel her heart rate was elevated. She didn't initially feel the cold, but once she was out on the sidewalk adjacent to the highway the breeze cut through her and she began shivering uncontrollably. She had slung her purse over one shoulder, but now hooked it against her stomach, held tightly against her with her crossed arms. Days earlier she'd dressed for a date with her boyfriend, and when in the warmth of Jason's truck, her skimpy attire versus the cold snap that had descended over Louisiana hadn't been a concern. Now she was underdressed, dirty from hiding in the swamp, and smelling of the room she'd vacated. There was just one benefit: she blended with the cheapest of cheap crack-whores lining the highway.

She even earned herself a honk or two of a horn, as passing curb-crawlers slowed to check out her butt and the tautness of her lithe calf muscles. She thought that if she could lower herself to their level, then she might be able to earn a living after all. She angrily shook off the thought: it wasn't even funny making jokes like that.

She hadn't made many forays into the local neighbourhood. She'd thought her own locale back in New Iberia was a bit on the rough side, but it was a peaceful haven compared to this one. She felt nervous simply walking alone at night, and the sooner she could get somewhere with more lighting and people with a full set of teeth the better. She was seeking an internet café, or maybe a public bar where she might find a payphone she could use. But there wasn't an establishment she felt comfortable entering: not without an armed guard.

She cut off the main highway and found a commercial strip. None of the dingy storefronts advertised what she was seeking, so she pushed on. A scruffy terrier dog, its rump enflamed and scabrous, watched her walk by, waited until she was past and then began yapping: the dog sounded insulted that she hadn't paused to pet it. She pitied the poor thing, but not enough to lay a hand on its mangy hide. She blew it a well-meaning kiss instead, and the dog cocked its head to one side, watching her now in silence. Some of the other pedestrians cast her similarly inquisitive glances. She knew why. She was a mess, but more so she was jittery with nerves. Out in the open like this, she half expected the Menons to drive by, bring their pickup to a squealing halt to grab her and bundle her inside. Her fear was exaggerated, but only until someone recognized her, and there was still the faint possibility of that happening.

When she had walked away from Rachel's house she'd had a plan to throw off any pursuit. She'd headed towards the bus station and bought a ticket to New Orleans. But only a couple of miles out of town she'd asked the driver to stop the bus, got off, took a cab back into Lafayette and then walked across town to the grim neighbourhood where she'd laid low the past few days. Anyone asking Rachel about her might trace her to the bus station, but from there they'd expect her to have travelled to New Orleans. She thought she was being clever, but now she realized she would have been better staying on that damn bus. Hiding in her own stomping ground probably wasn't the best idea she'd ever had, even if at the time it had felt like solid logic. What did she know about disappearing anyway? Everything she knew came from mystery books and TV programs. She should know from them that the one on the run was always found by her pursuers.

With unlimited funds, she could disappear permanently. But her available cash was meagre and growing shorter by the day. She couldn't survive out here alone like this. It was time to adapt her plan with that in mind.

The first bar she tried had a phone, but it required a credit card. She left the bar, and found another, but there was no working phone. Thankfully she found one in a convenience store at the next strip mall. She scratched around for quarters and dollar bills, and readied them: it was so long ago that she'd used a public telephone that it took her a few awkward seconds to figure it out.

She didn't think Zeke Menon had the ability to bug her family home, so felt safe enough ringing the house. She expected her mom to answer, it was usually a task assigned to her, but the surly grunt was her father.

'Papa?' She was barely discernible, a faint squeak.

'Is dat you, girl?' Darius Chatard's voice was loud and husky, testament of a fifty-a-day smoking habit he'd followed for as long as Emilia could remember. His Acadian roots also heavily afflicted his accent.

'Yes, it's me.' By contrast Emilia thought her own voice was higher-pitched than usual, the voice of a frightened little girl.

'Where d' goddamn hell you been?' Darius demanded, as if scolding her for being late home after curfew. She wasn't a teenager any more, and didn't have to answer to him, not normally. This time however she knew she owed him an explanation.

'Papa, I had to go away for a few days, you see . . .' She didn't know what further to add and the words stuck in her throat.

'Goddamnit, we been lookin' all over for you. Your brothers have been goin' mad, running all over town. You know how much trouble you causing us, girl?'

'I'm sorry, Papa, but I . . . I had no choice.'

'You had no choice? You had every damn choice! Your mama
. . . she needs you, and you're off on some goddamn bender
with that asshole junkie Jason Lombard. When I see him, you'd
better tell him, I'm gonna bust him upside his damn head for
turning you astray. You been on dem drugs wid him again, girl?'
As his anger grew, Darius's Acadian accent thickened. Emilia
knew that before long he'd be cursing her in French.

Instead of answering his accusation, she changed the subject.
'How is my mama? You said she needs me, Papa. Is she OK?'

Darius exhaled into the mouthpiece. 'Your mama is far from
OK, girl. You needs to git your skinny butt back here right now.'

'I . . . I can't come home, Papa. Not yet.'

'What's that you say? Can't come home? Now you listen to
me, and none o' your smart lip. Remember, you're not too old
to take a whupping, girl. Git yourself home right now afore I
come drag you back by your hair!'

'Papa, it's not that I don't want to . . .'

'Is it him? Is Jason stopping you? Put dat junkie fuck on d'
phone right now.'

'It isn't Jason.'

'Den it's just you being defiant. Home, girl. Now. Don't make
me tell you agin.'

'Papa, I want to come home. I really do.' Emilia couldn't
see clearly for tears. There was nothing more she wanted than
to go home, even if it was a place she'd felt unwelcome in
recent years. 'But I can't. Not yet. Please, Papa, trust me. I'd
only bring trouble with me.'

'Trouble? You think you know trouble. Continue defying me
and you'll see what trouble looks, and feels, like.'

'Papa, please stop. I know you're angry, worried, but please
listen to me. I can't come home, and you're going to have to
accept that for now. What about Mama? You said she's far from
OK? What do you mean?'

'Her heart give out.'

'What? Is she . . .'

'She's alive. Made it through, but she's failing, girl. So you
gotta git your ass back here now, before you too late to say yo
goodbyes.' Darius calmed a little. He had mellowed with age,

and the perpetual anger he'd once exhibited couldn't be sustained for long these days. His anger at Emilia, she realized, was through concern for his wife. *Her mom was dying.*

'I'm coming now, Papa.'

'There now, dat wasn't so difficult after all. What is dis trouble you wus talking about?'

'I can't come to the house,' Emilia said. 'Papa, where is my mama?'

'Your mama ain't here, any rate. She down d' hospital.'

Emilia clarified with him that Clara was at the Iberia General Hospital and Medical Center.

'Where else she be at, girl? Now where you? I'll have the boys come get you.'

'No, don't send them. I'll make my own way there. Papa . . . will you be at the hospital?'

'You know I got no truck wid dem places.'

Emilia didn't answer; she hung up before her money ran out.

SEVENTEEN

As he replaced the handset on his phone, the older man glimpsed up at his visitors and gave an almost imperceptible shrug of his wide shoulders. 'Kids, huh?' he growled. 'D' older they git, de more trouble dey bring ya.'

'Not a problem I've got,' said Zeke Menon. Then with an ugly twist of his mouth. 'None that I'll own up to anyways. I could have dozens of little bastards out there someplace, but they mean nothin' to me.'

Darius Chatard looked over at the hulking figure of Cleary Menon standing in one corner of his family room. 'Looks as if you have your hands full lookin' after that'n over there. Isn't he right in d' skull?'

Cleary's head came up and he stared balefully at Darius. Zeke adjusted the peak of his cap. He didn't give a shit if Cleary ripped the old man's head off his shoulders, but only after he'd finalized their business. 'Cleary's his own man, I assure you, an' doesn't need me to hold his hand,' he said and he heard a growl of agreement from his brother.

Darius Chatard pushed out of the chair he'd taken to answer the phone. He grunted, and both knees popped before he'd righted himself. He was ageing, fast approaching seventy years old, but was still a commanding figure. His large head was stacked on top of broad shoulders, and he had a barrel chest, only slightly rounder than his big belly. He wore a thick, drooping moustache, white as snow that seemed to glow against his weathered, sun-darkened skin. His legs were bowed slightly as he walked. 'Let's go out on the deck,' he announced. 'I got beer in the cooler, and I need a smoke.'

Zeke took a lingering glance at the phone. He wondered if he could check the last caller number, and trace back Emilia to her current location, without raising her father's suspicions about his motive. But why risk it? From what he'd overheard, Emilia was en route to her mother's bedside, and Zeke need only return to the hospital and wait for her. But he counted himself a resourceful man, who could benefit in more ways than one. He wanted to kill Nicolas Villere, but why not be paid for his trouble? It was what was called a win-win. 'C'mon, Cleary,' he said, and followed Darius.

To the immediate south of New Iberia, the Chatard property sat alongside one of many drainage canals – known locally as coulees – that took standing water away from town to spill into Vermilion Bay. Here the coulee was sluggish, and was almost obscured beneath a blanket of lily pads and detritus fallen from the overhanging boughs of trees. It smelled faintly of rotting vegetation. Not far away was the Port of Iberia, set on a network of waterways into which the coulee spilled. Zeke could hear the faint sounds of commerce, and smell the fumes from the industrial complexes. The unpleasant aromas, the faint yet constant din could spoil the thought of living there for some people. Nevertheless, the house and the plot it stood upon were picturesque. Surrounded on its borders by tall trees, there was no visual hint that it stood so close to the ugly industrial and shipping hub. Zeke envied Darius's home and aspired to own something similar. No, scratch that, something grander. Being a resourceful man, he decided that if a petty criminal of Darius Chatard's calibre could attain property like this, then he should have himself a Southern mansion in no time. After years of coasting along – towing his brother along with him – he thought it high time to begin climbing. He could do that via the clever manipulation of men who thought of him as a lowly hireling, someone to get his hands dirty on their behalf. Seemingly doing their bidding, they would never guess he was actually building his own legend, until he surpassed theirs. At which point there'd be no more taking instruction from old has-beens like Darius Chatard, and punks of Al Keane's ilk would bow and scrape to please him. Nathaniel Corbin would take some ousting, but nothing was impossible if you put your mind to the task, and never took a backwards step.

Bugs danced in the bright light that spilled beyond the deck and illuminated the trees on the opposite side of the coulee. There were chairs on the raised deck but nobody took one.

Darius fished cans of Budweiser from a plastic cooler box. Zeke accepted one and popped the tab.

'Beer,' said Cleary. The twist of his mouth said enough about his distaste for alcohol for Darius to dump the third tin back in the ice.

'Suit yoursel',' he said, and took a seat on the railing surrounding his deck. Cleary peered at him with small, piggy eyes, before turning away and staring out at the middle distance. Darius glanced at Zeke, who merely tilted his head in a 'beats me' gesture.

'Prefers soda?' Darius was deliberately snarky.

'As a matter of fact, he does.'

'I ain't got none.'

'Don't matter.' Zeke knew from the intensity of Cleary's stance that his attention had pinpointed on something in the nearby illuminated trees. Zeke took a quick squint, caught a flutter of brightly coloured plumage, and knew what Cleary was fascinated by. 'Can we get back to why I'm here?'

'That's the thing,' said Darius, as he wiped froth from his drooping white moustache, 'you just said you wus a man who could give me what I want. You a heart surgeon, bra?'

Zeke smiled at the sarcasm. 'In a way I am. I can cut the heart outta somebody and serve it to you on a plate.'

Darius eyed him. 'I've heard your name before. And his.' He nodded at Cleary, whose huge form was now bent at the waist as he stared intently across the coulee. Birds flitted in and out of the foliage. 'You're Isaac Menon's boys, right? I knew your daddy, once beat him senseless in a fistfight out back of Delancey's bar.'

A grunt of mirth broke from Zeke. 'Knowing my dad, he probably deserved it. There was a time or two when I'd have liked to beat him senseless too. He died before I got the chance.'

Darius gave him a sour look, then chugged down half the can of beer. 'You don't respect your old man?'

'Was he the type to deserve respect?'

'Fair point.' The beer was finished in another long swallow and Darius crushed the flimsy aluminium can in his fist. As he lit up a cigarette, he ambled across the deck and pulled out the Budweiser Cleary had declined. Popped the tab. He aimed the frothing can at Cleary. 'That why you're stuck with him? Nobody left at home to look after him?'

'Don't let Cleary deceive you. He's no dummy. Just has his own ways. In fact, if you know our names, I'm betting you've already heard that.'

'Heard that he's put the fear of God into some folks. By the looks of him, I can see why.' His thick Cajun accent was smoothing out now that he had calmed down. 'But I'm betting you're the one people should be warier of.'

'I'm far too modest to agree.' Zeke spat over the railing. 'But I can assure you that I don't make promises lightly. When I say I can deliver your enemy to you, I'm not blowing smoke up your ass.'

'I've plenty can do that for me. I've two boys of my own I can send. Plenty others I can call who'll kill Villere . . . without hiking up the bounty. What makes hiring you better value for my money?'

'You already lost two boys 'cause of Villere.' Zeke held up a hand to forestall the spark of anger that jumped over the old man's face. 'Hold on, Darius. What I mean is there's no need to risk another. Even if your sons finish him, they're the first the cops will come looking for. You want them behind bars for the rest of their lives? You can keep them outta this, let me do the job, and your family stays clean, untouchable.'

'You say Villere is in town? How's it you know this, and yet nobody else does? I've plenty people looking out for the bastard, but I've never heard as much as a rumour about him being here.'

'I saw him. Stood near enough as close to him as I'm standing to you now.'

'And you're positive it was him?'

'Would I be here otherwise?'

'I hear you bin working for Al Keane. What's his interest in this?'

'Keane has no idea who Villere is, or that I'm here. I told you Cleary has his own ways, well, so do I. I do some work for Keane, but I ain't on his leash.'

'Where is Villere?'

Zeke was about to mention coming across him at the hospital, but caution pinged inside him. Darius might wonder what the hell he'd been doing at Clara's room. He considered lying, spinning a line about visiting a friend and coming across Villere by chance. But lies were easily discredited: Zeke wasn't the type to visit sick friends. 'Credit me with some intelligence, please. If I tell you, you'll send over some of your punk-ass hired guns to do the job for less. You'll save yourself some cash, but only at the expense of their failure. Pay me what I'm asking; Villere will die. You can take that to the bank.'

'If he's around I guess I'll hear about it soon.' The back of Darius's thick wrist batted froth from his moustache. 'I'll pay you what you ask, Zeke. But I can't offer exclusivity. Somebody else claims the bounty afore you, it's your own fault.'

'That's why I want half up front.'

'You ain't gettin' it.'

'You gotta give me something for my time.'

'I am. It's called motivation. Go fetch me Nicolas Villere's head, and you git paid yer askin' price.' Darius grunted in sour humor, took a long drag on his cigarette, then allowed the smoke to leak from the corners of his mouth. He flicked away the burning stub. 'I can tell you're pissed. I don't care. You want paid, you get paid on delivery. You're worried I won't come through? Ask anybody. My word's good. Can you say the same for yours?'

Zeke held out his hand.

Darius put aside his beer can. He spat in his palm, and held out his.

EIGHTEEN

They came across the young man sitting out on his front step, smoking what appeared to be a cheap brand of cigarettes he didn't appear particularly fond of. Po made the introductions, while Tess stood slightly behind him. Pinky stayed in the van. Po asked about Jason Lombard. His roommate had missed Jason, but only because the spotty-faced guy was running short on weed and was pissed by his buddy's no-show. He was annoyed more than concerned for Jason's welfare, and to date hadn't raised an alarm. Apparently he wasn't his buddy's keeper: Jace came and went when he chose, as did his pal, and it wasn't unusual to go for a week or two without laying eyes on each other.

'So how do you know he hasn't been home lately?' Po asked.

'Food's still in the pantry, the place is too tidy, and . . . uh, well, I just know.' He was possibly about to add that their stash of weed hadn't been replenished, but once he'd laid eyes on Tess he'd assumed that mentioning his drug habit wasn't a great idea. It was understandable, because Tess still exuded 'cop' even after more than two years back on Civvie Street.

'So he only uses this place as a drop in?' Tess asked the young man. He had chosen not to let them inside the house, and had remained seated on the top step, blocking the open front door.

'We share the bills. Occasionally chill together, y'know. But we aren't really friends. I don't know what he gets up to and don't ask.'

'Does he ever bring any friends back with him?' Po asked.

The young man shrugged. 'Like I said . . .'

'Girls specifically,' Tess added.

'He scores now and again, yeah. We both do. We're young guys, y'know?'

Tess raised her eyebrows a fraction.

'Do you know Emilia Chatard?'

He rolled his head in thought. Then nodded sanguinely. 'Think so.'

'Has Emilia been here?'

'Not sure. I know Emilia from around, y'know? Think I've seen Jace with her, but can't say as she's been here. Not while I've been home.'

'What does Jason drive?' Po asked.

'He has a Ford truck. Black. Not new. Why d'you ask?'

Po didn't answer. He didn't push for a licence number, because Tess could easily find the details they needed. He shelved the information for later. 'Does Jason have any family in town?'

The young man shrugged. 'Like I said, I ain't his keeper.'

'Does he work?' Po said.

The young man's expression asked if Po was joking.

'So how does he pay his share of the bills?'

'Inheritance. He doesn't have to work. Had rich grandparents, I heard.'

'Where does he hang out?' Po went on.

'Around. Y'know?'

Tess took out a business card and handed it to the young man. 'If you hear from Jason in the next few days, can you let me know?'

He studied her card, and then looked up at her.

'You're a private investigator? All the way from Maine?' He frowned at the questions suddenly tumbling through his mind.

'Jason isn't in trouble,' she assured him. 'We're looking for his girlfriend, Emilia Chatard. She isn't in any trouble either, it's a private matter.'

He put the card in his trouser pocket. Tess doubted he'd find a need to take it out again soon, but nonetheless he had her number if Jason did show up.

Po wasn't finished.

'Who is Jason's dealer?'

Again the youth's eyes flickered on Tess.

'I don't give a damn if you smoke weed,' she assured him. 'We're only interested in locating Emilia. Perhaps Jason's dealer knows where we can find them.'

'He usually buys roun' town, but lately he got in with the Thibodauxs.'

'Who are they?'

'Just a couple of guys. They ain't heavy, if that's what you're worried about. Just some good ol' boys who got a line on some headies.'

Po stared at the guy. Waited. Finally the guy got the message. 'Wait on, I'll see if I can find where they're at.' He left them standing on his stoop and retreated indoors. Tess heard the murmur of a one-sided conversation on a cellphone, and then the youth came back out. He leaned in the doorframe this time, one hand on the door handle, hinting that his time was precious and they'd taken up more of it than they were welcome to. 'Hal and Jamie have a camp out near Bayou Chene, off Bayou Benoit Levee Road. I'd draw you a map, but that's all I got.'

Po nodded. He knew the area.

Tess said, 'Give us a call if you hear from Jason, OK?'

The guy closed the door without answering.

'Waste of time?' Tess wondered.

'Not completely,' Po said as they returned to the van. 'We've confirmed that Jason's missing too. He's probably with Emilia. We're not just looking for one missing person but two. Doubles our chances of finding them.'

'I'm not sure I agree with your logic, Po,' Tess said, 'but at least we've another lead to follow.'

'The Thibodauxs? It's why I pressed for a name. Even if Jason and Emilia are lying low for some reason, I'm betting Jace still keeps in touch with his dealers.'

'You're probably right. But the Thibodauxs aren't our priority.' They had Emilia's close circle of friends to speak with first, the young women whose names they'd gotten from the punks staking out Emilia's apartment: Jenna Cornell, Tracey Redding, and Rachel Paterno.

'I'm still tempted to go direct to Zeke Menon and beat some answers outta him.'

Tess exhaled. They'd gone over this more than once already. Zeke Menon didn't know where Emilia was. He might give up why he was interested in finding her, but more so she believed he'd cause a delay they couldn't afford.

'We don't have to waste time on house calls,' she said. 'I found Cornell's phone number. I'll speak with her, and take things from there. We should kill two birds with one stone, and go see these Thibodauxs before it gets too late.'

'Bayou Chene ain't a duck pond,' he pointed out. 'There's a lot of swampland between the levee road and the Atchafalaya River where the Thibodauxs might be. But I'll get Pinky on it.'

Pinky was in earshot. 'What do you need, Nicolas?'

They waited until they were back in the van before Po explained who they were looking for.

'OK, I have a few contacts roun' here, me. Let's get somewhere, and I'll start axing and see if we can pin those swamp rats down.'

He drove them to a diner he knew. On the way, Tess rang Jenna Cornell, and was rewarded when the young woman answered on the second ring. She explained who she was, and told Jenna she was ringing on behalf of Clara Chatard who was ill and needed her daughter at her bedside.

Jenna was concerned, but of little help.

She had the cellphone number for Emilia that Tess had already identified. The one that remained resolutely switched off.

'I haven't seen or heard from Emilia in weeks,' Jenna said. 'We don't exactly hang out like in the old days. I'm in a stable relationship, so don't get to run around with my girlfriends the way I once did.'

'I understand, Jenna. I'm wondering if you'd help me to contact some of your other friends. Maybe they've been in touch with her. Tracey Redding and Rachel Paterno?'

'Boreas.'

'Sorry?'

'It's Rachel Boreas now. She married and moved up to Lafayette with her husband and kids.'

'Do you have telephone numbers for them?'

'Tracey no. We . . . uh, well we had a falling out. She unfriended me on Facebook, so I returned the favour, blocked her in other ways too . . . the bitch. But if you hang on I might still have a contact number for Rachel.'

Dutifully Tess waited while the young woman found what she was looking for. Jenna recited the number, and Tess wrote it in the condensation on the van's window with a fingertip. She asked Jenna if she would contact her if she heard from Emilia in the meantime, and Jenna agreed, noting that Tess's number was in her call list.

Tess rang Rachel Boreas. The phone rang out and went to her voicemail service. Tess left a message requesting that if Rachel had a way to contact Emilia, could she inform her that Clara was desperately ill in hospital. Tess left her number, and asked if Rachel would please let her know when she received her message.

Two names were ticked off her list for now, so she set about finding contact details for Tracey Redding, but by then Pinky was parking at the diner. It prized itself on its authentic Creole cuisine, and offered po'boy sandwiches and bowls of gumbo – not to mention something called bowfin caviar that Tess decided would ever remain a mystery to her – as specialties. They'd eaten earlier from the sack of takeout food Pinky had brought to their motel, but they all agreed a strong coffee apiece was in order. Tess assumed it was going to be a long, restless night.

NINETEEN

Parked in the empty lot of an engine-repair shop on East Main Street, Zeke had a view across the way towards the hospital. He had pulled into a slot opposite the hospital so he could keep an eye on most of the approach routes. There was a one-way system on the surrounding roads, but he was situated in view of the two main entrances to the hospital's grounds. Evening visiting hours was over, and traffic entering or leaving the hospital minimal, so he felt confident he'd spot Emilia when she arrived. Ideally he'd have hung around in the corridors nearest Clara Chatard's room, but he would draw too much attention now that most civilians had left for the night: plus there was the chance he might cross paths with Nicolas Villere or his queer pal, Leclerc, again and things would kick off. He wanted his showdown with Villere to happen on his terms and on a battlefield he could control. Besides, he couldn't snatch Emilia in the hospital, and it would be best to grab her before she got inside. He'd come prepared, swapping the pickup for a nondescript panel van with no identifying decal and bringing backup in the form of two other men on Al Keane's payroll, who were parked further along the road should Emilia make a run for it.

Cleary sat alongside him, but he wasn't much good when it came to an extra set of eyes: his were fixed on a weighty paperback novel, the tenth volume in a sprawling fantasy epic he'd been reading. Zeke envied his brother's ability to get lost in a book; he didn't have the patience and hadn't read anything without smutty pictures in years. That wasn't entirely true. Lately he'd kept an eye on the newspapers and news websites, interested in the investigations into various killings that had occurred in New Iberia Parish. He paid less notice to the main-stream news, preferring the hysterical reporting of some of the websites proclaiming that there was a supernatural element to the deaths. When some of the more sensational reports had suggested that a rougarou was responsible for the slaughter of various animals, and even for a number of missing persons, he could only smile knowingly and squint sideways at his shaggy-headed brother.

There were many variations of the rougarou legend in Cajun folklore, and the manners in which a human could transform into the beast were as diverse and fanciful as in any other culture's tales of the wolfman. The name was a derivation of the legend passed down through generations of French settlers, of the *loup-garou*. *Loup* translated to 'wolf', and *garou* was 'a man who transforms into an animal'. Yes, there were actually folks out there positive that a werewolf was stalking the swamplands, eating their livestock, and cannibalizing missing people. Zeke could forgive them their mistake, because Cleary could easily be misidentified as some sort of ravening half-man half-beast, especially when consumed by one of his psychotic rages. He'd heard tales of rougarou linked to various medical and mental conditions, including porphyria, hypertrichosis, and even schizophrenia, and had to admit that Cleary suffered symptoms associated with all of those. But most often the rougarou was associated with lycanthropy – in itself a dubious prognosis – where sufferers exhibited the characteristics of a wild animal, primarily in the belief that they transformed into a wolf under a full moon. Then again, he'd heard Cleary baying and howling after his kills, and the sound had sent shivers up his spine. Anyone else hearing them could very well believe it was the victorious howling of a beast.

He knew that Cleary was responsible for the animal slaughters, and of at least one of the missing people: an old man walking his dog. Cleary had killed the dog when it had growled at him, and then the old man when he'd tried to come to its rescue. There were others – Hal and Jamie Thibodaux, Jason Lombard, and a female animal-rights activist – who had also fallen victim. They were yet to be missed, so hadn't been associated with the rougarou legend, but that was only a matter of time. So too Emilia Chatard when Zeke finally got his own claws on her.

'It's too dark.'

Zeke allowed his attention to slip from the approaches to the hospital to peer across at Cleary.

'We'll still spot her when she arrives.'

'Too dark in here. I'm not done reading.' Cleary held up the novel for emphasis.

'I can't turn on the light or we'll draw attention.'

'I'm not done reading.'

Cleary's bearded chin jutted, and his bottom lip was drawn back over his lower teeth. Zeke could spot the signs.

'Why don't you climb in the back and use that penlight I got you?'

'No seats.'

'You've a perfectly good ass to sit on, haven't you?'

'Huh. Perfectly good.'

'Then climb on back there. I'll need you there to open the door for me soon.'

'You said that thirty-three minutes ago.'

Zeke didn't question the timing. It was as if Cleary had a clock counting down in his head, and another of his specific quirks was being on the button when it came to keeping time. He could be damn infuriating though: Zeke couldn't say he'd be only a minute, because Cleary held him to exact timings and grew antsy if Zeke wasn't punctual.

'I've no control over when she comes, Cleary,' he said, and knew he was wasting his breath. Truth was, having no idea where Emilia was when she phoned her dad, and with no clue whether she had transportation available, he couldn't guess how long it would take her to arrive. The one thing he believed was that after hearing about her mom, Emilia would make every effort to get to the hospital as quick as she could. But there was the possibility that they could be camped out on watch all night. 'I hope it's soon. Besides, you're reading aren't you? Enjoy your book while you get the chance.'

Appeased by Zeke's logic, Cleary hauled his bulk over the seat and into the rear of the van. The vehicle rocked on its springs before the huge man settled down. A small penlight that could be clipped to his book came on, but the light made only a faint glow in the rear. Nobody passing on the street would notice it.

Zeke's cellphone buzzed. He checked the incoming caller ID and answered.

'Whassup, Ty?'

'Truck driver just dropped a young girl at the side of the road,' announced Wayne Tyson, one of the guys assisting with the stakeout.

'Hooker?' Zeke asked.

'Could be. Great ass, nice face: I'd give her my hard-earned. She fits the description of Emilia Chatard you gave us.' Tyson shared a murmur of conversation with his pal, Jim Croft, before coming back on the phone to Zeke. 'She's just come off of Gonsoulin Street, heading your way. You got eyes on her yet, Zeke?'

From his position Zeke didn't have a clear view towards the cross-street Tyson had mentioned. If it was Emilia and she was heading in on foot from there, it was the perfect opportunity to grab her before she made it to the hospital. 'Mark your spot in your book, Cleary,' he commanded over the seat, even as he turned on the engine and the van began to crawl forward.

'You said soon,' Cleary said. 'This is soon.'

Zeke ignored him, craning forward instead so he could scan the darkness to his left before pulling the van fully onto the street. Once committed to driving out of the lot, he might have to keep moving if he didn't want to cause the woman any alarm.

Distantly a figure trotted across the road, and up onto the sidewalk adjacent to the hospital. If she made it onto Haik Memorial Drive, a turning circle at the front of the hospital, grabbing her without attracting attention might prove impossible. He had seconds to decide to move.

He eyed the approaching figure. Was it Emilia or not? It was cold out, and yet he spotted bare legs flashing as the woman hurried along the sidewalk. She had her arms crossed under her breasts, clutching a purse to her stomach, perhaps in an attempt to stave off the chill. Her dark hair swung back and forth across her features, but it didn't matter, because he'd already recognized her clothes. She hadn't changed since he'd watched her sprinting for the swamp.

'It's her,' he announced into his phone, and to Cleary. 'Get ready to move. Tyson, Croft, you know what to do?'

'On it,' Tyson announced, and the phone went dead.

Zeke hit the gas, but only with enough pressure to set the

van rolling out of the parking lot. To avoid instantly alarming Emilia, he flicked on the headlights: a van approaching in darkness would set her hackles rising. If she were spooked before he got close enough, she'd run, and he knew from experience how fleet-footed she was.

He kept the van rolling, approaching at a moderate speed. Tyson and Croft appeared from the gloom behind Emilia. They strode along the street, one to each opposite sidewalk, moving to cut her off if she did turn and run. Croft was on the other side from Emilia, and he began crossing the road, walking fast enough to alert the girl. His helpers were in perfect positions.

Zeke hit the gas and the van shot forward.

TWENTY

D riving direct, Emilia could usually accomplish the twenty-five-mile journey from Lafayette to New Iberia in thirty to forty-five minutes, but it was entirely different when relying on the kindness of others. After hearing the news of her mom, her first instinct was to begin a fast clip south, but there was no way she could walk home, not if time was as short as Darius had made clear. She'd thought of returning to Rachel Boreas and begging a ride from her, but it still meant a walk across town. She'd called Rachel from the convenience store payphone to ask if she'd pick her up but she wasn't home. Emilia left a brief message asking her to call back on the store's number, but after only a few minutes she gave up waiting, and, defeated, left the store and began walking towards a shopping mall alongside Evangeline Thruway, where she recalled there was a twenty-four-hour 'drive thru' and perhaps a kind hungry stranger to take her home.

She lucked out with the first half-dozen or so, locals who were not prepared to go an hour or more out of their way for her. Then there was one man, so overly keen she feared he'd drawn the wrong impression from her skimpy clothing and desperate look. She thanked him for his offer, then told him to fuck off when he tried to grab and load her inside his car. A truck driver came to her rescue.

'I'm heading down to Morgan City,' he told her. 'You're welcome to jump in with me if you like.'

Emilia told him she needed to get back to New Iberia, that her mother was in hospital. The driver was a good man: he even left the highway to take her nearer to the hospital. On the drive down from Lafayette, Emilia had been thankful of the blanket the driver offered her, but she left it, despite his protestations when he dropped her at the curb. She only need walk down Gonsoulin, and then the hospital was a stone's throw distant; she wouldn't freeze.

It was evening, and already dark. The sky was still heavy with clouds, but thankfully the rain was holding off. She walked quickly to fight off the chill, but also through urgency to get to her mother's side.

Her relationship with her family was complicated. The one with her mother was much simpler. Clara wasn't the most loving towards her, in fact she wasn't the type to display her emotions unless they were anger or spite, but she was still Emilia's mom. Their differences were usually childish, easily set aside by Emilia, and for all of their blistering rows over the years Emilia still loved her. Hearing that she might lose the one person in her family she held any genuine affection for had come as a great blow, and she'd travelled from Lafayette in a state of shock. What if she was already too late? She rushed towards the hospital grounds, her purse clutched tightly to her body, the soles of her borrowed sneakers slapping the sidewalk. At first she wasn't aware of the footfalls matching hers for pace, because she thought them echoes of her own hasty steps.

Ahead and to the right of her a van pulled out of a vacant lot. It turned towards her. She paid it no heed. She swung her head round for a glance at the figure following close on her heels. It was a youngish guy with a sculptured beard, and his hair gelled flat to one side along a severe parting. The guy's face pinched when he caught her looking, and she caught his glance to the other side of the street. A second young male, heavier, clean-shaven, but wearing a stud earring in his right eyebrow, began striding across the road. For the briefest moment she feared they were trying to cut her off, but she told herself she was being paranoid. Haik Memorial Drive wasn't too far away now, she picked up speed, intending entering the hospital grounds by the first entrance.

The van swerved towards her, stopped fifteen feet away.

Emilia practically slid to a halt, a wordless question squeezed between her teeth as a sharp exhalation.

Behind the headlights, she couldn't make out the driver. But there was no good reason for him to swerve towards her like that . . . unless . . .

She knew who it was.

She should have run for the hospital, but her instinctive reaction was to flee.

Except the young guy with the beard blocked her passage. The other man was charging towards her across the road, and she caught the glint of his eyebrow stud winking in the wash of headlights from the van. His lips were open in a grimace, but his teeth were clamped together in determination.

Emilia danced from foot to foot, with no clue where to go. A wall enclosed the hospital grounds. Not tall. She lurched for it, was about to spring over, when a hand clutched her left elbow. She struggled to break loose, but another hand was now round her face, pulling her backwards, clamping down over her mouth to stifle her cries.

Emilia fought. She rammed her free elbow into the bearded man's gut, but it was ineffective, and he pulled her in tighter. The second man was on her in seconds, and he didn't pause; he scooped her up with his arms behind her knees even as the van crawled forward so it was alongside them. She got a glimpse of Zeke Menon grinning at her through the side window, his eyes flashing in triumph beneath the peak of his battered old cap. Emilia screeched behind the palm that forced her lips painfully against her teeth. Kicked and twisted. But the two young men had control of her and weren't for letting go. A door in the side of the van swept open, and two huge hairy paws reached for her.

She felt weightless in the brute's grasp, until she was hurled down on the bed of the van. Flattened cardboard boxes deadened the sound but took little of the brunt of the collision. It was as if she'd fallen from a great height. Sparks flashed across her vision, but darkness edged her mind. She heard Zeke giving curt instructions to the two thugs then the door slammed, enclosing her in almost total darkness with the shaggy behemoth that now crouched over her. Clipped to the front of his jacket was a small pinpoint of light, and Emilia felt her vision tunnelling around it, as if it were the promised light that would lead her to the afterlife.

'Don't kill her.'

She wasn't sure if Zeke's words were a blessing. The instant the van door had swept wide and she'd seen Cleary leaning forth like a grinning gargoyle, she'd thought her life expectancy could be counted in seconds. But she knew that continued existence would only mean horrendous pain and suffering at the hands of the Menons.

Zeke clarified things for his brother, if not for her. 'We need to hear where she's been these last few days, and who she's talked to, before you get to have her, bra.'

'Hurt her.'

'Not yet. Just shut her up, 'til we can get her outta here.'

'Then hurt her.'

'Yeah, then you can hurt your prize.'

Cleary's huge right palm smothered Emilia, covering most of her face, his fingernails digging painfully into her scalp behind her ears. Emilia bucked against him, but he flattened her out with a meaty slap of his opposite elbow. His palm ground her head down into the cardboard as if he intended squashing the breath right out of her. But in the next instant he yanked away her purse, threw it towards the back door of the van, and snatched up a pair of balled socks. She couldn't see what he was doing, but she felt his hand adjust on her face, and then he prized open her jaws and jammed the socks in deep. She gagged on the damp wool. In the next moment Cleary was wrapping duct tape round and round her face, securing the impromptu gag in place, matting and snagging her hair to her skull. Her nostrils were covered. She began to truly panic when her lungs jumped in her chest, begging for air. Cleary yanked the tape off her nose and she inhaled so harshly she was positive a train whistled its progress down inside her.

'You got her?' Zeke demanded from the front.

'Got her. Got her good.'

The van began rolling.

'Good. Now keep her quiet. And Cleary . . .' Zeke paused for effect. 'None of your goddamn howling 'til we're outta town, OK?'

TWENTY-ONE

'This has got to be the place, but I don't believe the Thibodauxs are home, me.'

Pinky's local network of contacts had come through, one of them offering directions to the trapping and fishing camp the Thibodaux brothers worked from. To Tess, the nearby shacks barely perceptible in the lights from Pinky's van, the scene was reminiscent of the set of one of those stupid horror movies where a group of hormonal teens visit for a weekend of debauchery only to be hacked limb from limb by a hockey-mask-wearing maniac. She wasn't keen on getting out of the van, but she followed the menfolk as they alighted and slowly approached the camp, both of them with pistols at the ready. Tess had left the gun supplied to her by Pinky in her bag, but was itching to take it out. She had great reservations about them arming themselves – especially illegally the way they had – but the second they'd entered the glade and spotted the ramshackle camp some of her disquiet had slipped, replaced by a worse feeling.

Her gaze darted around the edge of the clearing. Ancient trees strung with banners of moss hemmed it in. In the near-total darkness the forest appeared as impenetrable as a brick wall. She kept moving forward, placing her feet carefully so that they didn't break a twig underfoot.

'There's been a fire recently,' Po said, at much the same time Tess smelled the bitter aroma that only came from a bonfire dampened down by days of rain. She couldn't tell where the stench originated.

'Over that way,' Pinky announced, nodding towards the western boundary line of the clearing. 'You think they have a fire pit out there?'

Tess hadn't a clue. She wasn't familiar with the activity fur trappers got up to, but could picture what they might throw on a fire: the glistening entrails of forest creatures, spitting and popping as the fat was rendered down.

Po had made it to the stoop of the brothers' shack. He paused, one foot on the top step, a hand held behind him to halt Tess. She obeyed without comment. Pinky slunk off, circling towards the rear. Tess finally drew her gun, and racked the slide on the Glock 20 as silently as she could.

They weren't there for trouble with the Thibodauxs, only for information. But Po's advice that it was better to approach carefully than react after they were blasted at with a sawed-off shotgun made sense. Not that she feared ambush: the camp felt deserted.

'Hal Thibodaux,' Po called out. 'Jamie Thibodaux. If you can hear me, we're not cops, and we're not here for trouble.'

The shack creaked, but it was Po settling his weight on the porch. He stepped up. The door was ajar. He ignored it, took a quick peek through the nearest window, glanced back at Tess and gently shook his head. He touched the door with his pistol barrel, and the door swung in on squeaky hinges.

'Hello?' he tried again.

From the rear of the shack there was a corresponding creak, but Po wasn't concerned. Pinky materialized from the gloom of the left corner of the room, having entered through the back door. Po waved Tess up on the porch. 'They ain't home.'

Tess peered past him to where Pinky was moving slowly. 'Nobody has been home for a few days,' he said. 'Woodstove's cold. They'd have had a fire burning in this cold, them.'

It was an assumption, but one Tess could accept. She could see her own breath. People used to semi-tropical warmth would definitely be chilled in this icy snap. She wondered if that was why a bonfire had been lit outside.

Po went inside for a closer look with a flashlight. Tess stayed on the porch. She turned and again scanned the clearing for any clues to the Thibodauxs' whereabouts.

'The place is a wreck,' Po declared.

Tess watched him sweep the flashlight beam over a living space equipped only with the basic necessities. The few sticks of furniture were overturned and smaller belongings scattered on the floor. It reminded her somewhat of the state of Emilia's room when they'd checked it out, but more so that of Ron Bowen's house in Portland, where a disturbance had taken place and a man left dead. Underfoot the planks of the porch were sticky. She lifted her foot and felt the tug on the sole of her shoe.

'Can I see that flashlight a minute?'

Po returned to the stoop.

'Shine it here,' she said, stepping aside.

Po held the beam steady on a dark patch on the faded wood. He glanced up at her knowingly.

'Blood.'

She nodded in agreement, but for confirmation held up the sole of her shoe, which he bathed with light. There was a red tint to the sticky mess adhering to it.

'Blood,' Tess repeated back to him. 'But then we are in a hunting camp.'

'Nobody would butcher an animal on their porch,' Po told her. He nodded over at various trestles situated around the camp, where the carcasses of animals would be hung while the Thibodauxs flayed them before butchering them for their meat.

He swept the flashlight outward and found another glistening patch of moisture nearby. Deep ruts in the dirt indicated that a truck had recently been parked next to it. Po walked past Tess, and approached, again settling the beam on his discovery. He pushed his pistol into his belt and crouched, as Tess moved alongside him. Behind them Pinky had also vacated the shack.

'You smell that?' Po asked.

'Putrefaction.'

'A few days old,' Po suggested.

'You don't think . . .' Tess didn't want to say it.

'Emilia's blood?' He went silent for a long beat. Then shook his head. 'For all we know it's animal blood. You see the tire tracks? The Thibodauxs could have off-loaded a deer or hog they shot, and the blood got spilled then. I'm betting we'd find animal blood all over this property if we started looking.'

Pinky had progressed from the shack to join them. He peered down balefully at the wide stain in the dirt. 'I know you don't want to think about it, Nicolas, but it could be Emilia's blood. She came here with her beau to buy weed. What if the deal turned sour and bad things happened? You ax me it'd explain why there's been no sign of the girl or Jason Lombard since. Would explain why the Thibodauxs have lit out.'

Po didn't want to accept the possibility. He ran a hand through his hair as he stared down at the coagulated blood. Tess put a hand on his shoulder, kneading it gently. Po finally stood. Shook his head. 'Until I know otherwise, Emilia's still alive.'

'We should call the police,' Tess said. 'Something bad happened here, guys. There's no escaping it.'

'Call 'em,' Po said, 'but not while we're here. Do it anonymously. We can't afford to be slowed down by a police investigation.'

'The police could help us find Emilia quicker.'

'We still don't know if she has anything to do with this,' Po said, and indicated the sticky mess. 'I'm thinking the blood belongs to the Thibodauxs. There was a fight inside that shack. Someone died on the porch, another out here.'

'A fallout between the brothers?' As soon as she suggested it Tess knew she was wrong. 'If they killed each other, their bodies would still be here. They've been moved.'

'The question is who moved them? I've a good idea who that might've been.'

'Zeke Menon,' said Tess.

'We can't be sure,' Po cautioned, because it was a lot of extrapolation based on unsubstantiated facts around what might be pools of pig's blood, 'but it would explain his interest in finding Emilia.'

'You think she was here when the Thibodauxs were killed?'

He shrugged. 'I could be totally off track. Maybe she was here before blood was spilled, or maybe she turned up after. But we know from Jason's roommate that they were coming out here to buy weed, and neither Emilia nor Jason has been seen or heard from since. They witnessed something terrifying enough to send them into hiding. If Menon had a hand in this, he didn't hurt Emilia at the time. Not if he's so interested in finding her now. He was at the hospital today for one reason only; you guys stopped him from pressing my mom for her whereabouts. To me that means he's still looking, and Emilia's still out there some place.'

'So I don't call the police anonymously. Isn't it best that the police hear about Zeke Menon, and that he might be responsible for what happened here?'

Po nodded. But then changed his mind. 'We don't know he

had anything to do with this. But we do know he's chasing Emilia. Maybe for another reason entirely. I'd prefer to ask him why before he's taken off the street by the cops.'

'What about the Chatards?' Pinky asked. 'What's their part in this? You don't think that maybe they brought in Zeke to help find Emilia, the way Clara did with you?'

It was a consideration none of them had entertained before. What if Darius Chatard had hired Zeke Menon to search for her when he couldn't contact his daughter? There was only one way to find out.

'I've tried to avoid it, but I need to speak with the Chatards too,' said Po. Tess hung her head at what the foreseeable future promised.

TWENTY-TWO

O
n the return journey to their motel, Pinky pulled the van across from a gas station and Tess jogged to a payphone at the corner of the building, all of them avoiding the CCTV cameras. She used a tissue to hold the receiver, and another to feed quarters into the slot to ring the local police office, avoiding using the emergency 911 number, which would cause an immediate response from nearby radio cars. Affecting a hokey Southern accent she reported overhearing a disturbance and gave the location of the Thibodaux property. She left things at that, hanging up quickly and trotting back to the van. Because they had no way of knowing whose blood they'd discovered, she thought it best that identifying its source should be left to the professionals. Due to the low-key nature of her call, a cruiser would be dispatched to the scene to follow up on her report but not on lights and sirens, and it would be down to the attending officers to come to their own conclusion about what had occurred and bring in the manpower and equipment necessary for the investigation. She'd covered her moral duty and her ass by alerting the police to suspected foul play, but also bought Po some time for what he had in mind. The latter didn't sit as easily with her.

Back at the trappers' camp they'd ensured they'd left few clues as to their attendance, making sure any footprints they made had been obscured and anything they'd touched was wiped down. Their van's tire tracks they hoped would be buried under those of the responding police cars, but once they were back at the motel, Pinky decided it was time to swap out their transportation and looked into exchanging the van for something less identifiable. While he was gone, Po rang the hospital and asked about Clara. She was sleeping, stable, but still very poorly. He considered hinting that extra security should be placed on her room, but to do so would raise too many questions. He asked Tess to find him Darius Chatard's phone number, but before she got round to it her phone rang. She recognized the number, but not immediately who it belonged to.

'Hello?' she answered tentatively.

'Is that Tess Grey?' It was a young woman's voice, and Tess realized who it was.

'Yes. Is that Rachel Boreas?' she countered.

'Yes, I'm returning your call from earlier. You left a message. You were asking about my friend Emilia Chatard?'

'I was,' said Tess. She caught a glimpse from Po, and his mouth opened to speak, but she begged silence with a raised finger. She urged him over so he was close enough to hear the conversation. 'Rachel, you're probably wondering who I am and why a private investigator from Maine is interested in finding Emilia. You needn't worry, it's a private matter between Emilia and her mom, Clara.'

'Yes. So you said. You mentioned that Clara is in hospital.'

'Heart attack,' Tess confirmed. 'She's failing quickly, Rachel. It's why I need to find Emilia as a matter of urgency.'

'How do I know it isn't you Emilia's hiding from?' Rachel's voice held a trace of suspicion, but she wasn't buying her own accusation. If she thought Emilia was actually running from Tess she wouldn't have returned her call. Tess picked up the hint of something more important.

'Why do you think Emilia's hiding from anyone?'

'The way she acted when I last saw her.'

'You saw her in person? When was this, Rachel?'

'Four days ago. She asked me to tell nobody about picking her up, and I haven't until now. Tess, it has been tearing me up inside. I've been worried to death about her.'

'Emilia asked you not to tell anyone? Not even her family?'

'*Especially* her family.'

'She was frightened of them finding her?'

'No. That wasn't it. She was frightened, but from what she said, and the way she acted, it was more fear *for* them.'

'Was she alone, or was she with someone when you saw her?'

'Alone.'

'Do you know Jason Lombard?'

'I know him. He's a dick. I don't know what Emilia sees in

him. But if you're asking if Jace was with Emilia, the answer's no. She was alone. It looked as if she'd spent the night sleeping rough in the swamp.'

'You said you picked her up, Rachel. Is Emilia still with you?'

'I got a call from her early morning, asking if I'd collect her from Catahoula. I brought her back to my place, but she wouldn't stay. From what she said it wasn't safe for her – or my children – if she stayed with me. I've no idea where she's been since then, and I've been on edge worrying about her. Thank God she phoned me earlier.'

'She called you today?' Tess offered Po a brief smile and a nod, and she watched him deflate slightly along with a long exhalation of relief. 'When, where is she?'

'I wasn't home to pick up her call, just her voicemail message. She asked for a ride home to New Iberia. She said she needed to get back to her mom urgently. I returned her call and got some old foreign guy. He said Emilia had used the phone in his convenience store and then left before I could call back. He was annoyed that she didn't buy anything after hogging his phone all that time.'

'Do you still have that number?'

'Right here.' Tess scribbled it on a notepad. 'But I don't think the guy knows anything useful. From what I could tell, Emilia left to make her own way home.'

'Do you know where the store is?'

'In Lafayette, but on the north side of town. I've no idea why Emilia would be there.'

Tess decided it would be pointless calling the store for its address if Emilia had already set off on her return home. 'Excuse my ignorance; I'm not from round here. How far is Lafayette from New Iberia?'

'Twenty-five to thirty miles give or take. Depends on what side of town you're travelling to . . . a half-hour in a car maybe? But Emilia was on foot.'

Public transport was available to Emilia, and taxis. Or she could have hitched a ride home.

'When did Emilia call you, have you a record of the time?'

'I didn't check. It was while I was out with the kids at

McDonald's, so early evening. I only checked my messages after I got back, and had missed her at the store, but not by long. I got your message too, and tried calling you earlier, but you must have been somewhere with no signal.'

Tess cursed under her breath. Rachel had been trying to call while they'd been out in the swamp. She hadn't checked for missed calls being otherwise engaged with making the anonymous call to the police, and then getting tied up with Pinky's plan for alternative transportation and then Po ringing the hospital about his mom.

'So it's reasonable to say that Emilia could be back in New Iberia now,' she said.

'Easily,' Rachel said. 'From what she was asking about a ride, I think she'd have gone directly to the hospital to see Clara.'

That's what Tess thought too. It was also where she and Po should go without delay. She thanked Rachel, and assured her she'd call and let her know that Emilia was fine as soon as she found her. 'Forget ringing Darius for now,' she told him, 'we need to get Pinky back here and over to the hospital.'

TWENTY-THREE

The tap of Zeke's heel on the floorboards was like the constant tock-tock of a metronome. The sound wasn't distracting, it soothed him, helped him clarify his thoughts. He was sitting in an old office chair, his right leg crossed over his left. His arms were folded across his chest and the peak of his lucky ball cap was pulled low on his forehead. His smile was faint, but cruel. Directly opposite him, Emilia Chatard watched him over the top of the duct tape that still concealed most of the bottom half of her head. The breath rasping through her nostrils was in time with the rhythm he'd set with his tapping heel. Her cheeks were streaked with tears and dirt, her forehead blanched of colour, and her turquoise eyes burned, feverish with terror. Each time his boot heel rapped the floor, her eyelids twitched. The sound wasn't half as soothing to her. He uncrossed his legs and settled his feet firmly, leaned forward so that his elbows were on his knees. Halting the slow torture wasn't a consideration on her behalf.

'I bet you're wondering why you're still alive?'

Emilia didn't answer. She couldn't.

'You saw something you shouldn't have,' Zeke went on. 'You can't be allowed to tell anyone.'

Emilia said something behind her gag. It was a garbled moan.

'I guess you're trying to convince me you've told nobody. I believe you. But you won't convince my employers that will always be the case. They're not as confident in your trustworthiness as I am.'

Emilia moaned again.

'You don't believe I'm being honest? I am. I can see that you're terrified of the consequences; I know that you wouldn't go telling tales because of what *will* happen. But those guys, with their nice suits and two-hundred-dollar haircuts, they don't believe the integrity of poor white trash like me and you.' Zeke wiped his mouth with the back of his wrist. He placed his arm back on his thigh, leaned closer. His face crinkled in pleasure. 'Then again, maybe you have a good right not to trust me. I'm a killer, right? You witnessed the aftermath of what I did to the Thibodaux brothers. How can you trust the word of a killer?'

He stood sharply, his palms cracking loudly on his jeans.

'I'll tell you why.'

He walked around her. Emilia was sitting in a chair too, but hers was a thing of metal tubes and pre-formed plastic. Her arms were bound behind her, secured to the back legs of the chair with more duct tape. Her ankles were secured to the front legs. She remained gagged, the balled socks still behind the duct tape, but she had freedom to move her head. She didn't follow his progress. She allowed her head to shy away from him, digging her chin into her sternum.

Zeke curled his fingers over the back of the chair and leaned close, so his lips were alongside her right ear. 'You can trust me because I've no reason to lie to you, Emilia. See, I warned what would happen if you mentioned a thing about what you witnessed. I'm happy that you've upheld your side of the bargain, and you know what, I'm happy to uphold mine.'

He stood and walked away. He faced a blank wall of the small windowless room.

'But there we have a contradiction. Right?' He turned to observe her and saw that she hadn't moved. She was still curled forward in her chair. 'I've told you conflicting messages, so can see how you might be confused. But hey, stick with me and I'll explain.'

Again he strolled past her, approached his original chair but didn't sit. He used the back of the chair to lean on so he could bend and meet her gaze. Fresh tears had welled, making cleaner tracks down her exposed but dirty skin.

'You upheld our bargain,' Zeke went on, 'and I've upheld mine. You didn't speak about me to anyone, so I haven't killed you, and I haven't touched your family. But here's the quandary. I've recently received further instruction from my employers, and they are explicit in their instructions that you disappear. The new bargain trumps ours, Emilia. So you see, you have to die, despite obeying my previous warning to the letter. You, my girl, have to go and join your boyfriend out in the swamp.'

Emilia quaked. Her head shook as if with palsy. Her words were muffled.

Zeke snorted at her. Even if her pleading words weren't distorted out of shape by the gag, they'd have been a waste of breath.

He thrust the office chair aside, and it clattered against the nearest wall. Zeke straightened, and adjusted the brim of his cap.

'It's pointless struggling against the inevitable,' he said. 'The question is how you're going to die.' He deliberately edged back the front of his denim jacket, and watched her eyes widen at sight of the knife hilt jutting from a sheath on his hip. 'There's the quick, silent method, or I can call Cleary back in here.' He grinned maliciously, and then clacked his teeth together with the same metronome rhythm as he'd tapped the floor before. Now Emilia reared back in her seat, her head whipping side to side. Zeke chuckled, pleased with the result.

Suddenly he planted the heel of a palm to his forehead. 'Oh, wait! What a dummy I am. I can't kill you yet. There's more I want to explain to you.'

Emilia stared at him. He watched a bubble of mucus pop in her right nostril. Her gaze was anything but bemusement at his antics, but he didn't care. The play-acting was for his amusement. Tormenting her was far more enjoyable than simply taking the edge of his knife across her throat, although that was a prospect he looked forward to.

'I went to see your momma today,' he announced glibly.

Emilia bolted high in her chair, and this time her cry was barely deafened by the gag. The chair rocked to and fro.

'Hey, settle down. I didn't do her any harm. In fact, I didn't get to even say hi. See, she already had some other visitors. Do you know who Nicolas Villere is?'

Emilia was suddenly silent. Her gaze now intensified with other emotions.

'Oh, that's right,' Zeke grinned. He creased the bill of his cap, resettled it on his brow. 'Of course you know who he is. He's the guy who killed two of your big brothers, right? It got me to wondering: what the hell was Nicolas Villere doing at your momma's bedside? But then I remembered something I heard way back. Your momma is also his momma. I thought I came from a dysfunctional family, but let me tell you girl, yours takes the biscuit. Villere is your momma's son, but he's your father's worst enemy. Ol' Darius hates him so much he's willing to pay to have Villere killed. And can you just guess who he went and gave the job of killing Villere to?' He placed fingers to his chest, as if he couldn't believe it either. 'Now how is that for an unexpected kicker?'

Moving within a few feet of her, he crouched, resting the heels of his palms on his knees. 'Do you believe in karma, Emilia? See I never placed much faith in all that Eastern voodoo bullshit, that our lives are preordained. But certain recent events have kinda got me challenging my faith. Who'd've thought that such random and diverse events surrounding the laying of a new pipeline would bring everything together in such a neat bundle as this? Makes me wonder if indeed there's a greater power at work, y'know? Hmm, I can tell you think I'm nuts. You don't lay any credence in any of it. Well let me tell you . . .'

The door rattled, and swung open.

Wayne Tyson glanced once at the back of Emilia's head, before his gaze found Zeke, where he crouched before her.

'What?' Zeke demanded.

'Keane wants you.'

'Doesn't he know I'm busy? Tell him I'll call him back.'

'He isn't on the phone, Zeke. He's here. Wants to see you urgently. He looks worried, man.' Tyson also looked worried. He chewed at his bottom lip, making his sculptured beard bob up and down. He held Zeke's gaze for a moment longer, before he blinked and looked away.

'Tell him I'll be right there.' Zeke stood slowly from tormenting Emilia. He inhaled deeply. 'Go on, Ty. I'm just gonna finish up here first.'

Tyson closed the door behind him.

'Talk about an untimely interruption,' Zeke said to nobody in particular. But then he returned his attention to his captive. 'You might think that karma is bullshit,' he said, and his smile grew broad again. 'But you should thank it all the same. It's just won you a stay of execution, girl. I can't go murdering you just yet, not when I intend taking money from your old man. But it's not through any sense of misguided loyalty. Oh no. See, I don't trust Darius Chatard one bit. I fully expect him to try to twist out of our agreement when it comes to payment, so I gotta have a contingency in place. What do you say, Emilia? D'you think he'll pay as much for his daughter's head as he agreed to for his enemy's?'

TWENTY-FOUR

I t took a little persuading of the nursing staff for them to allow Po back at his mother's bedside, but he'd convinced them he was Clara's son, and that he would be no trouble. But when he returned to the parking lot Tess could tell from the frown riding his forehead that Emilia was still a no show at the hospital. They'd arrived twenty minutes earlier, and after gently arguing their way past the nurses' station on the intensive-care ward, Po had disappeared inside Clara's room while Tess retraced her steps to the entrance. She stood where she'd last watched Zeke Menon drive off in a pickup. Pinky wasn't along with her this time; he was still swapping out his wheels when they called him from the hotel, though he promised to be back as soon as possible. But Po couldn't wait, so they'd hailed a cab. Pinky was due to swing by and pick them up once he'd collected the alternative vehicle from one of his contacts. Tess had decided to station herself at the front of the hospital: should Emilia arrive, she hoped to speak to her first, to warn her she'd nothing to fear from the stranger she'd find in her mom's room. Emilia would know of her supposed half-brother by reputation, but it would be one painted black by her parents and other siblings. By explaining Po's good intentions, Tess hoped to avoid a confrontation at Clara's bedside, where emotions could override good sense.

But Emilia hadn't shown up.

'Clara's still sleeping,' Po announced. 'Didn't want to disturb her, but I spoke with her nurse. Nobody has visited my mom's room but for us earlier today.'

'Maybe she swung by her apartment,' Tess suggested. 'Or maybe she has gone to see her dad before coming over here.'

'Step-dad,' Po corrected. 'And I doubt it. Rachel said she sounded desperate to get to the hospital, right? So what's keeping her?' He thought hard, then took out his cell. Hit buttons. 'Pinky, you got a vehicle sorted yet? OK. So as soon as you're mobile again, do me a favor, bra? Go on over to Emilia's place and check she hasn't come home yet. Any of those bozos hanging around like earlier; you have my blessing to see 'em off. Me an' Tess are gonna wait here.'

'You just want to wait out here in the open?' Tess asked. She'd donned a thicker jacket, but was still chilled.

Po pulled out his cigarettes.

He walked away from the hospital towards the main road. Stood at the gateway and lit up. Tess watched him smoke, shivering in the frigid air.

'We're going about this all the wrong way,' she said.

'How so?'

'We should bring in the police.'

'I recall you criticizing me for suggesting the same thing not so long ago.'

'That was different. Ron Bowen was dead. He wasn't going anywhere, and I only wanted some time to think things through before the cops arrived and kicked us off the investigation. Emilia isn't dead, but we both know she's in danger. Look at what happened to those hunters.'

'We don't know if anything happened to the Thibodauxs. We found blood, but maybe there's always blood there.'

'You don't believe that any more than I do. I know it's putting too much emphasis on a hunch, but I'm under no illusions and I don't think you are either. Emilia witnessed something bad happening there and ran away. It doesn't take a rocket scientist to figure out who she's running from, other-wise why would this Menon character have his goons looking for her. It's no coincidence.'

Po inhaled deeply, and allowed the smoke to leak from the corner of his mouth. Finally he nodded.

Tess went on, 'I know you're burning to go and front things out with him, and I know it's only because I'm here with you that you haven't yet. You don't want to cause trouble for me, and I appreciate that, but we've been over this before. I'll back you to the hilt every time, Po, but not if I think you're doing the wrong thing.'

'He needs stopping.'

'I agree. But he can be stopped in ways that don't send you

back to prison. We can come clean to the cops, explain we've been looking for Emilia and it led us to check out the trapper camp where we found all that blood. The police weren't involved before because neither Emilia nor Jason Lombard have been reported missing, but it's different now. If the Thibodauxs were hurt . . . no, let's face it, if they were murdered, and I'm beginning to believe that something bad has happened to Jason too, we need the cops. We have to let them know that Emilia's in danger from whoever hurt them. With their resources, they can help protect Emilia and take down the people threatening her.'

'Emilia's not missing, she's on her way here.'

Tess returned his gaze.

'You can't hide it from me, Po. That strong, rocky facade doesn't fool me one bit. You're worried.'

'She should've been here by now,' he agreed. 'But what if we're wrong? What if Emilia didn't witness a thing, and the reason Zeke Menon's looking for is for an entirely different reason, like we thought, that maybe Darius asked him to find her? Maybe he has nothing to do with the Thibodauxs, or anything other than that Emilia and her boyfriend owes him money. From the sound of things Jason is heavily into the drug scene, so maybe Zeke was his dealer and he's hiding from a bad debt. Would explain why Emilia could have run off with him.'

'Jason wasn't with her when Rachel picked her up in Catahoula. She said Emilia looked like she'd spent the night sleeping in the swamp. How far is Catahoula from the Thibodaux place?'

Po walked away, to flick his cigarette end into a storm drain. It was also to give him time to think before answering. As he returned to her, he dug out his packet again and fed another cigarette between his lips. He stood, peering at the hospital over Tess's head while he lit his second cigarette. 'You're right,' he said.

'About calling the cops.'

'About her possibly spending the night in the swamp. About the Thibodaux camp being too close to Catahoula to be a coincidence. About Zeke Menon's interest in her being something more. And about me being worried. But the thing is, we don't *know* anything for certain. If we call in the cops now, you know who's going to spend the next few days answering awkward questions, don't you?' He watched her for a response, but all she did was lower her head and stare at the sidewalk. 'We'll be put in the frame for the trouble at the Thibodaux camp. I know it can easily be refuted, once they get the forensics back on the blood, and how old it is because we've strong alibis being half a continent away when they died, but that will take time. I'm not sitting in an interview room, or a goddamn cell, while Emilia could be on her way here. I'm damned if I'll do it if she's in imminent danger.'

Tess wasn't as concerned by the prospect of being treated as a potential suspect, but he had a point. They'd have to explain why they went to the trappers' camp, and that would lead the investigation back to Jason Lombard's roommate who'd sent them there, and she didn't trust the junkie to play straight with the investigators. He could even lie, and say that they had been threatening towards him, and had been angry with the Thibodauxs for selling drugs to Po's sister. It would be a possible motive for Po to exact retribution on the dealers. He would be locked up while things were straightened out. They'd also want to know what had led them to Jason Lombard, and who they had learned the boyfriend's name from. Tess could show she'd identified Emilia's girlfriends through their social-network activity, but not where she'd got their names from in the first place. God help Po if the cops learned of the armed confrontation he'd had with the thugs staking out Emilia's apartment. And there was also Pinky's inclusion to consider. He was offering his assistance selflessly, and it'd be unfair to drop him into the centre of a police investigation that could have repercussions on him.

'OK,' she finally said. 'So phoning the cops might not be my most inspired plan. What do you want to do?'

'If Emilia isn't here by the time Pinky gets back, we do what I originally planned. I call Darius Chatard, ask him if Zeke's his man, and if not . . . well, I call Zeke.'

Tess shivered again, but this time it wasn't due wholly to the cold.

An ambulance drew their attention. Its flashing lights came

on, followed by its siren, and as they watched it go, Tess
wondered if it was streaking to Emilia's assistance. She forced
down the horrible notion and didn't mention it to Po, because
she suspected he had had a similar thought. She watched him
glance sourly at the burnt stub of his cigarette, before he flicked
it away into the curb.

Behind them another vehicle approached, turned into the
hospital, mere yards from them, and suddenly braked. It was a
silver Toyota Camry XV50, one of the most popular models of
passenger car in the US. Before Tess got a good look at its
occupants, it pulled away again, and drove for the parking lot.
Po watched it go, but he seemed unconcerned by the driver's
sudden stop then acceleration. Maybe, as they were, the driver
expected to see someone they were looking for at the hospital
and had pulled up sharply before realizing his mistake.

They waited for Pinky to return for them. But neither expected
an imminent arrival, not if he'd followed Po's request to swing
by Emilia's apartment first. He was at least fifteen minutes out.

They kicked their heels, occasionally glancing along the main
road in hope that Emilia would materialize out of the gloom.

After a while Po lit a third cigarette.

Tess exhaled.

'You want a coffee or something?' he asked. 'Help warm
you up while we wait for Pinky.'

'You want anything?' she offered.

He held up his cigarette. 'I'm good.'

Tess headed inside. While in the lobby she used the public
facilities, washed her hands, and then checked out the coffee
machine. She fed dollars into the slot and waited while the
machine worked its magic. She chose a black coffee with extra
sugar. A caffeine kick and the extra calories were very welcome.
Finally she wandered outside again, sipping gratefully on the
hot coffee and wondering if by now Po was on to his fourth
cigarette in quick succession.

He was nowhere to be seen.

TWENTY-FIVE

'**Z**eke! For God's sake! Are you totally insane?'

Al Keane's face was slick with perspiration, despite the cold. He was seething, and not a little terrified of the consequences of Zeke Menon's actions.

'It has been suggested before,' said Zeke, and offered his employer a snarky smile that tugged at one side of his mouth. 'But before you get yourself all bent out of shape, I've thought everything through, and everything's under control.'

'Are you freakin' kidding me? You've got a goddamn witness who could potentially bring us all down locked in one of my offices!'

'She can't cause us any trouble from in there.'

'You were supposed to shut her up, Zeke, not bring her here. It's bad enough you made a mess of clearing up the Thibodaux problem, you've gone and made it ten times worse by not silencing all the damn witnesses. What were you thinking, bringing her here?'

'Where would you suggest I took her, Al?' Zeke's tone had lowered.

'Out in the damn swamp, where you've taken everyone else.' Keane ran his hands over his face, and sat heavily in the chair behind his walnut desk. 'If she's traced here, I'm finished. Corbin's finished. And you can bet your damn ass you'll be finished too, Zeke. And don't think you can escape. Corbin will have you hunted down like a dog wherever you go.'

'You always were prone to exaggeration, Al. Chill a moment. Let me explain.'

'Don't be so patronizing,' Keane snapped. 'You're not talking to a frightened young woman now.'

Zeke grunted in mirth. 'Am I not?'

Keane's fists came down solidly on the desk. 'It'd do you good to remember who signs your damn paycheck! Watch your damn mouth, why don't you, and show some respect?'

'I earn my money,' said Zeke, and left the suggestion that respect should be earned too for Keane to realize. But he wasn't in an argumentative mood, so shrugged in something approaching apology. 'Al, I can understand your frustration, but you haven't thought things through clearly. Emilia has been running around for the last five days, and who knows how many people she's talked with. I brought her here because before I put her in a hole I have to question her, and make sure that her loose tongue doesn't unduly affect your and Nate Corbin's businesses. I could easily give her to Cleary if you wish; my brother would love to take her out in the swamp as you suggest, but what then? This is about damage control, the very thing you employed me to take care of. So I really don't see what you're concerned about.' He thumbed at the doorway. 'What? You thought I was going to dismember her in there or something? Forget about my insanity crack from before, I was just yanking your chain. I'm not mad. When I'm positive that we've nothing to fear from Emilia Chatard, I fully intend doing my job. She'll disappear. But not until I've dragged the names of everyone she's been in contact with out of her.'

Keane nodded, but was still worried. He again pawed sweat from his brow. 'Mr Corbin might take some convincing. It's why I'm here. He's coming to see what the hell is going on, and wants answers. What the fuck is the deal up at the Thibodauxs' camp?'

'What do you mean?'

'Corbin got a call from one of his contacts in the New Iberia Police Department. They've received an anonymous tip-off about a potential murder at the camp. The NIPD and IPSO have teams out there now, and are treating it as a potential crime scene. What the fuck happened, Zeke? You were supposed to sterilize it, not leave pools of blood for the cops to find.'

'So there was a little blood left behind. So what? The place was a goddamn slaughterhouse as it was. Given a few more days the rain would've completed the clean-up for us, and failing that the site is due to be dug up by your construction crews. This anonymous tip? I grant you, it couldn't have come at a worse time.' Zeke glanced at the door, wondering if Emilia had called the cops when she phoned Darius Chatard and learned of her mother's plight. Perhaps she had doubted his warning about talking to anyone, and had realized it was her only option if she intended returning home to her mother's bedside. Stupid bitch had been wrong on that count. He'd warned her what he'd do to her loved ones . . .

Yet he wasn't prepared to do harm to any of the other Chatards just yet. He fully intended having his reckoning with Nicolas Villere, and being paid handsomely for the privilege sweetened the deal for him. He was an opportunist, yes, but also a player in the bigger picture. If he was careful, and as fearless as ever, then he could use the fuck-up at the Thibodaux site, and the fallout involving Emilia, to his benefit. Until now he'd relied on generating terror based on his and Cleary's ferocious reputations, but wouldn't it be neat if he actually toppled those who believed him their superiors through the manipulation of events?

'The blood at the camp won't prove that the Thibodaux brothers are dead. I'm confident their corpses will never be found, and without their bodies I'm doubtful the cops will launch a full murder investigation. This tip-off from Corbin's guy in the NIPD, did it mention murder?'

'No. Come to think of it they just said there'd been some kind of a disturbance,' Keane replied.

Zeke shrugged at the less than hysterical report.

'So they might find some blood. You know Cleary, he gets kinda carried away at times, but as I recall it wasn't excessive. Couple of puddles here and there, but somebody could bleed that much from a busted nose. Cops could assume this disturbance was down to the Thibodauxs having a fallout, throwing punches and curses at each other. Do you really think they'll take things seriously and treat it as a major crime scene?'

'And when they can't find the Thibodauxs?'

'They're renegades, drug dealers who have no truck with the law. The cops will assume the brothers are lying low or have disappeared into the bayous on another hunt.'

'They aren't stupid,' Keane warned.

'Just predictable. Look, let me reassure you, Al. The Thibodaux brothers are history in the best sense of the word. Period. The stupid kid that stumbled into the scene when we were doing clean-up, history. His girl in there . . . well, her days are numbered. Then she'll go where we put the others. Their cars are all chopped and crushed and on a truck to a scrap-metal dealership in New Orleans. There's nothing out at the camp that can tie me to it, so neither you nor Corbin need worry I'll lead the cops back to you. With the Thibodauxs off the land, Corbin can assure his investors that there'll be no further delays in getting that pipeline of his in place. I've done what was asked of me, so I don't know what you're both so upset about.'

'You got those squatters off our land, as you promised. But did there have to be so much blood? After all the recent news stories, it's bound to attract attention. Especially if the media get onboard.'

'News stories that people aren't taking seriously. For fuck's sake, Al. Even the *Daily Iberian* ran copy with headlines about a freakin' werewolf. Nobody but some of the most superstitious Creoles out in the swamp are taking that shit about a rougarou seriously.'

Grunting, Keane finally stood. Some strength had returned to his shaky knees. He glimpsed around. 'Talking of werewolves, where is the big dummy?'

'Please don't call my brother that. He's not dumb.'

'You know what I mean.' Keane, along with the strength in his legs, was regaining some of the firmness of his balls. He pointed a finger at Zeke's chest. 'You need to get a handle on Cleary, Zeke. I'm telling you, man, you can't let him go on like this. You might laugh at those stories, but if he keeps up these killings, those superstitious Creoles you just flipped off will be hunting him through the swamps with dogs and flaming torches.'

Zeke adjusted the peak of his cap, and grinned at the future painted by Keane in grim strokes. 'Remember what I warned about exaggeration, Al? Cleary's under my control. The only one who has to worry about him losing it again is that young woman back there. Now if we're done here I'd like to get back to her.'

'Do what you have to do,' said Keane, in an effort at re-establishing their pecking order. 'Try to get this mess cleared up before Mr Corbin arrives. He's not happy at having to come here in the middle of the night with some of his investors, so I'd like to give him some good news to share when he gets here.'

'His multimillion-dollar deal moving ahead isn't enough for the asshole?' Zeke turned his back on him, dismissing Keane.

TWENTY-SIX

'**P**o, you arrogant, wooden-headed son of a . . .'

Tess was back outside the hospital again. Dumping her coffee minutes ago, she'd rushed back inside, on the chance that she'd missed Po in the lobby while she'd visited the bathroom, but all the time in the knowledge she hadn't. She hurried to Clara's room, attracting a scowl from the night nurse on the reception desk.

'Ma'am, I told you already . . . visiting hours have ended.' The nurse's expression was practiced stern. 'Hours ago.'

'Has Clara's son been back?'

'He left about a half-hour ago. Mrs Chatard has been disturbed enough for one evening . . .'

'I'm sorry.' The light inside Clara's room had been turned off, and the blinds drawn on the door. Clara was sleeping, as she recalled. Po hadn't returned to his mother's side, but she had never believed he had, only hoped. 'I won't bother you again.'

Passing through the lobby she ducked her head inside the men's bathroom, calling Po's name, but it was deserted. She knew she was wasting time looking for him there, but she had to cover all the bases. She swept outside again, jogging towards where she'd last seen him near the exit gate. An unsmoked cigarette smouldered at the edge of the sidewalk. She looked both ways along the street, and even checked Po wasn't strolling about in the parking lot of a machine-repair shop across the road – he was a mechanic by trade, and she didn't put it past him to go for a poke around at the machinery on display in the forecourt. She rang his cell but he had switched it off.

She cursed him for being a stubborn fool, and after a second quick scan of the street in both directions turned and looked back at the hospital's parking lot. She couldn't see Po, and there was something else missing. The silver Toyota Camry XV50. She should have known!

The way the driver had stamped on the brake as he drove past should have warned her. He had recognized Po, and Po had recognized the threat he posed. Goddamnit if he hadn't sent Tess inside for a coffee to get her out of harm's way. The stupid, stupid man! Sometimes he infuriated her with his old-fashioned male chauvinism. Not that he looked at things in the same way; he came from the old school where chivalry towards the fairer sex was a given. If he weren't so morally sincere about molly-coddling her she'd slap his face for being such a damned misogynist. If he appeared right now she would do just that, but only after hugging him out of relief.

She pulled out her cellphone.

Ringing him again would be pointless. He'd sidelined her and would ignore his phone even if it were switched on now. She called Pinky instead.

'You're not going to believe what that stubborn idiot has gone and done now!' she said as soon as Pinky picked up.

'Uh-oh. I dread to think, me.'

'He's left me standing . . .'

'That I do believe. He does make a habit of disappearing, him.'

'I think he took off on one of his damn solo missions,' she went on, 'the trouble is I don't know who he has gone after first.'

'Emilia hasn't been home,' Pinky said. 'I'm on my way back to you now, pretty Tess.'

Usually when he used the affectionate term of endearment for her it gave her a gentle thrum of pleasure, but hearing him call her pretty now only rankled. Could a gay man be as misogynistic as the lout she'd fallen in love with? She didn't challenge him on it; she knew he was only trying to calm her. 'Please hurry, Pinky. You know that damn fool even better than I do. And I know he's gone and stirred up trouble.'

'I'm a few minutes out. Is there anything you can do to find him?'

'I've tried phoning but he typically isn't picking up. Damn him, Pinky, why is he always so stubborn?'

'It's that wooden head of his, it's in Nicolas's nature.'

'Where the hell could he be?' Tess regretted not demanding

Zeke Menon's phone number off Po earlier, but she had noted Darius Chatard's. She should warn him what would happen if he harmed as much as a hair on Po's head. She thought again about the silver Toyota Camry. Who had been driving it? Zeke Menon? Another of those he'd paid to watch for Emilia? If it were Menon he'd swapped out his wheels since earlier: she recalled the beaten-up pickup truck, the decal on its sides, and its registration number. 'Pinky, I have to hang up.'

'No worries. Be with you in no time.'

She called a contact in the DMV and within two minutes she'd confirmed the pickup was registered to a large construction company based in Louisiana, matching the details she recalled from the side of the truck. She had to check; what was to say Menon wasn't driving a second-hand vehicle without removing the decal, or that he had stolen it, even switched out the plates?

A huge Chevrolet Tahoe roared along the one-way system towards her, its headlights flicking up and down. Under no doubt about who was driving, she stepped out, waved it down, and Pinky brought the SUV to a halt alongside her. She hopped in the front passenger seat.

'Anything?' Pinky's eyes were wide, hopeful, reflecting the dim glow from the instrument panel.

'It's a long shot, but I think I might have an idea where we can find Zeke Menon. I'm betting if we find Zeke, we'll find Po.'

'Tell me where,' Pinky said, already pulling away from the curb.

Tess brought up the web browser on her cell. 'I'll have the directions in moments. Hang on.'

'You hang on,' Pinky announced and the SUV surged onward.

TWENTY-SEVEN

P o was in a large SUV similar to Pinky's. But unlike Tess, he was lying face down across the bench seat in the rear compartment, his hands cinched behind him with thick nylon rope. There was a sack over his head. It was an untenable position to be in, and that was discounting the fact that a man sat on his legs, holding him still, while another threatened him with a sawed-off shotgun. It was over-kill, considering he'd offered no resistance to his captors. He'd have happily sat up front, chatted pleasantly to the driver while he was escorted to whatever destination they had in mind: it was his intention to go there anyway and his kidnappers had only speeded up the process.

He was taking a stupid risk. But he wasn't stupid, and understood the consequences. On any other occasion he would have fought tooth and nail, but when they'd swooped on him with tires screeching and dire promises made at the end of the shotgun, he'd merely flicked aside his unsmoked cigarette and held his empty hands out to his sides. One of them found the gun tucked in his belt and spirited it into his, before two of the three men from the SUV grasped him and bundled him towards it. The third ensured he didn't resist by jamming the gun in the small of his back. One of the two men from the silver Toyota Camry, having sped from the parking lot to offer support to the snatch team, wore a gloating expression before he spat in Po's face. Watching the saliva dribble over Po's mouth, who had no option for wiping it away, the spitter laughed nastily, and went as far as lifting a fist to punch home his hatred.

On a main road outside a hospital wasn't the ideal place to deliver swift justice, and the man stepped out of the way so Po could be thrown across the back seat. One of the men clambered in on top of him, pulling the evil-smelling sack over Po's head then yanking his arms behind his back so he could loop the rope around his wrists. Taunts and curses were directed at Po from all three who got back in the SUV, and he took a couple of hard digs in his kidneys from the one in charge of his immobility. He took the blows stoically, pleased that Tess wasn't along and being similarly roughed up.

As soon as he'd spotted the driver of the Toyota, when the man had injudiciously stamped the brake in disbelief, his immediate future was set. He had remained calm, allowing the driver time to make his preparations. He had given Tess no reason to suspect what was on his mind, so that when he suggested she head inside to warm up and grab a hot drink it would sound agreeable. His timing had been close, because Tess had no sooner disappeared within the hospital lobby, and he had turned off his phone and lit up another cigarette to add to his nonchalant, unsuspecting pose, than the SUV had coursed along the road towards him, and the Toyota had zoomed from the parking lot in a pincer move. Tess wasn't going to be happy when she learned of his subterfuge, but he'd take the ear-bashing gladly, it was nothing compared to what might happen if he couldn't convince his abductors of a course of action other than slowly beating him to death.

He hoped she wouldn't go and do something stupid when she found him missing. She'd assume a lot, probably come to the wrong conclusions. The last he wanted was for her to follow her old instincts and think that the cops could sort out everyone's problems. The inhabitants of his world didn't obey the laws of the land, but were governed by ancient ones akin to medieval feudal rule and Old Testament justice.

He didn't bother asking where he was being taken, just kept his peace and tried to control his breathing through his mouth so he didn't retch on the stench of the sack.

His abductors' mood changed to disbelief at their luck, and then celebration. They still cursed, but now it was to colour their triumph and the lurid pictures they painted of Po's future. Speaking to them was now off the cards, because he'd nothing to say to minions. He'd save his breath for the bosses. The Toyota would be following them, with its driver and front-seat passenger. Five men in total to take him, but there'd be more where he was going.

Of course he could have made a miscalculation concerning numbers, and where he was being transported. If these punks had instructions to take him out into the swamp and execute him then he was supremely fucked. He'd fight back then, but with his arms tied behind him and a sack blinding him he didn't credit his chances. Perhaps he should have given Tess and Pinky a heads up after all. No. He couldn't think that way. He had to be confident that the men who'd ordered his capture also wanted to be in on his punishment. Stay positive. He actually grunted in mirth at the inanity of his warning. And took another punch in his kidneys for what was perceived as resistance.

Whatever the future brought, whatever his fate, he wouldn't end things until he'd paid back some of the delight his rough captor took in beating him.

Time passed achingly as he was transported from alongside Bayou Teche to the hinterlands surrounding the Port of New Iberia. As the crow flew it was no great distance, but the drivers of both the SUV and Toyota took things easy, obeying the posted speed limits and traffic lights. There would be NIPD patrol cars on the road and nobody, including Po, wanted to be pulled over while a captive was trussed in the back of the SUV; that would spoil everyone's plans. Finally he sensed the terrain change beneath the wheels of the SUV, from smooth asphalt to a rutted gravel trail. Small pebbles rattled off the undercarriage as the SUV crept forward. Finally he felt the front rise up, and a moment later the rear wheels completed the manoeuver and the car rolled to a slow stop on some kind of platform.

The engine shut off, and his back-seat companion grasped the sack, bunching a handful at the back and yanking up Po's head. 'Give me any trouble, bra, and you're history. Don't forget, you got a twelve-gauge aimed at your ass.'

The evil-smelling sack rubbed at Po's features, tugged at his hair. He didn't reply; the sooner he was outside and the bag removed the better. As the door was thrown open, he heard the Toyota prowl by before coming to a squeaking stop. Doors were thrown open. Boots scuffed on decaying concrete. Men's voices began calling back and forth, some from a little distance away. Po was manhandled out of the SUV, and forced to one side. A boot to the back of his knees folded him with a groan to the concrete. Shards of perished concrete jabbed his knees.

Po struggled up again.

'Get on your fuckin' knees!' the man controlling him barked.

'Have your buddy pull that trigger,' Po snapped in response, 'I'm kneeling for nobody.'

'On your knees . . .'

Po stood straight, resisting the hands that tried to force him down. A fist pummelled his gut, landing squarely where he'd been stabbed not so long ago. He wheezed, bent as his abdominal muscles contracted but then forced himself upright again.

'You and me, asshole,' Po hissed to the man holding him, 'are going to have words after this.'

'Ha! Try saying that again when you've no teeth left in your face.'

Again he was forced to one knee, but he struggled against his captors, and made it upright. He was pushing his luck, but if they intended shooting him they'd do it whether he was on his knees or not. He preferred not to give them the satisfaction of seeing him debased. His over-exuberant captor punched him in the lower back again. 'Kneel down, or I swear you'll be pissing blood!'

'That's enough, Rocco,' growled another voice. 'Let him stand, and get dat sack off his head. I want to look d' fucker in his eyes.'

The man's command was obeyed instantly.

The sack was yanked backwards, the bottom pulling and scraping at Po's lips and nose, leaving his skin raw. His vision was bleary with tears. He blinked hard as he sucked in fresh air. Not so fresh: the atmosphere was pungent with rotting vegetation and diesel fumes. Finally he squared up and faced the thickset figure standing ten feet away. In his peripheral he counted six figures milling close by. Another two men stood behind the leader like personal bodyguards. Po ignored everyone else.

'Hello, Darius,' he said.

'Been a long time,' Darius replied.

'Should've been longer. I didn't come here for you.'

'I know why you're here. Dat mother of yours, I never could control her, even wheezing out her last breaths she's still a wilful bitch.'

Po didn't reply. He studied the two men looming behind Darius, watching their expressions as their father maligned their mother's character. They didn't like Clara being badmouthed,

but not at the expense of challenging their father. He hadn't
laid eyes on either man in years, but recognized them as Francis
and Leon Chatard, the two surviving brothers of the men he'd
killed. The driver of the Toyota Camry, who'd spat in Po's face
earlier, and who was now standing to Po's left, was their cousin
Jean Chatard. When Jean had arrived at the hospital, no doubt
on some errand at Darius's request, and spotted Po standing by
the entrance gate, he must have almost messed his pants in
surprise. He'd stamped the brakes, and blinked in open-mouthed
recognition. The instant Po got a look at that face he'd planned
his reunion with the Chatard clan.

'You've got steel balls showing your face roun' here,' Darius
said. He nodded his large, square head in respect of Po's bravery,
but Po didn't buy the sincerity in the gesture.

'You expected I wouldn't come?' Po asked.

'I had you down for a coward. I thought you'd keep hiding
your face for d' rest of your life. You should have.'

Po checked out the men gathered around him. They were
standing on a platform alongside the sluggish water of a coulee.
Parallel metal rails had been sunk into the poured concrete. It
was a jetty, but it hadn't been used for a very long time. Across
the water there were a number of industrial buildings, all
deserted this late in the evening. Nearby lights flooded over the
top of the treetops, casting a sickly yellow pall on the low-lying
clouds. He could hear the distant sound of traffic passing along
a highway. He was encircled by his enemies and in a location
removed far enough from potential witnesses so that any screams
for help wouldn't be heard. Not that Po would ever scream for
help.

'There's nine of you,' Po pointed out. 'Who are the cowards?'

Darius smiled grimly. 'There's nine of us, yes. And each and
every one owes you for what you did to their kin.'

Po had already assumed that most of the gang members were
close relatives to the three standing directly in front. He didn't
know their faces, but then most of them would have hardly
been born before he went to Angola. He eyed the one referred
to as Rocco. For all Po knew he was the grown-up son of Roman
or Lucas Chatard, the brothers he'd originally come into mortal
conflict with. Then again, probably not: otherwise the level of

punishment Rocco doled out during the car ride would have been worse, and delivered more passionately. Rocco was most likely a cousin's boy. The young thug had learned his hatred.

Po nodded at Darius's surviving sons.

'I understand you guys having a beef with me, not so sure about any of these other punks. Whaddaya say we cut these ropes and we'll sort things between us?'

Francis and Leon stirred aggressively. Darius held a palm back towards his sons. He took an extra step towards Po. 'You don't think I have a right to avenge my boys?'

'You're an old man. I wouldn't insult myself by punching you in the face.'

Darius rolled his neck. He curled his fingers and braced his wide shoulders: he was still a formidable man even in his later years. 'Old man, huh? I could still rip your head off your skinny neck.'

'Face it, Darius. When my dad called you out you wouldn't meet him like a man, you sent Roman. So let's not kid each other. You're not going to do anything now. Not when you can sic all these young ones on me.'

'Let us fuck him up like you said you would,' Francis argued, with a nod at his brother, who looked equally eager to get stuck in. But Darius ignored them. He smiled again at Po, his white moustache bristling.

'I'm tempted to cut you loose and see . . .' Darius shook his head. 'But you're right. It'd be selfish of me to kill you all by myself. I will give all dese boys what they want.'

'That's what this is about for you? Killing me?'

'What else?'

'You haven't grasped the bigger picture.'

'The bigger picture is putting you in a grave.'

'And where does that leave you then? You know I've friends who won't let this drop.'

Darius laughed bitterly. 'Take a look around. Do you see any friends? Where you're going nobody will ever find you. Dey won't have a clue what happened to you.'

'You don't think when I came here I didn't have a contingency in place?' Po was lying through his teeth, but Darius couldn't know that. 'Didn't you think it was maybe a little convenient the way I was just standing out in the open like that, confident that once you heard Emilia was on her way to the hospital, one of your "boys" would be sent over to pick her up? You heard somehow, right, and you sent Jean to meet her? I knew he'd spot me—' he turned and smiled sarcastically at Jean Chatard – 'and being as dependable as any trained mutt he'd get straight on the phone to round up a few of your boys. I allowed myself to be taken. Don't you maybe think I'm more in control of this meeting than any of you realize?'

More than one of the men surrounding him glanced nervously around, imagining Po's allies – or worse, the cops – suddenly announcing their presence in this remote place. It was a desolate location alongside a bend in the coulee, but effectively it offered little escape back up the trail they'd come down. If a raid was launched, their only option of escape was to dive headlong into the water and swim for it.

Darius didn't buy Po's story. He was thinking about what Po had just said but with another emphasis. 'So if help's coming for you, maybe we should get on with dis.'

'Would better serve you to hear me out, Darius.'

'There's nothing you can say would change my mind, even if you begged me. Francis, Leon. You know what to do.'

The sons came forward.

Po had hoped it wouldn't come to a fight, but the situation wasn't under his control at all. He steeled himself, planning if nothing else on getting in his licks with the few weapons remaining to him. His hands were still tied, but he had feet and a head that he'd use to give him some room to manoeuver.

But the brothers didn't come on. They waited until one of their cohorts had fetched twin axe handles from one of the vehicles parked nearby. Francis accepted one and gave a couple of practice swings. The wood whistled to his satisfaction. Leon grasped his axe handle across his chest, studying Po for where a blow would hurt most.

'Don't go hitting him in d' head,' Darius cautioned.

His instruction had nothing to do with pity; he didn't want Po knocked cold before he was sufficiently punished.

TWENTY-EIGHT

A scream of frustration threatened to overwhelm Tess, but she fought it down. The last thing to do now was lose it, but she was burgeoning on a blow out, and finding it more difficult by the second to deny her instinct to call the police. Po hadn't wandered off alone for some private thinking time. He'd been taken, and knowing him and how he would ordinarily react to a threat it would have been under violence. The prime suspect in his abduction was Zeke Menon. So that was who she concentrated on finding: where Menon was, then so would Po be. Except she wasn't positive she'd found Menon at all, although she'd tracked the pickup he'd driven earlier in the day back to this swathe of churned-up land to the east of Catahoula, adjacent to Bayou La Rose. Heavy terraforming of the swampy landscape was underway, with construction crews laying culverts and something akin to a raised levee on which concrete stanchions had been poured to support the pipeline destined to cut through the area, before skirting New Iberia to hook up with the existing pipelines bringing light sour-crude from the Gulf of Mexico to the off-shore oil port at Houma.

From the front seat of Pinky's SUV she could see Zeke Menon's work truck parked alongside similar pickups all bearing the construction company's logo, but of the tall man in the grungy baseball cap there was no hint. She had to ask herself: why would Menon even be here this late in the evening when his workday would have ended hours ago? Likely he'd parked the pickup and gone off in another personal vehicle, but she'd been unable to identify a ride belonging to him from any DMV records. She had found no contact details for the man, and repeated calls to Po's cellphone in the hope that *somebody* would pick up had found it turned off.

There was unexpected activity on the site. A small convoy of vehicles had arrived minutes earlier, and men had decamped to enter a large compound that must serve as a temporary operational base. Several of them looked like important business people, wearing suits and ties and shiny shoes – totally inadequate wear for the muddy site – while others looked as if they might be private security contractors. Tess assumed that some sort of managerial meeting had been called to deal with an emerging problem: she hoped said problem wasn't Po. She doubted it, but how could she be certain without taking a look?

Pinky was all for invading the construction site, and Tess was with him. But caution held her back, and therein lay most of her frustration. Po could be in immediate danger, and she wanted nothing more than to rush to his rescue, but what if they were wasting time here when her partner had been taken elsewhere?

'And won't we look stupid if we drive away from here without checking, pretty Tess?'

Pinky was as equally frustrated.

She gripped the front of her jacket, bunching it in her fists. 'I know, Pinky. But what if we're wrong? What if Po isn't even here and we go poking around where we have no right? Those guys by the cars, they look like they mean business.'

He checked out the trio of tough-looking individuals who'd remained outside the temporary office buildings. One of them had grabbed the opportunity to have a smoke; the other two were kicking back, sharing jokes while they waited for their charges to reappear. They were suited, their jackets a size too large to cover the concealed weapons they carried. 'Glorified chauffeurs, them,' Pinky announced. 'They're too busy talking BS to notice us if we sneak inside.'

'I wouldn't underestimate them if I were you,' she said. 'They don't look overly alert, but they'd have to be blind to miss the two of us.'

The ground surrounding the compound had been stripped raw of cover, with just an occasional heap of dirt to offer concealment within a dozen yards. The only reason Pinky had gotten them this close without notice was because they'd arrived prior to the convoy of vehicles and parked two hundred yards from the front gate, their lights extinguished. But as soon as they moved the car, or even got out, they'd be spotted.

'So we wait until their backs are turned. We find another way inside other than strolling in through the front gate.'

Tess studied the tall fence surrounding the compound. It had never been designed with the intention of withstanding an assault; it was more a boundary marker than anything. 'You think you can climb that thing?'

'You should know by now, I'm not built for aerial acrobatics, me, but I'm pretty sure I could use my other attributes to bust a way inside.' Pinky made a long sweep of the visible perimeter. 'You see up there . . .' He indicated a spot where the fence sagged inwards. 'Bet you a dollar to the cent I could pick that up enough for us to scramble under. It's out of the line of sight of the Three Stooges over there.'

'We have to.'

'You're going to get muddy, you.'

'Least of my worries.' She was more fearful of Po getting bloody.

'You still got that gun?' Pinky asked.

Tess had considered leaving the gun behind at their motel when she and Po returned to the hospital, but had buried it deep in her purse instead. She dug it out, and quickly checked it over. It was a Glock 20, with a Bar-Sto precision 10mm barrel, loaded with 10mm Hard Cast ammunition: serious stopping power, some might even argue overkill. She hoped she didn't need to use it beyond a threat.

'You OK handling a Twenty, Tess?'

'I've fired ten mil before. I'll handle it.'

Pinky had armed himself the same. The recoil from such a powerful handgun was no problem to him, and he wouldn't have worried about Tess if she had full use of her damaged shooting hand. It was a cannon for someone who'd almost had her wrist severed only a couple of years ago. 'If the worst comes to the worst, throw the frickin' gun at 'em.' He winked to punctuate his joke.

'If it comes to it, I'll throw you at 'em,' she countered. 'At least that way I'd be confident of hitting my target.'

Pinky laughed, but it was grim humour. 'If any of them have hurt Nicolas . . .'

'Let's try and stay positive,' said Tess, feeling anything but.

They waited. An opportunity to move came a few minutes later when the smoker offered his buddies his pack. They bunched together, sharing the single lighter. While they were huddled against the breeze blowing off the bayou, Pinky slipped out the car and went immediately around the back. Tess ducked out too, and joined him, keeping the SUV between them and the trio of guards. They backed away until they were obscured by the deeper night, then immediately tracked across the road and into a copse of trees yet to be torn out by the excavation equipment. It wasn't easy going, undergrowth snarling their every step, brittle branches strung with Spanish moss clawing at their heads and shoulders. Tess felt something squirming in her hair. She ignored it, fighting the qualm of disgust that shuddered the length of her spine. They were making enough noise to alert the guards as it were, without voicing her revulsion at what was worming its way towards her scalp.

Finally they crouched at the edge of the copse. Tess dug for the critter, even as Pinky also wiped bugs off his face, and thumbed at the corner of one eye. 'Well, that was unpleasant,' he whispered.

They were now at an angle where the buildings within the compound concealed them from the view of the guards. Open ground stretched between them and the fence, but if they hoped to get inside and search for Po they'd no option but cross it. Pinky went first, staying low, his feet digging deep into the churned earth. Once he was at the fence and had tested its integrity, he waved Tess over. She followed the deep plough marks her friend had already made in the muck, so the going was a bit easier for her, yet still hard going. She crouched beside him, breathing deeply at the exertion. Mud clung to her sneakers in clumps and stained her jeans almost to the knees. Pinky was filthy, and had managed to wipe mucky fingerprints down one cheek. 'If Nicolas is in there,' he whispered, 'I'm going to kick his tight ass for making me crawl through the dirt for him.'

'Take a ticket,' she replied, 'and join the queue.'

She checked her weapon, ensuring none of the invasive dirt had found its way into the mechanism. It was all in order. But crawling under the fence with the gun in her hand was impossible. She'd left her bag in the SUV, so tucked the gun inside her jacket and deep in her waistband. Pinky dug under the edge of the chain-link, and heaved up. There was plenty clearance for Tess to squirm under. Once she was in the clear, she stood, got both her hands on the fence and reared back. Pinky squeezed through, the twisted loops of the lowest links scraping his back and leaving small punctures in his jacket. He got through with his hide intact, but was filthy to his elbows and mid-thighs. 'Dump Nicolas, stick with me,' he said, 'I'll take you to all the interesting places, me. Can't promise we won't get as filthy. He-he!'

Tess shook her head at his shameless flirting. Moments like this and he was still going for laughs. But that was what she enjoyed most about his company. If she'd been here alone she'd be fraught with worry, and on reflection she realized she was no longer as frustrated with the unknown as she was eager to put a lid on it. She took out her gun again, and after checking that they hadn't been observed they jogged together for the side of the nearest building, a modular pre-fabricated cabin on skids. The other buildings were similar mobile structures, and large metal shipping containers. She assumed that as the pipeline progressed the mobile hub of activity would follow.

The first window she peeked through showed her a deserted canteen. There was no hint of Po or that he'd ever been inside. She was more intent on taking a look in the largest unit, where the recent arrivals had gone, but to get there unseen was pushing their luck. Floodlights surrounded it, and the lights inside were so bright that it was difficult looking directly at it. Surrounded by barren earth the building had the look of an alien spaceship that had touched down on a desolate planet. Approaching it they would be in the full wash of its lights. Tess was smaller, fleeter than Pinky. 'Watch my back?' she asked. 'I'll go take a snoop.'

'If he's in there, you tell me, and I'll come on over.' Pinky moved towards the front of the unit and settled himself at the corner where he could watch the trio of inattentive guards. He held his Glock 20 alongside his right thigh. Tess mimicked him, wedging the barrel alongside her thigh as she moved rapidly for the next building along. Because of the floodlights bringing day to the area around the main cabin, it offered deeper shadows alongside the nearest building and she used the concealment they offered to move closer. The final few yards would be traversed in the light, but there was nothing for it. She checked for the guards but couldn't see them, and Pinky was no longer in sight. Trusting that if she couldn't see them then she too must be invisible, she crept forward and placed her back against a wall. She was five feet from the nearest window. She moved for it, sliding gently along to make as little profile of her silhouette as possible.

A venetian blind hung slightly askew when she bobbed up for a peek. It helped her, because she wouldn't easily be spotted by anyone inside chancing a glance her way. The suited men she'd watch arrive were gathered around a central table or leaning against filing cabinets set along the opposite wall. One silver-haired businessman looked familiar, but only in a cookie-cutter manner that made diplomats and politicians alike. She knew instantly he was the highest-ranking individual in the room. He was wearing a faint sneer, as he listened to a man sitting kitty-corner to him at the table. Tess couldn't get a good look at the speaker's face, but she picked up on his body language, his gestures and mannerisms and knew he was uncomfortable with his report. In identifying the company to which Zeke Menon's truck was registered, she'd checked out who was helming the local project and assumed that the uncomfortable man was the project manager, Alistair Keane. Her research hadn't been in-depth enough to identify the silver-haired man, and assuming any of these people had a clue what a minor player like Zeke was up to might be stretching credibility beyond its breaking point.

Their conversation was too muffled to make anything out, but she listened keenly for any mention of Po. She thought she heard Cleary mentioned once by the man she believed to be Al Keane, but he could have said 'clearly': besides, the name meant nothing to her . . . or did it? Hadn't the thug to whom Po introduced his knife tip to his nostril mentioned someone called Cleary in relation to the Menons? The driver had acted fearful of Cleary as she recalled, but had been at pains to call him a retard too. It wasn't important. Po was all that mattered, even Emilia's unknown fate meant little to her at that moment.

She moved away, skirting the building. At the rear the illumination was ambient, allowing her easy progress but also more

cover. She checked more windows at the back but the small
anterooms were empty. She began to think that she was wasting
time, yet she couldn't leave without checking the other buildings. She'd never forgive herself if she neglected to find her
lover, locked in one of the cabins or shipping containers. To
save Po she would do whatever it took, which came as an
epiphany as bright as a detonating flare. Apparently it didn't
take much for her to put aside years in law enforcement when
she was prepared to push her way inside that building at gunpoint
and demand her partner. She was tempted, but again had to ask
if she were wrong about Po being there.

Low-key approach, she cautioned herself. Check and see.
Then base your response on your findings.

The trio of guards, chauffeurs, or whatever they were, were
still engrossed, so she slipped across to the next cabin, which
looked like a site office, and to a side window. There was no
light from within and the window was encrusted by dust stirred
by machinery. She used her sleeve to wipe away some of the
grime, but it didn't help much. No . . . that wasn't entirely true.
She could see dim light coming from under a door in the
rear. She couldn't ignore it.

She crept round the side of the cabin, but making a full circle
around the building she found no window for the adjoining
room, and certainly no door. She placed an ear to the wall and
listened. She could swear she could hear laboured breathing,
until it occurred to her that she could hear the breath whistling
in her own lungs, and her raised pulse inside her head. Had she
heard a subdued murmur, a brief scuffling? When she glanced
down, her jacket had caught on splinters on the wall. She gently
eased away. Disappointed at failing to find Po, she turned to
scan the other buildings. She could see now that most of the
shipping containers weren't locked, and some doors stood open.
They continued various items of equipment she couldn't identify,
others were stacked to the roof with boxes of what she surmised
were parts used on the pipeline or the excavation vehicles. She
couldn't see one that raised her suspicion about what it held.

Po wasn't there.

Most likely he had never been there.

She turned back to retrace her steps and almost walked

directly into a huge figure who'd stepped around the corner. He towered over her, a massive blot of darkness defined by a wild mop of hair that shrouded his broad head. The wash of flood-lights set him in shadow, but a nimbus of light played around him, adding to his weird and startling appearance.

Tess emitted a yelp, and took a step backwards.

The giant grunted, almost as surprised as she was, but then he bent at the waist towards her and she could see clearly enough as his mouth opened in a wide grin, ambient light sparking highlights on his slab-like teeth. 'Who are you, sweet girly-girl?' he rumbled.

Snatches of the conversation Po had had with the thug outside Emilia's apartment streaked through her mind.

'*Who is Cleary?*'

'*Zeke's brother, man. He's not right, you get me? He's scary wrong.*'

As his words came back to her, Tess almost echoed more of the thug's sentiment as she stared at that horrid mouth that widened in delight: *Cleary will eat me alive.*

Too late she brought up the barrel of her gun, silently commanding him to back off.

To anyone else, the Glock 20 would dictate immediate respect, but Cleary Menon swatted it aside with one hand, while his other reached to grab her.

TWENTY-NINE

Miles away, Po took the jab of Leon's axe handle to his gut. There was little he could do, other than fold over the handle in a paltry attempt at absorbing some force from the blow in his clenched abdominals. It didn't help, and left him exposed to the whack dealt across his right thigh by Francis. The strike to his leg was worse by far, and he buckled. The next smack of wood came across his rounded shoulders.

'Sons of bitches,' he growled at them, and fought to yank his hands free of the ropes.

Leon jabbed him in the chest, and it brought him back to his toes, his teeth clenching. Leon laughed in derision. One of the cowardly cousins behind him kicked Po in the backside. The pain that flared down his leg was white-hot. He used the pain to energize him, turning quickly and throwing a kick of his own, but it fell short and earned him a hoot of laughter at his ungainliness. It also left him vulnerable to another smash of a handle alongside his thigh. He suffered the most intense Charley Horse he could ever recall, and no way could he remain standing. He collapsed sideways. The boots of several of his baiters rained in, and he wheezed with the effort to breathe. He should have stayed down, taken the kicks, but it wasn't in his nature. Impulse forced him up again, and he limped to one side. An axe handle was whipped into his ribs, and he felt something give.

'Bastards!' He bent and retched up his last meagre meal.

He won an extra round of taunts for his noisy vomiting. But also a few seconds of respite from the physical torment.

He snapped his bleary gaze around on Darius. The old man's mouth was turned up at one side, as much a sign of derision as pleasure at seeing his enemy beaten. Young Rocco took Po's inattentiveness as his opportunity to deliver a dig. He slashed the palm of his right hand across the side of Po's head, splitting the skin where his ear met his jawline.

'Don't hit 'im in d' fucking head!' Darius roared.

Rocco was furious, but equally cowed. He stepped back, and good job because Po swung for him, hoping to drive him off with his shoulder. Again he was vulnerable to the axe handles and took two solid clumps to his sides. Absurdly, Po was thankful in that moment that his arms were still bound, because his fore-arms saved his kidneys from terrible punishment.

The eldest of Darius's sons, Francis, glanced at his father for further instruction.

'Keep at him, boy. I want that piece of shit beggin' for forgiveness before he's done.'

'Isn't . . . going to happen . . .' Po's face was twisted up in agony, but his denial was greater. 'Roman murdered my father and got what was coming to him. You, Darius . . . *you* sent Lucas after me in Angola. The fucking coward tried to blind me with a shiv, and we know where that got him. Their deaths are on you.'

None of the extended Chatard clan – especially Darius – was ready for the truth. Po's words only encouraged a renewal of the attack, and this time it was driven by more ferocity. However, the scramble to punish him was oddly to his favour. There were too many of them trying to get kicks, punches, and whacks of the axe handles in for any blow to land cleanly. Against Darius's commands some of the fists and elbows scuffed his face, and the back of his skull, and blood dripped from both nostrils and one eye began to swell. The kicks to his body hurt like hell, but his legs were so numb they were almost immune to further punishment. If he got through this, walking was going to be a chore for the foreseeable future. He went down on his side on the decaying concrete of the jetty. The crowd skipped around, pushing and shoving at each other for clearance. Po tucked in, his hands beneath his backside, heels pulled up, protecting his vitals. He took more scuffing kicks to his back and legs, but nothing was as debilitating as before.

'Let me see!' Darius moved in, pulling and shoving his younger kinfolk aside. Reluctantly, they backed away, still forming a circle around the viciously beaten man. Now that Po was sufficiently softened up Darius wanted to eat his slice of the revenge pie. He bent over the beaten dog, grabbed him roughly by his chin, and twisted Po's face towards his. 'Are you ready to beg yet, asshole?'

'No,' said Po, his jaw working against the crushing fingers holding it in place. 'Why would I? You're the one who's gonna be sorry . . .'

He abruptly wrenched around onto his back so he was staring up at his would-be tormentor. Darius no longer had control of his head, unless he bore in closer. He didn't. He snapped upright, stunned to see Po's hands free, trailing the cut rope. From Po's right hand jutted the blade of the knife he'd surreptitiously slipped from his boot to sever his bonds while seemingly cowering from the beating. One man with a knife, against nine armed with a collection of clubs and even a shotgun should be at a total disadvantage . . . and Po was. But he was no longer constrained, and now able to begin swinging the odds in his favour. With a wordless shout he stabbed down.

Darius roared at the burst of agony, and tried to wrench away. Momentarily he couldn't move. The knife driven through his foot effectively pinned it to the decaying concrete. When Po yanked it out trailing blood, Darius went over on his back with a holler of dismay. Po swarmed over and climbed the old man's body. Cutting Darius's throat at that instant would have been simple, but it was never his intention. Neither was using the man as a hostage. He stayed close to Darius because nobody dared attack when they could inadvertently harm the Chatard patriarch. Po used him as a springboard to launch up at the nearest men. They were too stunned by the sudden turn of events to react effectively.

Po's body was racked with pain, and his limbs were leaden, but he was driven by white-hot rage that commanded obedience from his tortured frame. He made a wild slash at the nearest men to get them moving, and they scattered. The next few seconds were dominated by chaos, as those who moments ago were engaged in the assault now feared for their lives. Francis grasped his dad's arms to try to pull him clear, and in the shambles dropped his axe haft. Leon stood over them both, swinging his club as protection, but doing nothing to halt Po. Po ignored them for now. He went after the man with the shotgun, who couldn't shoot for fear of tearing holes in his kinfolk. Po jabbed the blade at the man's face, and as he reared away, dropped his line of attack in an unexpected fashion and kicked the man's ankles out from under him. Before he'd fully sprawled on the gritty floor, Po wrenched the shotgun out of his grasp. He grasped it by its shortened barrel, a heavy club in his left hand. He snapped his attention on Rocco.

The young man tried to throw a punch into Po's throat but missed, and was rewarded by the stock of the shotgun rammed into his mouth. Teeth, and jawbone, shattered. He fell to his knees, cupping his face, trailing strings of bloody saliva. Po kicked him over with a boot to his chest. He lay on his back, moaning through his ruined mouth. Perhaps in that instant he thought about the threat he'd aimed at Po only minutes ago: *Try saying that again when you've no teeth left in your face.* The thought didn't occur to Po, but Rocco's punishment was karmic.

Po kept moving, slashing with his knife, swiping at skulls with the stock of the gun. The others fell back, gasping for breath, eyes red hot, all of them still dangerous but wary now their victim was mobile and armed.

Leon screeched and came at Po, his axe handle scything the air. Po ignored the handle, swung for the hands grasping it. The shotgun stock smashed Leon's right thumb to pulp and impacted fully on the fingers of his left. The handle jumped from his grasp. Po stamped on it, pinning it to the floor, even as he used another clubbing blow of the shotgun to knock Leon aside.

Francis stood guard over his father. He looked ready to die in Darius's defence. Po juggled round the shotgun, so it was now in his right hand, and the barrel pointed directly at the two men. All around him, men barked curses and threats, the injured moaning and trying to crawl clear. Po ignored them, fixing his stare on Francis even as he aimed at Darius, who wasn't flexible enough to reach his injury, so lay grimacing, and trying pathetically to kick the pain out of his impaled foot.

Blood streamed from both Po's nostrils, got in his mouth. He dashed his lips clear with a swipe of the back of his left hand. It still held his knife. He spat, so he could speak. 'I could kill you now, you sons of bitches.'

'So fucking do it!' Francis snarled. He had tears of frustration dripping down his cheeks. 'You've already murdered two of my brothers, why stop now? You've hurt my father, my little brother . . .' He looked for Leon, who was sitting abject and forlorn, cradling his broken hands to his chest as he rocked back and forward. He snapped a glance at Rocco, but didn't linger on him long. He looked for Jean, his other closest relative, but Jean was standing off to one side with his mouth hanging open in dread: after all, he had led them to this moment where nothing had ended as they'd planned. 'There's only me left to get your revenge on,' Francis went on. 'So if you're going to shoot, shoot now, or go an' fuck yerself.'

'Trust me,' said Po, 'I'm tempted. But if you stupid fucks stopped and thought for one second, you'd have realized I came here to speak.' He used the barrel of the gun as a pointer at the others still milling just out of his immediate striking range. 'Y'all got your licks in,' he returned this aim to Francis and Darius, 'and so did you. Then again, I got in some of my own too, so I'm happy. What happened before was a fucking lifetime ago, d'you really want to take this fucking feud to your graves? If so then so be it. I'll kill you, use up both barrels, and then your kin here might get me . . . might not, but more of us will be killed f'sure. But if you're ready to see sense, this can be the end of it.'

Francis swore, but his words were unclear. But Po noticed Darius's hand grasp his son's leg, urging caution. Po held the younger man's gaze. 'My mother's dying,' he announced. 'Yeah, I'm talking about Clara, the woman who has also been your mother for the best part of a quarter-century. You think she wants any of her children to die? When she left me, I hated her. I've held onto that hatred for decades. But y'know, for her and somebody else's sake, I've put that hatred aside.' He couldn't help the sneer on his face as he made his next announcement, but it was aimed inward rather than at the Chatards. 'I've even given up hating you assholes.'

'Help me up,' Darius commanded.

Francis glared expectantly at Po. The gun barrel jerked up and down.

Francis hauled the old man up, with much grunting and straining from both. Darius supported his weight with an arm around Francis's shoulder, his injured foot held off the floor. Blood dripped from the sole of his boot. 'I gotta take some weight off. Can we go over dere and speak?'

'F'sure. Was my intention to speak all along.'

'And you expected us to sit round playin' happy families?'

'Not for a second. It's why I let your boys give me a beating first, so's you could get some of that pent-up anger out of your systems.'

'You're a smug son of a bitch,' Francis said, but his father patted his shoulder.

'Can it, son,' Darius warned.

'Look what the bastard did to Rocco and Leon, Papa: we going to just let that go? Look at what he did to *you*!'

'I don't need reminding; my foot hurts like a sumbitch. But things coulda turned out much worse. So, hush now. Let d' man with d' shotgun speak.'

'I'm hoping I don't need this at the negotiating table now,' Po said, with a nod at the gun, 'but I'm not about to throw it away either. Drop the attitude, Francis. And these others, they need to get the fuck outta here. Would offer a place for Leon at the table, but I think he needs to go see a medic. If y'all want another able-body with you, Jean can stay. The others, our business has fuck all to do with any of them, so they can leave.'

Darius nodded, and against Francis's whispered advice, the old man overrode him. 'You lot. Git d' fuck outta here. You've had yer fun, and now it's over. Take Rocco and Leon home, and make sure they're cared for, y'hear?'

Po followed as Francis assisted his father to one of their pickup trucks and Darius thankfully lowered his butt on the flatbed in the rear, his knee bent to lessen the pressure on his injured foot. Po had put away the offending knife, but still cradled the shotgun. He ensured he could see all three of the remaining Chatards, and that the others were leaving now that they'd helped their injured kin into the SUV. It reversed away, leaving only Jean's Toyota Camry parked on the raised dais they'd used for a makeshift arena.

'OK. Now that we can speak without all the posturing for their sake, let's get down to it,' Po said. 'I want to know what interest Zeke Menon has in our Emilia.'

'Whaddaya mean, *our* Emilia?' Darius demanded.

'I always thought you were an asshole, Darius, but I never took you for a fool.'

Darius frowned. 'So you know?'

Francis squinted sideways at his father, but Darius didn't explain.

Po said, 'First time my mother showed me a picture and I saw Emilia's eyes, I knew they didn't come from you. Emilia has turquoise eyes like mine, like my father's.'

Now Francis was scowling, his mouth working silently. Darius laid a hand on his son's shoulder. 'It don't change a thing. She's still your sister, son.'

'She's also *my* sister,' Po emphasized.

Darius scowled, but then his face worked on what else Po had just asked about, his eyelids twitching, his nose scrunching up. 'What was dat about Zeke Menon? The fuck would dat lunatic have any interest in my daughter for?'

'That's what I was hoping you could tell me. I'd have preferred to dispense with all the drama, but that was never going to happen. Hopefully we've cleared the air now and can get down to what's really important. There's a frightened young woman out there, and I mean to find her before Menon gets his hands on her.'

THIRTY

I f Tess could have heard Po's words, she would have shaken her head at the irony. Cleary Menon was so huge that one forward step had brought him directly over her, and she shrank beneath him. His left hand still warded off her Glock, while his huge right hand teased and plucked at her hair, lifting the curls and allowing them to slide silkily from his fingertips. 'Pretty girl,' he murmured under his breath, 'pretty hair.'

Tess didn't know what to do.

She could probably lurch away, get a bead on him, and pump a few shells into his massive body. But two things stayed her. First, she wasn't confident that even 10mm Hard Cast ammo would be ample stopping power to fell such a brute, and mainly because she had no reason or justification to shoot him. Being touched unbidden in such an intimate manner caused a qualm of mortification to run through her frame, but at the same time Tess could sense no lasciviousness in his fascination with her blond locks. His attention wasn't sexual; she felt more like a yellow Labrador being petted. Surreptitiously she moved the gun aside and hid it behind her right hip.

When first he'd appeared from the gloom, she had assumed the worst, that Cleary had recognized her as an intruder and was intent on capturing her. Yet he didn't appear suspicious, and the gun in her hand didn't alarm him. Either he was always around weapons and had become desensitized to them, or the presence of the weapon – and her reason for carrying it – hadn't registered in his mind. His grin, which at first had reminded her of the maw of a predator, had begun jumping up and down before it set again, and his gaze had darted and finally alighted on her pale hair. Tess knew her hair must be a mess, snagged with Spanish moss and tree litter from the copse and likely dotted with mud from jogging and crawling around in the dirt, and yet Cleary appeared mesmerized by it. At any other time the flattery might have caused her to blush, and yet nothing about his innocent-sounding compliments felt genuine. An unwanted compliment often felt dirty, and that was how his words made her feel.

'Pretty hair,' he said again, and this time tugged a lock so it stood high above her forehead, he allowed it to drop and it curled on her brow. His fingers flicked it up again, and Tess lifted her own hand, and pressed his to his chest.

'Please don't touch me,' she asked.

'Pretty girl.' Her request must have fallen on deaf ears, because he immediately reached out again and his fingers stroked up the side of her head. Tess moved aside, but the giant barely shifted his stance to keep her within the circle of his reach. His face was still set in the same grin, but his gaze lowered, tracing the slope of her nose, and the slight up-tilt in it at the end, before it settled on her mouth. In the ambient reflections of the floodlights she watched him studying her, but felt as if his focus was elsewhere, seeing more than what she physically presented before him.

'Please. Excuse me, but I must be going,' Tess said, and attempted to duck past him.

Cleary squared up before her, blocking any route past. 'Sweet girly-girl has sweet-girly lips,' he announced.

Tess changed her mind. This was beginning to feel like violation. If he tried to kiss her she'd shoot him in the face. Meanwhile she continued to try tact, because the racket would bring the others running from their meeting and then she would be in a worse predicament. 'Thank you for the compliment,' she said. 'But please, I have to be getting on.'

She moved to the right, and when he adjusted his huge frame to block her, she skipped back a step and then spun away. Cleary grabbed at her, but she swerved out, ducking under his elbow, and then was past him. The skin between her shoulder blades puckered in anticipation of his shout, but it didn't follow. Trying to continue with the charade that she had a good reason for being on the site, she headed past the portable office as if making for the meeting room. Only when she believed she was clear of him did she glance back, dreading the thought that he was stomping along behind her. She could no longer see him. His disappearance brought no relief. The fact that the giant could

move so silently and stealthily was worrying, because where
the hell had he gotten to?

She was so intent on searching him out she forgot about
the trio of guards, almost walking directly out from the front
of the meeting hall in her urgency to escape. She skidded to a
halt in the mud and one of the men turned towards her. He eyed
her momentarily, but luck was with her. He had no reason to
recognize her, and being a stranger to the site must have taken
her for an administration worker or something else, because he
returned his attention to his buddies, catching the punchline of
a joke, and joining in with the laughter. Keeping up her act,
Tess moved as if she intending entering the meeting room, but
once she was almost at the door and certain none of the chauffeurs were paying attention she angled away, and around the
corner where she could hide in the shadows. She set her shoulders against the wall, only a few feet from where she'd recently
peeked inside the window, and breathed a sigh of relief.
Adrenalin made her hot and shaky.

The glare of the floodlights bathed the next cabin along; it
was the canteen, as she recalled. Beyond the canteen Pinky kept
guard, but she'd no hope of spotting him from her position.
Suddenly she longed to see the big guy again, almost as much
as she did to see Po. Unsolicited compliments came thick and
fast from Pinky all the time, but they were in direct contrast to
those recently endured from Cleary Menon.

'Hoo-hoo! Girly-girl!'

Tess's knees turned to water.

Her head swivelled to the source of the voice, her mouth
open in a silent exclamation.

'Hoo-hooooo!' The call was almost the howl of a wolf.

Cleary's large, shaggy skull jutted around the far corner of
the building in a crazy game of peekaboo. He guffawed out a
laugh when she caught him spying on her. Inside the meeting
room the babble of voices stilled abruptly. Pressed up tightly to
the wall, Tess saw light and shadow flash as someone teased
open the blinds for a glimpse outside. The person inside couldn't
possibly spot her from there, but it might only be a matter of
seconds before they came out for a better look. She had to move,
but couldn't get past Cleary. There was nothing for it . . .

She ran across the intervening space in the full wash of the floodlights, and across the front of the canteen building. Behind her, Cleary bayed like a hound dog on a scent and came after her. She heard the door of the meeting room snatched open and feet thud out onto the small porch formed of packing crates. Voices were raised in confusion, some even in alarm when they heard Cleary's hunting call.

Somebody spotted her.

'Hey! You there!'

Tess didn't bother looking back; she was a stranger and an unwelcome one at that. She ran, slipping and stumbling on the clods of churned-up earth. Down near the cars, the three chauffeurs also turned to watch, but she ignored them too.

Where was Pinky?

She could spot neither hide nor hair of her friend.

More importantly, where was Cleary Menon?

His howling was curtailed, but only because he'd flushed her out and now intended stealing on her more stealthily again. She couldn't fathom his intention – was this a game to him or something more sinister?

She had to assume the latter, and prepare for it.

She gripped her Glock tighter, and for one insane moment considered halting, swinging the gun on her pursuers, and demanding to know where Po was. But pointing a gun at a bunch of men, some of them most definitely armed, could invite a deadly response. She couldn't do that: not if she were wrong and Po wasn't here, and all she'd stumbled on was a genuine and lawful gathering of businessmen. She'd be at fault if bullets began popping. But if that damned crazy man tried to lay hands on her again . . .

Cleary skidded out from the other side of the canteen. His grin was back, fixed now in a shark's toothsome smile. Tess dodged to the left to get around him, and her feet went from under her. She landed heavily on her side, and her Glock flipped from her hand. It disappeared in the deep tracks left by an excavator. She crawled after it, pushing aside clumps of sticky muck.

Cleary moved to stand over her. One boot was either side of her thighs as he bent at the waist. Tess flipped over so she could face him, and thrust one hand towards him. He halted, and she watched his grin flicker and disappear as he studied her.

'All muddy now,' he said. 'Not sweet girly-girl.'

As his hands reached for her they'd lost all the tenderness they'd previously exhibited.

'Get away from me!' The heel Tess drove between Cleary's legs punctuated her yell.

The giant huffed out a breath.

If she got him fully in the testicles, he didn't react the way she'd hoped. He seemed to shake off the nauseous turmoil he should have been experiencing in his lower gut with a judder of rage that fired him up. Tess yelped, kicking again, trying to scramble backwards. Cleary snatched at her right ankle, lifted it high in the air, and Tess was borne up with it, dangling in his grasp as he lifted her clear of the ground. Cleary barked, snapped his arm hard, and Tess felt the whip-crack go through her. For the briefest instant it felt as if the kinetic force was about to rip her head from her shoulders, but then she was flying through the air a few feet above the ground. She landed on her shoulders and her body folded into a graceless heap, her knees smacking down brutally on her lower chest. The twin impacts forced every molecule of oxygen from her lungs as she unfurled and lay stunned in the dirt.

She had landed two full body lengths away from Cleary.

He stamped towards her.

Grabbed both her ankles this time and suspended her before him. She was facing away from him, a convulsing wreck as she tried to suck air into her lungs. Tears filled her vision, and the blood thrummed through her brain. She could barely make sense of the group of figures gathering around them, or their words: except they sounded as stunned as her at Cleary's antics.

'Cleary,' a voice rang out. 'Put her down.'

'Mine.'

'Put her down. You don't want to hurt her.'

'Do. She hurt me.'

'Put her down, bra.'

Through her bleary gaze, Tess could see the nearest figure. He was tall, wiry, and wearing a frayed ball cap. Zeke Menon.

'Mine,' Cleary stated again, and he released one ankle, but

only so he could wrap a forearm around her waist. He pulled her in with crushing force, then allowed her legs to fall over his shoulders. Her lower spine was bent achingly. She tried to roll back out of his grip, but Cleary wasn't for letting go. Her legs windmilled either side of his head: horribly his mouth was close to her most intimate parts.

Tess prized at his arm, but there was no freeing herself. She tried to appeal to those around her, but everyone – even Zeke – appeared too wary of challenging Cleary for his prize.

'These are the kind of maniacs you have on your payroll?' It was the suited man with silver hair who'd spoken. He was glaring at the man Tess had tentatively identified as Alistair Keane. 'No wonder everything went to shit. You told me there'd be no more delays in the work schedule, that there'd be no more problems. Then what the hell is this about?'

'I . . . I've no idea who she is,' Keane bleated. He stared at Zeke for clarity.

'I've got everythin' under control,' Zeke Menon assured his bosses. 'Cleary will listen to me. Just give me a minute, Mr Corbin . . .'

'You'd better damn well sort this,' the man referred to as Corbin snapped, 'or there'll be repercussions.' He turned away to console some of the shocked individuals behind him. He began ushering them back towards the meeting room, reminding them they'd previously endured trespassers on their sites, and that environmental activists occasionally tried to sabotage their machinery, convincing them that Tess was one such vandal caught in the act. His scowl was aimed directly at Al Keane, who covered his mouth with one hand, before trudging after them. Keane paused, looked wearily at Zeke. 'Sort this mess, for fuck's sake!'

'Cleary,' Zeke said to his brother, showing the giant both his open palms. 'Put the woman down.'

'Mine,' Cleary growled.

'No, this isn't the girl I promised you, bra. Look at the mess of her, why would you want to play with something as ugly as her? Put her down, and you'll get your sweet girly-girl as soon as I'm finished with her, just like I promised. OK, bra? Are you listening to me?'

'Not mine?' Cleary held Tess out, studying her.

'No. This one isn't yours.'

'Messy,' Cleary observed.

He dumped Tess in another bone-jarring heap at his feet.

'Good. Now go and read your book, Cleary. I'll call you when it's time to get your prize.' Cleary moved away, bent at the waist as he took off in a loping gait. Zeke looked down at Tess, adjusting his cap while shaking his head. Tess pulled herself over onto her backside and sat up, cradling her ribs. When she returned his gaze there was no thanks in her eyes for saving her: she was seething. He frowned, studying her closely. As Corbin had pointed out, the pipeline had attracted the attention of some activist groups concerned by how the route was damaging the local terrain and displacing indigenous wildlife, and more than once he'd had to chase objectors away from the site, and one of them into a grave. But this woman didn't look like a tree-hugger. She was filthy; her features were puffy, flushed and streaked with dirt, but otherwise she looked like a normal person. But he thought he recognized her from somewhere. He couldn't think where he had seen her before but it was recent.

He bent over her, peering closer.

Then stood upright, adjusting the rim of his lucky hat in thought.

'I saw you at the hospital earlier,' he said in sudden recognition. 'You were with that sumbitch, Nicolas Villere!'

'She was,' said another voice, 'and she was also with me.'

Zeke snatched at the knife hilt protruding from the sheath on his hip, while spinning quickly to confront his other old enemy.

'Too slow, you,' said Pinky as he battered the barrel of his Glock down on Zeke's head.

THIRTY-ONE

A frantic five-minute drive later, Pinky pulled the SUV off the levee road and onto a bridge that took them over the still waters of the bayou. Once on the opposite side, he found a secondary road that skirted a neighbourhood of suburban housing, and pulled up in the deserted lot outside a strip mall. All the stores and businesses had closed for the night, except for one fast-food joint at the far end from where they sat. There were no customers entering or leaving, but even if any came they were far away enough to avoid prying eyes. Pinky switched on the overhead light so he could study Tess.

Tess still looked beaten to hell. Her features were slack with shock. She didn't look at him.

'Are you OK?' he asked, leaning towards her. 'That was something you just went through, you.'

'We shouldn't have left,' Tess said. She still wouldn't look at him.

'I had to get you outta there, Tess. There was nothing for it, not with them other guys coming over.'

'Twice in one evening I've been slung over someone's shoulder like a sack of corn,' she said. She glimpsed sideways at him this time, and Pinky's face constricted in a frown.

'I took a bit more care about carrying you than that crazy brute did.' Pinky stared forward, his gaze settling in the far distance. His mouth worked silently. He looked over at her again. 'What in God's name was that?'

Tess shook her head, and the motion followed as a qualm down her spine. She gripped her knees to stop shuddering. 'That was Cleary Menon.'

'You sure? He looked more like the Wolfman, him.'

Tess didn't argue. Cleary had been reminiscent of some monstrous creature out of legend. His shaggy hair, deep-set eyes, and tusky mouth gave him the appearance of something primal, but it hadn't been his looks that had left her shaken.

His strength went beyond anything she'd ever experienced in a human before, but it wasn't even the way he'd manhandled her as if she was an insubstantial doll filled with feathers that had left her reeling. It was the unfathomable process of his mind that she couldn't come to terms with, his weirdness that left her feeling as if she'd been touched by something uncanny. 'I don't believe in werewolves,' she said lamely, but she couldn't convince herself. There was something decidedly wrong about Cleary Menon. She could have as well been the plaything of a carnivore toying with its catch. Reasoning with him would have proved impossible.

'I should have been there to protect you,' Pinky groaned in apology. 'I didn't get to you in time. I'm sorry, Tess.'

'It wasn't your fault,' she reassured him.

But he wasn't done apologizing. 'I lost sight of you, was watching those fools at the cars instead. Didn't know that you were in trouble 'til I heard that crazy man howling like a loon. By the time I spotted you, he was holding you upside down, inspecting you like a fish on a line. I was gonna pop him right then and there, but then all those other guys in suits gathered round. What could I do: shoot them all? Couldn't do a damn thing, me! Not 'til they went back inside and left you alone with Zeke. Shoulda capped that fucker, instead of knocking him out.'

'There was nothing else you could do,' Tess reassured him again. 'It's not your fault, Pinky. I put myself in danger, poking around too long. I should've been more careful, but I let Cleary corner me. You got me out, and that's all that's important.'

Pinky shook his head. His jowls hung low, and his chocolate eyes were dull; he was deeply sad and it was not a look she was familiar with from the usual jovial guy. He felt that the roughhousing she'd endured was down to him and would take a lot of convincing otherwise. Tess reached over and folded her hand into his. He patted her hand with the fingers of his other hand.

'If you'd come to my rescue any sooner I wouldn't have learned what I did,' she announced.

She was being jerked around like a ragdoll in the hands of a boisterous child, her brain rattling and her thoughts all over the place, and yet she'd still absorbed some of what was going on around her. In as few words as she could, she explained to Pinky about the meeting of businessmen, and that the top man in the room had been referred to as Mr Corbin. Corbin wasn't too pleased with his lackey, Alistair Keane, or with Zeke and Cleary Menon for that matter. The three were obviously on his payroll, and were supposed to avoid any further problems and delays. It didn't take much figuring out: they were tasked with keeping the pipeline construction on schedule. Keane was the building contractor, so his responsibility was in the overall management of the project, whereas the Menons' had a different focus. Theirs, she suggested, was to ensure that nobody got in the way of the job, and it didn't take too much imagination figuring out how. They were troubleshooters in the most literal sense. If anyone got in the way of progress, the Menons removed them. She thought of the trapper camp they'd recently visited, and how the Thibodauxs had sequestered themselves on land the pipeline was scheduled to cut through. She wondered if the Menons employed various tactics to run off troublemakers, perhaps with bribes, threats or beatings, but to what lengths would they go to if the more recalcitrant of people dug their heels in? Those pools of blood they'd found spoke volumes.

There had been no hint that Po had been at the site, although Zeke had mentioned seeing her with him at the hospital earlier in the day. From the way he spoke Po's name, it sounded as if he hoped to meet him face to face, but hadn't yet had the pleasure. She was thankful for that small mercy, but it left her with a more worrying thought. If Po hadn't gone after Zeke then it left few others that he'd have sloped off for a reckoning with. He hadn't suddenly been inspired by where to find his missing sister, he'd gone after her father and brothers. She didn't care to dwell on what Po had done . . . and positively wouldn't think about what could have gone wrong.

She turned to Pinky again, and told him the most important thing she'd learned from her run in with the Menon brothers. 'Zeke convinced Cleary to drop me in exchange for another "prize". He said something about another girl he'd promised to give to Cleary as soon as he finished with her.'

'So he does have Emilia?'

'He didn't mention her by name, but who else could he have been talking about?'

'He actually said he had her?'

'No. Just that he wasn't finished with her yet. That could mean he's still looking for her, but . . .'

'You think he's holding her somewhere, but hasn't finished having fun with her before handing her over.'

'It's not a pleasant thought.'

'But she's not at that site, her?'

'I couldn't find her. But I didn't get to check everywhere before Cleary surprised me and the chase was on.'

'I should've dragged that son of a bitch Zeke back here with us. I'd make the piece of shit tell us where Emilia is.'

Pinky's hands had been full toting her semi-conscious butt to safety without trying to carry an unconscious man as well. The chauffeurs, thankfully bewildered by the sudden activity on the site, had come to investigate, but had backed off when Pinky waved his Glock at them, winning enough time and space to throw Tess over his shoulder and jog with her through the gate and along the track to their car. One of them had run to alert those in the meeting room, while the others had gone to assist Zeke. Pinky had driven them away at speed before any pursuit could be mounted.

'One good thing has come out of this,' Tess reasoned. 'If Zeke was talking about Emilia, it tells us she's still alive. It's not too late to save her.'

'Want to go back?' Pinky dug in his shoulder holster for his gun.

'I'm unarmed,' Tess admitted. 'I lost my gun back there in the mud when Cleary was throwing me around.'

'I can get more guns,' Pinky said.

'It's not guns we need.'

'Nicolas,' he stated in agreement.

Mention of his name acted like some kind of summoning spell. Tess heard the familiar ringtone of her cell squawking away in the purse she'd left in the car. Po. She dug out the phone, and answered.

'Hey,' said Po.

Relief washed the shivers from her body, but it also caused

her chest to hitch, as if kick-started by a jolt of electricity. Her voice was as sharp as a slap to the face. 'Hey? That's all you've got say for yourself? Where the freakin' hell are you, Po?'

'Had something I needed to do,' he said.

'And as usual you ran off and did it all by yourself! Jesus, Po, we've been looking all over the place for you. Do you realize how worried I've been?'

'I have an inkling.'

'A fucking *inkling*?' Tess turned and stared at Pinky, who softly shook his head. A smile rode his lips again; he was as happy to hear from Po as she was. But he wouldn't berate Po for his disappearing trick the way she was happy to.

'You sound pissed,' Po said, and grunted in mirth. 'I guess it's understandable. But at least you're safe and uninjured.'

Pinky's head came up, and was in danger of saying something, but Tess held up a hand and shook her head. She didn't want Po to know what she'd just gone through. The focus should stay on him until he'd damned well explained himself. Then his words forced a way past her anger.

'Please tell me you're not unsafe and injured.'

'Well, one out of two ain't bad.'

'Where are you, Po? We're coming.'

'I'm back at the hospital. Before you get all twisted out of shape, I'm not getting stitched up. Just looking for you guys.' The way he spoke, did he really expect that she'd hang around at the hospital while he was off who knew where?

'We're on our way back.' She looked at Pinky who fired up the engine and shoved the SUV into drive. 'What were you thinking of, going off on your own like that?'

'Best for everyone,' he replied, and she knew he wouldn't be moved on his reason. 'I went to see Darius.'

'Tell me you didn't . . .'

'Took a new approach for a change. Wasn't it you that once encouraged me to give diplomacy a chance?'

'It worked?'

'It hurt.'

'Sometimes you have to put aside pride to get the result you're after.'

'It's not my pride that's hurt. I mean literally. I tried diplomacy,

Darius and his kin weren't for listening.' Po cut off her squawk of alarm. 'Don't worry. Got him to see my point of view in the end. We buried the hatchet, so to speak, for the sake of finding Emilia.'

Tess closed her eyes. The only thing that made her feel easier was his relatively easy manner. He was injured, but not too badly, and hopefully the same could be said for the Chatards. 'You can tell me all about it when we get back. How's Clara?'

'Couldn't get in to see her, but she's not faring too well. Only Darius has been allowed in.'

'You're there with Darius?'

'You expected me to walk all the way back?'

'I didn't expect you to run off in the first place. If I did, would I have let you out of my sight? OK, never mind all that. We're coming.' Tess looked at Pinky for clarification.

'Fifteen minutes,' he said.

'OK. Hang tight,' Tess told Po. 'And you'd better be there when we arrive. There's a lot you need to hear about.'

'Tell me.'

'Not on your life. If I tell you now, you won't wait for us.'

'Tess . . .'

'Nope. You're not going off on another damned solo mission.'
She hung up.

THIRTY-TWO

Blood trickled from his scalp, tracking a meandering route down Zeke's forehead, before taking a sharp turn over the top of his ear and down towards the collar of his shirt. Al Keane shoved a handful of paper napkins towards him. 'Clean yourself up, goddamnit.'

Zeke balled the tissues and dabbed at the blood, wiping up towards the rim of his cap.

'Take the damn cap off, Zeke. You need to stem the flow not just mop it up.'

Ignoring the advice, Zeke shoved the wad of tissues under the rim, and left it in situ to catch any further leakage. 'This cap once saved my life; pretty sure it just did so again. If I wasn't wearing it, I'm sure that sneaky nigger woulda smashed my skull.'

'Don't you ever take it off? What do you do when you wash your hair, suffer separation anxiety?'

'Who says I wash my hair?'

Keane's face twisted in revulsion. 'Keep the fucking cap on.'

Zeke snorted in disregard.

He was seated on one of the chairs recently vacated by Corbin's business associates in the meeting room. He'd made it there under his own steam after being dragged back from unconsciousness by the chauffeurs who'd run to his aid. His head was throbbing, and a sharper pain marked where Pinky Leclerc's gun barrel had impacted on his skull. He could taste copper in the back of his throat, and nausea roiled in his stomach. He was certain that if he tried to stand too quickly, his legs wouldn't support him. He was in no mood for Keane's bullshit. Though, to be fair, Keane was only trying to help. He was also intent on briefing Zeke before Nate Corbin returned. Their boss was currently outside bidding farewells and trying to forge continued relations with his investors.

'I told you Cleary was out of control,' Keane bleated. 'Look at where he's gotten us now.'

'I think you owe Cleary a debt of gratitude, Al. If it wasn't for him, none of us would be any the wiser that we'd been spied upon.'

Now it was Keane that snorted. 'He should have raised the alarm, not gone after that woman like he did. We could have caught her and her friend, and sent them on their way without giving them any cause for suspicion. Cleary attacked her, Zeke! What do you think is going to happen now?'

'If you're worried she's gonna go runnin' to the cops, think again. She was trespassing on private property. Her and her pet nigger were armed. You really think they're gonna complain to the law?'

'That's the thing! Why were they here, armed like that?'

His question was moot.

'They've no idea that Emilia's here.'

'How do you know?'

'I just do.'

'And what the hell brought them here in the first place? It's that mess you left at the Thibodaux camp. Somehow they've tied that clusterfuck to *me*! You assured me that the Thibodaux brothers would disappear quietly, that there'd be nobody in the way of the pipeline's progress. Look at where that's gotten us! Cops swarming all over their camp, and now . . . I don't know who these people are, but they're obviously looking for Emilia. And crazy-fucking-Cleary only went and gave them more reason to believe we've something to hide.'

'Don't call him crazy.'

'Have you a better definition of his actions? What the fuck was all that howling about?'

'What can I say? He enjoys expressing his enjoyment.'

'Are you yanking my chain?'

'Just telling it like it is, Al.'

'What would he have done to her if you weren't there?'

'Best you never know, Keane. Just in case the cops do come here.'

Keane was already pallid, but now the blood drained out his features, leaving almost translucent skin on his temples and upper lip. He sat down heavily in the chair alongside Zeke.

He placed his face in his hands and groaned. 'A moment ago you were confident the cops wouldn't be called.'

'There's always the possibility. If the Thibodauxs had just fallen off the face of the planet like I always planned, there'd be no reason for the cops to look for them. Could be different now. I'm thinking that bitch that Cleary got his hands on was the one to tip the cops off about the blood at the camp. Wouldn't be surprised if she made a similar anonymous tip-off about some naughty goings on here. Under the circumstances the cops probably will follow it up.'

'Then the sooner Emilia's out of here the better.'

'You've got that right, Al. Just need a minute or two to shake some of these cobwebs loose, and then I'll get on it.'

'And what then?'

'Then you can tell Corbin you can carry on digging. The best way to avoid suspicion is to keep on going as normal, Al.'

'Corbin's business partners witnessed that madness. What if they speak about it?'

'I'm sure Mr Corbin has enough influence to persuade them otherwise. Besides, if the cops do turn up, you tell them that you had some trouble with environmental terrorists and had to chase them off. Convince them that the anonymous tip-off has come from one of them hoping to cause you further delays. Then you demand action from the cops, that they do something to stop the damn tree-huggers from harassing you. Believe me, Al, if they think you're adding to their workload, you won't see them for dust.'

'The cops aren't stupid . . .'

'Al, you're not gonna get a visit from a Homicide detective, just some shit-kicker from the Iberia Parish Sheriff's Office at most. In my experience Sheriff's deputies are the dumbest of dumb fucks, and lazy with it.'

THIRTY-THREE

Tess was conflicted.

She came from a family dedicated to law enforcement, with two brothers still serving. Her father used to be a cop, and her grandfather before him. She'd served too, attaining the rank of sergeant with the Cumberland County Sheriff's Office before her injury sidelined her from duty, and since then she'd made a living as a private investigator, hoping to right wrongs in the only way left to her. Her career plan had always been to follow the family tradition, and if fate hadn't intervened she would still be a Sheriff's deputy, albeit higher up the ranks by now. Following Po's action plan flew in the face of everything she had ever stood for. Those that enforced the law did not applaud vigilantism. And yet, despite the prickling of her moral centre, she was with him this time.

She wasn't sure about the confederates Po had recruited, though. Darius Chatard, his son Francis, and a nephew called Jean had all expressed their interest in getting Emilia safely home, and were due to rendezvous with them near to the construction site she and Pinky had recently fled. Jean had even loaned Po his car – the silver Toyota Camry she'd watched skid to a halt earlier that evening outside the hospital. Apparently when the Chatards had lifted Po, his gun and cellphone had been taken from him and dumped in the car's trunk. He'd since liberated both, along with the keys to the car.

Because Pinky's SUV was identifiable to those at the site, Po had driven the three of them to a picnic area alongside Bayou Chene in the Toyota Camry, to wait for the Chatards to arrive. They had to wait while Darius had an injury patched up.

They had got out of the car, Po and Pinky both checking their guns, while Tess stood feeling like an amateur having lost hers. Given time Pinky could have replaced the gun for her, but time was against them. Po didn't offer her his knife. She wouldn't have taken it. As crazy as it sounded, she could shoot someone, but never stick them with a blade.

'And you're positive we can trust them?' Tess asked, and it was simply the rewording of similar questions she'd aimed at Po since he'd informed her about their new allies.

'If this were simply about finding Emilia, I'm not so sure,' he said, 'but when Darius learned that Zeke Menon was trying to work him over for cash, he hit the roof. Would you believe Zeke went to Darius and offered to kill me for him: the caveat being that Darius doubled the bounty on my head? As bad luck would have it, Zeke was with Darius when Emilia phoned home to say she was going to the hospital. I think Zeke went straight from Darius to the hospital and grabbed her there. Darius is of the same opinion, and is spitting bullets about the guy's nerve in asking for double the money when he was planning on snatching his daughter.'

'Says a lot about how much he cares for Emilia . . . not.'

'Yeah, he has a skewed way of looking at things. Been that way for decades, so it's hardly surprising.'

He'd already described what had happened since allowing the Chatards to snatch him. If he hadn't, the bumps and bruises he carried would have explained what kind of parley he'd endured with Darius and his kinfolk. His right eye was almost swollen shut, and he'd a cut above his right ear, and enough scuffs and bruises about his face that made her fearful to check out his body. He walked stiffly, and favored his right arm, and she'd noted him rubbing at sore ribs more than once. He was in no fit state for a fight, but then she was hardly top of her game either. He looked like an extra from *The Walking Dead*, but had shooed off any attempt she made at soothing his injuries. He was more concerned about hers.

He'd looked mortified when she'd earlier slid from Pinky's SUV and gone to him. She was building up to give him a good scolding, but when she'd spotted his disarray, and the bruises and marks on his face, her demeanor had changed and she'd dropped any admonishment in favour of a hug. He'd hissed in pain as she squeezed him, then gently pressed her away so he could study her under the Toyota's headlights. She was shaken, a bit achy, but otherwise had gotten off lightly.

Pinky had apologized to him for allowing her to fall into the clutches of the Menon brothers, but it was unnecessary. Tess assured Po that Pinky's intervention had most likely saved her life, and Po was under no doubt his friend had done everything he could for her. She told him then about what Zeke had promised his brother. The woman who would be Cleary's prize just had to be Emilia, right? Who else could it be?

Nobody was under any illusion. By seeking Po at the construction site, Tess and Pinky had inadvertently stumbled on where Emilia could have been hidden. But they'd made a mistake and alerted Zeke Menon to them. He had no idea that Po had been missing, and would assume that they were there looking for his hostage. If he had any sense he would move Emilia without delay . . . or do something far worse to her. He could give her to Cleary as promised, but that might take too much time: for all any of them knew he could have slit Emilia's throat and buried her under one of the concrete pilings being poured to support the new pipeline.

It was the early hours of the morning, full dark. Po had left the headlamps on to see by, and thousands of bugs swarmed in the dome of light. As they waited for the Chatards to arrive Tess again suggested calling the police without delay.

Po wasn't confident they could help in time.

'Down to us,' he said, 'and I promised Darius I wouldn't make a move without him.'

'Suddenly you owe that prick?' Pinky asked, looking shocked by the suggestion.

'I guess I do. He's known all along that Emilia wasn't his, but has raised her all the same. So he wouldn't win any father-of-the-year awards, but he could've been an asshole about it and kicked her and my mother loose. He didn't differentiate between her and his other kids, didn't even let slip to any of them that Emilia wasn't their full sister. Didn't want any of them taking out their hatred of me on her.'

'He's a real saint, him,' said Pinky, unconvinced.

'Play nice when they get here,' Po warned.

'They been hounding my best friend for years, now I've to smile and pat them on their backs, me?'

'If I can do it you can.'

'What's to stop them turning on you after this is over with?' Tess said.

'We shared spit,' Po said.

'You did what?'

He mimed spitting on his palm. 'We shook. Feuds run long round here, but so do solemn promises.'

Tess shared a frown with Pinky.

'Apparently gullibility isn't in short order either,' she said, and Po actually grinned at her wit.

'If Darius intends reneging on the deal, then there's not much I can do about it now. Let's wait and see. If he comes through for us, then I'll stick to my side of the bargain.'

'What exactly did you promise him?'

'Told him I wouldn't nail his other boot to the ground.'

'His other boot?' Tess stared at him.

'Stuck my knife through his foot. Only way I could pin him down and get him to listen to me.'

'He-he! That's what you meant when you said he was hopping mad,' said Pinky. 'It had nothing to do with hearing Zeke Menon was playing him for a fool.'

'I had to break Leon Chatard's hands, and shut up some dick called Rocco so's he'd keep his smart mouth out of things. But all came right in the end. I think we can trust Darius, and if not, well he's bringing along others who can be counted on. Francis is Emilia's brother, Jean's her cousin, and they genuinely want to help her. Y'know, if not for everything that has gone between us, I could grow to like those guys.'

'You're shittin' me,' said Pinky.

Po only served him with a quick jerk of his lips.

'If nothing else, they'll do for cannon fodder, them. Or chum to feed to that shark called Cleary. I guess I can keep my peace while they have their uses.'

Tess scratched at an insect bite on her right cheek. Swatted at some multi-coloured bug that fluttered in her vision. 'If we don't get out of here soon I'm going to lose it completely,' she snapped. 'I'd rather wrestle Cleary Menon again than put up with these damn bugs any longer.'

'Be careful what you wish for.' Po eyed her, and she got the message. He wasn't being flippant. 'When we get there, stick close to Pinky.'

'I won't let that rougarou-looking fool touch you again, pretty Tess.'

'Rougarou? That's something like a werewolf, isn't it?' Tess would take anything to keep her mind off the present, where she was equal parts harassed by the swamp life, sore in her joints, and nauseous with anxiety about what was to come. She'd heard tales about the Louisiana Boogeyman before, but had taken only a layperson's interest in the subject. 'Is there any truth in the legend?'

Pinky beamed his pleasure at her. 'It's total bullshit, you ax me. But there are some ignorant inbred folks aroun' here believe in the supernatural.' He winked over at Po for emphasis.

Tess glimpsed at her partner. He shrugged. 'Seen some strange things in those swamps when I was a boy. I'm not closed-minded like some folks I can mention—' he gave an exaggerated look at Pinky – 'and besides, it was *you* that brought up the subject of rougarou.'

'Well, I can assure you Cleary Menon is very real, me. Won't need to cap his ass with silver bullets, if that's what you're worried about.'

'I'm not worried about him or his brother, I'm looking forward to putting both of them down.'

'I'm not sure we should be planning on capping anyone's ass,' Tess cautioned. 'Cleary has something wrong with him, without a doubt he's psychologically challenged. It makes him unpredictable and dangerous, but it doesn't give us the right to shoot him like a sick dog.'

Neither of her companions replied. They took a different stance than she did. A flash memory engulfed her of Cleary holding her aloft, studying her like a tasty morsel he was about to chow down on. Who knew what would have happened to her if Zeke hadn't intervened at that moment? He had mental problems, and ordinarily she would have pitied him, but given the alternative, if Cleary got his hands on her again she would shoot him rather than let him sink in his teeth.

The growl of an engine announced the arrival of their unlikely allies.

Pinky held his gun down by his thigh, but didn't put it away, still unconvinced of the Chatards' trustworthiness. But Po had shoved his Glock in his waistband and didn't take it out now. Tess stood so that she was partly hidden from view; the wash of headlights bathed them as a Dodge Ram truck pulled into the picnic area. There was nobody riding on the back, the only people apparent the trio that filled the cab.

Whenever Tess had pictured Po's enemies before she'd always conjured images of rednecks in flannel shirts, bib-and-braces dungarees and scuffed work boots, John Deere ball caps and perhaps cross-eyes. As the three clambered down, the third man leaning heavily on the door for support, she saw she was wrong. All her preconceived notions of the Cajun family were thrown for a loop when the three men presented themselves before Po and looked like they had dressed for a relaxed, informal supper in open-necked shirts, jeans, and sneakers. The anomaly that picked them out as unusual was in the bandaged right foot of the eldest man. To help protect his dressings from contamin-ation, Darius Chatard had donned one of those plastic overshoes available to surgeons in operating theatres and CSI techs at crime scenes. If Po had recently rammed his knife through his foot, the injury didn't appear to be troubling him too much. He limped, but not overtly. Tess guessed that a mixture of pain medication, anger, and anxiety was keeping Darius moving, the way it was her partner.

Darius didn't look like the ogre she'd pictured. He looked like an old man, and a father worried about his child's welfare. Francis Chatard, dark-haired, wearing a day's worth of stubble, was handsome and statuesque, and could have made a living as a model if he'd been given the openings, while Jean, fairer-haired and round-faced, was the type of bland guy you passed in the street without noticing. It was hard to imagine that any of them had ever entertained murdering her lover, or even paying someone else to do it on their behalf, but it was the truth. You didn't have to look like Cleary Menon to be a monster.

She was judging them unfairly. When all was said and done, they were kin to two men who'd fallen victim to Po's venge-ance, and even Po had admitted that if the shoe were on the other foot, he'd want to see him punished too. She had to put aside the enmity she'd bred for these people, if they were going to work together to bring back safely the one person who might mend the rift between the Villere and Chatard families.

Po made the introductions. Pinky remained cool towards the trio, even when Darius looked him up and down as if he couldn't believe what kind of person he'd allied himself to: black, gay, and unwilling to put away his gun, Darius couldn't decide what he disliked most about him.

'Chill, bra,' Pinky sneered at Darius. 'I'm not too keen on lame-assed whip-crackers either, me. If I had my way, there'd be no kissin' and makin' up, but this ain't about me.'

Tess sometimes forgot how scary Pinky could be when he switched from cuddly teddy bear to illegal arms trader mode. She got a hint of it now, and so did Darius, who bit down on the retort that was building on his lips.

Instead of responding, Darius pulled a gun from his belt. 'I'm lame, thanks to Nicolas, but I won't be a dead weight. Are we going to go and see Zeke now?'

'Before you straighten things with him,' Po reminded, 'I need to speak with him. We go in first, you and your guys come in when we give you the sign.'

'What is the sign?' Darius asked.

Po's smile was grim. 'You'll know it when you see it.'

THIRTY-FOUR

Emilia had worked diligently at loosening the strips of duct tape that bound her to the chair, but all that she had managed was to rub the skin raw at her wrists and ankles. She'd forced a little give in the bonds holding her arms, but not enough that she could worm free from them yet. With more time and effort, she was confident that she could pull at least one hand free, and from there loosen her other restraints. She was prepared to put in the exertion, but knew that time was not on her side. If only she'd been capable of more movement earlier, she might have been able to raise the alarm, and let the unknown woman outside know she was a prisoner. She had heard the woman prowling around, and had cried out, but the balled socks still jammed in her mouth and taped in place had stifled her, and when she'd tried scraping the chair across the floor had found the sound deadened by the spongy plyboard. What little noise she'd made was covered by the murmur of voices from another nearby building, and the woman had moved off, continuing her search elsewhere.

She only knew the seeker was female because shortly after she'd made her way around the cabin she had fallen foul of the monstrous Cleary. The woman had tried to be polite at first, and then assertive, but there was no getting through to the brute unless you were called Zeke. Then the woman had been forced to run, and Emilia knew this because she'd listened with a tremor racking her frame as Cleary howled and took up the chase. It was the same demented call he'd made when stalking, and ultimately tracking to ground, her boyfriend Jason. The chase had taken him to the other side of the construction site, and Emilia had no idea what had befallen the woman. All she could be sure of was that her appearance had thrown confusion among those who'd gathered – to determine her fate? – in the nearby cabin. There had been a lot of activity since, and she had listened to the excitable voices of people intent on making a rapid getaway, and the sounds of vehicles leaving the compound in a hurry. She hadn't heard the woman's screams, but maybe Cleary didn't give her the chance. She couldn't count on any assistance from the mystery woman, so getting away was all down to her own efforts now. If anything the woman's interference had possibly trimmed what time she had left. Zeke would return, and probably sooner than he would have if the woman hadn't caused the flurry of panic.

She hadn't heard Cleary since he'd grabbed the woman. But she was certain one of the voices she'd heard filtering through the walls of her prison belonged to Zeke. Her tormentor had not finished with her yet: a small blessing. Because she was certain that once he was done questioning her, then it would mark her final seconds of life. He had threatened her with a knife before, and she only hoped that when the time came, he'd do her the small mercy of cutting her throat decisively. Rather that than be handed over to his brother for disposal.

Other voices she'd heard were those of men she didn't know, and hadn't laid eyes on yet, but had surmised were Keane and Corbin. Keane was a whining coward, Corbin a snappy, arrogant asshole. Neither of them personally planned her death, from what she could overhear, but that didn't surprise her. They had the Menons, who'd dirty their hands on their behalf. Her boyfriend had been murdered, and she was next. Who knew what had become of the woman from earlier. All this trouble because they had stumbled into a business arrangement built on profit and greed. From what she'd gathered from the snippets of conversations she'd overheard, Zeke had been employed to bribe, coerce, or force away any opposition to the progress of a damned pipeline. A swathe of swampland designated for its route wasn't officially owned by Hal and Jamie Thibodaux, but they had a historical claim on it, and weren't for moving. Enough money wasn't offered to convince them to move, not when they were suddenly rolling in cash from the sale of illegal drugs, and they were too stupid to be coerced, so Zeke had employed a heavier hand: in fact the heaviest type. The Thibodauxs were slaughtered, and that would have been the end of the problem, if Emilia and Jace hadn't witnessed the aftermath. Zeke told her that the land was due to be bulldozed within a week, and any trace of the camp and the Thibodaux brothers' remains would have been buried without trace. But her interference had gone and spoiled everything. Before the crime scene could be sanitized someone had gone and tipped off the cops, and Zeke wanted to know who the hell she had squealed to. Emilia couldn't convince him that she'd kept his secret, and she doubted she ever would now that the unknown woman had come snooping around. Who was she? What was her interest in the site? Was she looking for Emilia or something else? All questions without answers.

Whomever, whatever, the woman had been seeking, she'd found neither, only violence at the hands of Cleary. Emilia couldn't count on the woman, so had to get on with freeing herself.

She fought with her bonds, groaning at the effort. More skin was chafed raw. She rocked the chair back and forth, but if it toppled what then? This tubular steel and plastic construct wouldn't come apart easily, so she'd be left lying on the floor, without any leverage available to pull and twist at her bindings.

The more she strained the harder it was to breathe. Sweat poured from her hairline, got in her eyes and in her nostrils. As she exhaled a fine mist sprayed before her. In her mouth the foul socks were sodden, but that made speaking more diffi-cult as the material cleaved to the roof of her mouth and rubbed her tongue raw. Water hadn't passed her lips since she was in the truck on the way to the hospital. She was growing dehy-drated, and her exertions only sped up the process: she could sense an oncoming headache like a hungry predator about to pounce.

A headache's the least of your problems, she reminded herself. Get loose or die.

She struggled, and finally, with a sawing motion of her right hand found a gap opening in the tape on her wrist. She fed her fingers into it, pulling and tugging, and got a tear going. The tape zipped apart, but it was only one strip of many. She continued writhing, ripping, and yanking, and with a final wrench her right hand popped free. Gasping, she pawed for her

other hand, but couldn't reach it easily. She tore at the length
of tape fastening her to the headrest, but didn't waste time
loosening the gag. Screaming would get her nowhere fast.
Instead she leaned forward as far as possible and began tearing
apart the tape around her ankles. Once they were free she was
able to stand, move around the chair, and start on loosening her
left arm.

She was so intent on the task, she'd no idea that Zeke had
re-entered the office until the key turned in the lock. She reared
up, dragging the chair still attached to her arm, as Zeke threw
open the door.

'Well, ain't you the spirited one?' Zeke crowed as he eyed
her from the doorway.

Emilia clutched the chair before her chest, the legs aimed at
him, as if she were the modern incarnation of a circus lion
tamer.

She gurgled a warning through the gag.

A snort of derision was her only reward as Zeke stepped into
the small room, grabbed the chair, and yanked it savagely to
one side. Bound to it still, Emilia staggered, and Zeke caught
her hair in his left fist. In his right the knife had appeared. He
sat the flat of the blade alongside her left eye as he leaned in
close. His sour breath washed over her. In that moment she
expected instant death, and as defeat assailed her, her gaze fell
on the dried blood around his ear and gathered under the rim
of his stinking cap. More of his blood stained his shirt collar.
Zeke hadn't had it all his own way with the woman Cleary had
chased. That simple nugget of knowledge was enough to give
Emilia hope.

Had the mystery woman escaped after all?

Was she bringing help?

It would explain the panic and urgency that had flooded
through the others who'd quickly evacuated the site.

'After all the trouble you've caused me I should kill you right
now, bitch,' Zeke snarled. 'But I ain't gonna. No. I've something
better in mind for you.'

He turned so abruptly that she didn't know she'd been cast
aside until she crumpled against the doorframe, caught up in
the office chair. Zeke grabbed it, hauling it up and away from

her, and swiped once with the edge of his knife. Her left arm sprang loose, trailing the severed duct tape like a pennon shredded by gale-force winds. She was now free of the damned chair, and there was an open door right beside her. But before she could gather herself to lunge through it, Zeke's fingers were in her hair again and she was hauled on her hands and knees into the office.

One of the men who'd assisted in her capture blocked the exit. It was the stockier of the two with the shaved head and the stud in his eyebrow.

'Did you bring up the van like I said?' demanded Zeke.

'Tyson's on it, bra.' The young man's face was creased with worry as he stared at Emilia.

'Good. Put her in the back.' He slung Emilia to the other man, who clasped both hands on her shoulders. 'And Croft, don't fucking let her out of your sight for a second, do ya hear me?'

'Got her, Zeke.'

'What about Harry and Rory?' Zeke said.

'Ty phoned Harry, but he didn't pick up.'

'Doesn't surprise me, Harry's a useless piece of shit. I gave him simple instructions, told him to watch her place and stay close to his phone, and the sumbitch can't even do that. When was the last time you heard from him?'

In the act of pulling Emilia into his embrace, Croft was a beat slow in answering. Once he had his captive under control, Emilia's arms pinned in the circle of his, he looked back at Zeke. 'I haven't heard from him in hours.'

'What about his fuckwit buddy?'

'I've no reason to speak to Rory.'

'You have now. Those two ass-bandits are like conjoined twins. Once you get her in the van, tell Tyson to call Rory and ask him what the fuck's going on with his buddy. Then have Tyson tell him they better get their lazy asses to the dumpsite to give us a hand. Make sure Tyson tells them they better not let me down, there's plenty more space in the ground for them too.'

Nodding, Croft backed out of the door with Emilia.

Her eyes were huge, the whites almost luminous around the

turquoise as she stared back at Zeke over her gag. He met her gaze, but his was pitiless. He dragged at the peak of his cap. 'And where the hell has Cleary got to now? He won't want to miss this.'

THIRTY-FIVE

H er earlier incursion of the construction site had shown Tess that it was neither impregnable nor heavily guarded. Of the people she'd seen only the chauffeurs were armed, but they weren't regular attendees, being present only because they had driven their charges to the meeting. Those guys most likely had no inkling of the crimes that the Menon brothers or their employers were involved in. She urged her confederates to avoid hurting any of them. But her point proved moot, because by the time they arrived back at the construction hub, all but one of the visitors had fled the scene and with them their cars and drivers. There was no way of telling until she got eyes on him, but she suspected the man who'd stayed behind was the silver-haired guy called Corbin. She had also cautioned Po especially about other possible innocent workers on the site. Although she'd seen nobody that fit the bill, there could still be a few of the regular construction workers around. She doubted it, because it was obvious to her that the meeting wasn't the type the attendees would wish to be overheard. Perhaps anyone not involved with the criminal element of their business had been given the night off. She hadn't noticed a uniformed security presence, which struck her as odd. At the very least she thought Keane would hire nightwatchmen. Due to the delicate nature of the meeting, she assumed any security guards had been sent to patrol the pipeline: currently work was underway along a large stretch of land, and there were other pockets of activity where excavation and construction equipment was vulnerable to thieves and vandals.

Tess, her friends, and their unlikely allies had gathered on land a few hundred yards to the west of the construction hub, choosing a different approach than the one used by her and Pinky earlier. The land was slightly elevated, and the forest sparse enough so that they could overlook the site, and the excavated swampland beyond it.

'Anyone tries to stop us, they're fair game,' Darius growled in response. But Po shook his head, supporting Tess's logic.

'We don't go in with guns blazing. We check first that Emilia's even here.'

Darius stared at Tess. 'Your girl here said Zeke promised Emilia to his crazy brother.'

'He didn't actually mention her by name,' Po said.

'He said Cleary could have the "sweet girly-girl" as soon as Zeke was finished with her,' Tess clarified. 'He promised to call his brother when it was time to get his prize. It tells me there was a woman being held close by.'

'And who d' hell do you think he was referring to?'

'Even if it wasn't Emilia he was talking about, there's some poor girl in danger,' Po agreed.

'I don't care about some other girl,' Darius growled.

'We do,' said Po.

'Suit yersels, but we're here for Emilia. An' for dat puke-ball Zeke Menon. Don't know who dat sumbitch thinks he is . . .'

Francis Chatard, who was twenty feet away, keeping an eye on the site, gave a low whistle. He waved them over. All but Pinky and Jean moved towards his position. Darius grumbled under his breath as he negotiated the undergrowth with his game leg.

'A van just turned up,' Francis informed them. 'Y'see it?'

A panel van had entered the compound and driven close to one of the portable structures. Though the floodlights brought false noon to the site, the distance, and the angle, thwarted them from seeing who got in or out of the van.

Tess quickly calculated her earlier progress through the site, following the point from where she and Pinky had entered under the chain-link fence, and past the cabins she'd designated as a canteen and then a meeting hall. 'I checked that hut out earlier,' she said, 'and it looked like an office. But there was a smaller anteroom I couldn't get a look inside. I thought it was a stationery or store cupboard, but the odd thing was there was a light on inside it. Now when I see it from this angle, the dimensions look bigger than I thought.'

Emilia, or some other unfortunate girl, could have been inside that room all along, and it irked Tess to think she'd crept away without making sure. She had been seeking Po at the time, not a

young woman, and had been eager to check out the metal shipping containers – more viable structures to hold a tough guy like
him. Now she thought about it, she believed she'd heard breathing,
and a brief scuffling sound that could have come from within the
closed room. Damn it! She'd written off the sounds at the time
as her own breathing and her clothing catching on the wall.
Although, how could she blame herself for the hostage's predicament, when at the time she had no idea anyone but Po was missing?
Back then she'd just learned from Rachel Boreas that Emilia was
most likely en route from Lafayette, so had no inkling that Zeke
could already have snatched her, so she could be forgiven for
ignoring the signs at the time.

'I'm going down there,' said Po.

'I'm going with you,' Francis said.

'Not yet. Let me check Emilia's here first.'

'She's my sister,' Francis said, and glanced at his father with
undisguised anger. When he looked at Po his expression hadn't
softened. 'And you don't get to make all the decisions, Villere.'

Po faced him squarely.

'Stick to the plan, Francis,' he said.

'The one where you're the big hero?' Francis challenged.

'The one where you get Emilia safely outta the way. Going
down there and getting in a fight with the Menons won't be worth
shit if Emilia has already been moved. I'll go down there like
we planned, find her, and if she's there I'll give you the signal
to come get her.'

Darius's tone was low, and measured as he said, 'Listen to
him, son. Villere knows what he's talking about. Let him do
his stuff, then we'll do ours.'

His words held an unsubtle promise, and Tess wasn't sure
that the threat was solely aimed at settling a score with Zeke
Menon. The enemy of an enemy wasn't always a friend.

Francis looked once again at the site, picking out the roof of
the van that was barely visible beyond the office hut. 'We probably need to get mobile,' he said. Without another comment to
Po, he headed back with Darius towards where they'd left their
Dodge Ram. He waved Jean to join them. Moments later, they
drove away, heading to block the route to the camp from the
north.

'I'm not happy about you going down there alone,' Tess said.
'It's better I do.'

What he meant was that he couldn't look after her and another
woman. Ordinarily she would bristle at the idea he thought
she was a weakling in need of mollycoddling, but that wasn't
what he suggested. He was simply stating a fact. He knew Tess
could handle herself, but shit happened, and he'd enough to
handle without worrying if Cleary had gotten his hands on her
again while he concentrated on rescuing his sister.

'So where do you want me and Pinky?'

'Need you to the south.'

'OK. But, Po . . . be careful.'

'Careful is my middle name,' he assured her – and offered
her a brief wink at the irony.

She pecked a kiss on his lips. 'I mean it. You're trying to
hide it from those others, but I know the Chatards hurt you
more than you're letting on. Avoid getting into it with the
Menons if you can. I know you're a tough guy, but that Cleary,
well . . . he's something else.'

'Don't worry, I won't underestimate him.' He turned her
around and patted her backside to send her on her way. 'But
the same goes for you. Stick with Pinky. Don't go after anyone
by yourself.'

'Kettle. Pot.' She aimed a smile at him over her shoulder,
but then picked her way through the undergrowth to where
Pinky waited alongside the Toyota.

'I don't trust those Chatards, me,' Pinky announced the second
she was in earshot, making their family name sound like a
Cajun swear word.

'Me neither. If it's any consolation, neither does Po. Best we
all keep our guard up, eh, Pinky?'

He tapped the barrel of his Glock alongside his nose, and
said, 'He-he! I'm on it, me.'

When they both turned to look for Po, he'd already slipped
away into the night.

'Let's get going,' she said, and slid into the driver's position.
She was more useful as the driver: being the one with the gun,
Pinky required both hands free.

THIRTY-SIX

Using the forest as cover, Po approached within fifty feet of the compound. Distantly he heard Tess and Pinky drive away to take up a position on the approach road, out of sight but within hailing distance to respond quickly when he called. He knew he could rely on them, and though he couldn't control what any of the Chatards might do, was reasonably confident that they would deliver their end of the bargain, possibly with interest. He wasn't stupid: his alliance with Darius, and especially Francis, was shaky at best, and his little get-even stunt from earlier hadn't been as effective as he'd hoped. Pride was important to those men, and by giving them an opportunity to beat the shit out of him would have appeased them more if he hadn't subsequently busted up a couple of their boys and stuck his knife through their patriarch's foot. But things had turned out the way they had. He couldn't trust them to bury the death threats they'd aimed at him for years, but all he needed was for them to set their enmity aside while they all concentrated on getting Emilia safely home.

Earlier, Darius had asked him why he gave a hoot about a girl who hated his guts as much as the rest of them, and Po had told him the basic truth. 'Blood's thicker than water.' He felt no hatred for Emilia, and that was before he'd learned from Clara that she was his full sister. Any hatred she had of him would have been learned, and based on lies. He hoped one day that she would see that for herself, and maybe put aside the enmity and learn new behaviour based on her own experiences. When all came to all, she was his kin, and he'd be a poor example of a human being – let alone her big brother – if he turned his back on her at her most desperate time.

It was just his way. He was loyal beyond a fault. He had never met Emilia, had only seen her briefly in the photo shown to him by Clara, and on a Facebook stream brought to his attention by Tess, but it made no difference to him. She was his sister. And as he'd already proven, both to his father's memory, and in taking a knife in the gut for Tess, those he cared for he'd protect with his life. It begged the question, though: did he care for Emilia? It was a question he didn't need to ask.

He moved rapidly across the fallow earth between the edge of the forest and the perimeter fence. His thighs were stiff, felt heavy, and the pain in his ribs made running at a crouch difficult, but he ignored the discomfort. Once he was moving, and in the zone, all his aches would be forgotten. Once Emilia was safe, he could take the time to recover then. As if to prove a point, he clambered over the chain-link fence with disdain for the pitiful barrier. As soon as he was within the compound, he drew his blade. At this stage he wouldn't encumber himself with his gun, because he was unsure he'd choose to pull the trigger. A gun was good for two things only, it could be a deterrent, or it could be used to kill. In his opinion a knife was far more versatile and not as noisy.

He hoped to rely on stealth to get close enough to Emilia to free her. Once she was out of harm's way, then it wouldn't matter about how much noise was made. He headed directly for the office-cum-cabin Tess had pointed out at a loping run. Now that he was closer he could hear men's voices, but still had no view of them. Tess cautioned him that not all people at the site were involved in snatching his sister, but it wasn't a consideration. He'd argued down Darius earlier, but if pressed he had to admit the old man's point: if anyone tried to stop him, they were fair game.

A van door slid shut, slamming loudly.

A couple of the voices grew muffled, sealed within the van, and there was a solid thump as something shifted inside. He began creeping alongside the hut. Another voice rang out. 'Go on, get the hell outta here!'

There was someone in the hut. The van's engine roared to life. He heard the timbre of its growl change as it pulled away in a tight arch. Through the gap between the office and the meeting hall he spotted the rear end swing around, the lights flaring briefly as the driver touched the brakes. Then it changed direction, the driver having completed a 'Y'-turn to point the van at the exit gate from the compound, and began to crawl for the gate, its thick tires struggling for traction in the churned muck. Clods of dirt rained behind it.

Tempted to dash after it, Po paused to take stock. He had no idea if Emilia was in the van, or if it had anything to do with her. But if she were inside then he had to stop it. That meant he'd have to run past the guy in the hut, and if it were one of the Menon's and armed, then he'd be inviting a bullet in his spine. He chose a different tack, quickly pulling out his cell and speed-dialling Pinky.

'The van's leaving, and, hold on . . .' He waited to be sure. 'It's turning your direction. Are you in position to stop it?'

'We're just about there, Nicolas. You leave it to us.'

Po hung up and immediately rang Francis.

'I was expecting an explosion at least. This your big sign you said I wouldn't miss?'

'Change of plan. The van's leaving, heading away from your position. I need you to back-up Tess and Pinky.'

'Is Emilia in the van?'

'That's what I need you to find out. If she's there, you need to get her out.'

Darius's voice chimed in. 'Where's Zeke? I want him too.'

'Just stop that fucking van,' Po snapped in answer. He hung up before Darius could respond. He realized he'd spoken too loud. So much for his stealthy approach. The person inside the hut had fallen silent, and Po feared it was because he'd been heard. He quickly retreated, moving towards the rear of the cabin again. Footsteps from within told him that the person was walking in the opposite direction, towards the exit. Po took a quick peek through a window and glimpsed the back of a tall male wearing a baseball cap, just before he stepped outside and closed the door behind him. If the man was Zeke Menon, he had grown since Po had seen him last. Then again, Zeke had barely left his teens when Po had smashed his collarbone with the wrench, so he'd had a few years to mature and fill out. He was tempted to go after him and check; and beat Emilia's location out of him. But he couldn't make the same mistake Tess had earlier, when she'd ignored the possibility that the anteroom of the office could be Emilia's holding cell.

He took another peek inside the office. The separating wall held only a single door and it had been pulled to. Tess said that a light had burned behind it earlier, and it did now. He could have sneaked around the front, checked that all was clear, and entered by the entrance door, but he had his knife. He used it to spring the window lock, and swarmed inside. Once inside, he knew he'd just missed Emilia because of the strips of torn duct tape littering the floor, following the path taken moments ago by the tall guy in the hat. It took no figuring that the duct tape had formed the bonds on a prisoner and they'd been cut or stripped loose when she'd been loaded into the van. He also spotted a wad of discarded napkins that were bright red with blood.

Emilia's blood? He couldn't know, but he'd place a bet on it that it was. More than ever he wanted to chase down Zeke Menon.

He scanned the site for any sign of him, but couldn't see him. He chose to go to his right, because that was where the meeting room was, and if Zeke had gone anywhere it would be to report back to his superiors. Tess had mentioned a couple of ass-hats called Keane and Corbin. If Zeke wasn't in the meeting room, he was sure one or other of them would be, and they deserved his wrath as much as anyone.

But before he reached it, he heard voices from his far left. He immediately swung around, dropping into a crouch so that he was mostly hidden behind a parked saloon car. He was under the full wash of bright floodlights, around which swarmed thousands of bugs. But the two men were hidden by the gloom at the far side of the compound. He had no way of telling who the voices belonged to: perhaps they were innocent construction workers. He glanced once at the meeting room. Yes, there seemed to be people within it, but again he couldn't tell who without looking. He ignored the two distant men and quickly turned back for the meeting room.

He went into the gap between the cabins. Towards the front, the cabin had been jacked up on metal legs to level the floor, but Po was tall enough to spy through the venetian blinds. There were two individuals. One of them was a middle-aged guy who looked as if he had the woes of the world on his shoulders. He was struggling with the weight of his thoughts, judging by the way he propped his head in his hands, his elbows on a central large table. The second man was suited and had a tie knotted at his throat. His silver hair looked almost blue beneath the overhead strip lights as he paced back and forward, talking animatedly into a cellphone. Keane and Corbin, Po guessed. There was a third guy just out of his line of vision, and Po wouldn't have noticed him if he hadn't shifted on the chair he'd taken in one corner, and only then could he make out the man's laced-up black shoes and the bottoms of his suit trousers. Probably one of those chauffeurs Tess had mentioned from earlier, waiting patiently for his boss – Corbin – to finish up and leave. The chauffeur could also be a bodyguard. The third man's presence didn't worry Po, but had to be taken into consideration. He slipped away his knife in the sheath concealed in his high-topped boots, and drew the Glock supplied to him by Pinky. Deterring and killing were uses for a gun, but he had to admit they were also useful when it came to controlling a number of people too, generally commanding more respect than a single blade.

His best move? Go in through the front door, surprise the trio, and have them corralled within a few seconds. With a gun to their heads, one of them would quickly give up Emilia's location. He'd also be able to force the full sorry story about their criminal scheme from them, for when they were handed over to the police. Po and his friends would require an ace card when it came to protecting their own liberty after conducting an unlawful rescue attempt like this. Decision made, he headed for the front.

His cellphone vibrated in his shirt pocket.

He was about to ignore it, because taking a call might upset his forward momentum, and allow the situation to change against him. Yet he slipped out the phone and checked the caller ID: Pinky.

Hopefully his friend had some good news for him, but a worm of unease worked through his mind. Pinky was calling sooner than expected.

'You get her?' he whispered as soon as he picked up.

'We didn't get in place in time, Nicolas. The van got through.'

'Damnit . . .'

'Must have beaten us by less than a half-minute, them. We blocked the road, but the only ones turned up was them Chatards.'

'There are no other turn-offs between you and the site?'

'Not that we know of, us. But we're checking. My guess is the van got through, and that's what Darius thinks too. Them Chatards just took off like frat boys on a beer run, think they can chase the van down, them.'

'Damnit,' Po said again.

'Should we come back for you, Nicolas?'

Po thought about the men inside the meeting room. Pinky and Tess could help him to compel Emilia's whereabouts out of them, hold them prisoner until the police arrived. But things had grown more time-sensitive. He believed there was only one reason why Emilia had been removed from the site, and it was not a good one. He thought about urging Pinky back, but to pick him up so they could take up the chase too.

Voices from across the site caught his attention. Not the words, but a single wolf-like howl of excitement. He rushed to see what was happening, and spotted two men approaching one of the construction-crew pickups. The first was a thick-bodied giant, with wild hair. The second was a tall man, but he looked diminutive and austere by comparison. He wore a ball cap. Instantly Po recognized the Menons from Tess's description.

'Don't come back here,' Po told Pinky. 'Get on the Chatards' trail: I think Emilia is definitely in that van and it needs stopping.'

'What about you?'

'Don't worry. I'll arrange my own ride.'

THIRTY-SEVEN

To Tess, Maine felt a million miles away, and as distantly removed in time as it was by location. She could hardly believe that it was less than twenty-four hours since she'd boarded the flight out of Portland International Jetport, so much had happened since. There'd been little opportunity after arriving at the hospital in New Iberia to gather her wits, what with all the jumping around they'd done in the meantime. When Po had gone missing, and she'd charged around with Pinky hunting for him, she wouldn't admit to anyone that she was frantic with worry for her lover, and failing to find him had almost burned her out. The manhandling she'd suffered at Cleary's hands had left her rattled, aching all over, and no less stressed, but more so because she'd realized the dire peril that Emilia was in if she had fallen into the clutches of the Menons. Now it seemed that the worst-case scenario was true and she didn't feel any less fraught. She was strung out, riding on fumes, and although it was a contradiction, she was also re-energized by necessity to get the young woman safely home.

As she concentrated on driving, she could feel the small hairs prickling on the back of her neck, and the skin on her face felt too tight. Adrenalin and anxiety bubbled inside her. Even at speed the Toyota Camry handled the levee road easily enough, but had shown its limitations as a cross-country vehicle when they'd almost got bogged down trying to block the road. Pinky had to jump out and help shove the car clear of boggy ground, and thankfully he kept them moving, but the delay had meant they were now having to play catch-up. Pinky hadn't admitted the delay to Po, because it was pointless: they were late and that was that. They'd gained ground on the Dodge Ram, its lights winking like a demon's baleful glare from the distance, but had no idea if the Chatards had eyes on the van yet.

As they were supposedly working in tandem, they had swapped cellphone numbers with the Chatards. Pinky rang

Francis. It was Darius that picked up, because as Tess was, Francis was concentrating on the chase. Pinky put the phone on speaker mode.

'Can you see them?' Pinky demanded.

'They're aways ahead,' Darius said, 'but we're catchin' up. We'll have dem in minutes. That you behind us?'

'It is.'

'We're not waitin' for you. We catch 'em, we're takin' Emilia back wid or widout you.' Darius's accent had thickened with emotion.

'You should wait,' Tess cautioned. 'The more of us there the better. We can help stop the van safely.'

'We're supposed to wait while you catch up? Fuggedaboutit . . . first chance we get we're stopping dat van.'

'And how do you plan on doing that, you?' Pinky demanded. 'You gonna ram it off the goddamn levee? Cause I can't see how y'all gonna do it otherwise.'

'Wait 'til we get there,' Tess said again. 'One of us can overtake, the other move in close behind. Together we can box it in and stop it safely.'

Muffled argument arose in the Dodge Ram, the words coming too fast and thickly accented for Tess to catch, but it was clear the Chatards didn't appreciate her knowledge – or past experience – of bringing a moving vehicle to a controlled halt.

'We're doing it wid or widout you,' Darius proclaimed again. 'If you wanna be in on it you'd best get your butts movin'.'

'We are coming.' Tess flattened the gas pedal to the floor and the Toyota surged forward in response. 'Just don't go doing something stupid, OK?'

Francis's voice broke in. 'They're turning left, taking the bridge over the bayou. Looks as if they've picked up another tail.'

'Cops?' Tess asked hopefully.

'No. Shit-kickers in a truck,' Darius corrected.

'Could be an innocent coincidence.'

'No,' Francis said, 'they flashed their lights at each other and the pickup stopped and let them cross in front of them, then followed them over the bayou. Looks like a prearranged meeting to me.'

'Then it's even more important that you wait for us, otherwise you'll be outnumbered.'

'We've enough bullets for all of dem,' Darius growled.

'Stop being a dick, old man,' Pinky snapped, 'and let Francis do the thinking.'

'I've enough bullets for one more smart-mouthed nigger,' Darius warned.

'Fucking Klan peckerhead!'

'Keep it up, faggot, an' I'll have Francis stop and I'll wait for you after all.'

'Gentlemen!' Tess's voice rang sharply. 'This really isn't helping, is it? Let's just drop the macho bullshit and concentrate on saving Emilia, shall we?'

'So now we've a girl callin' all d' shots?' Darius snarled, but this time Francis came to her assistance.

'She's right, Papa. This is about Emilia. Let's keep focused on her.'

'See . . . at least one of them ain't a dipshit,' said Pinky, and Tess snapped a frown on him. He got the message: his attitude wasn't helping. He held the phone nearer her as she continued powering along the levee. The Toyota rose and fell as it crested small humps in the road. Ahead of them, Francis applied the brakes on the Dodge as they approached the turn-off for the bridge.

'Do you know what's on the other side of that bayou?' Tess asked.

'Wilderness,' Francis replied as he negotiated the narrow span over the bayou. 'Swamp and pine forest all the way over to the Atchafalaya.'

A new voice cut in: Jean Chatard.

'There's more construction going on out there. I saw something on the news about it, some activists were demonstrating about the damage they were doing to the environment. Some of the land has been prepared for the pipeline coming through. They had to cut out a path, get levees and culverts in place. I think the pipeline takes a sharp turn to the east there so it goes around Attakapas Island . . . it's a wildlife refuge area.'

'You throw a stick anywhere out here it lands on a goddamn wildlife-management area,' Darius put in, and it was evident his tone had taken on a different edge. He was worried. 'An' I'll tell you somethin' else. You throw a stick it'll probably land on a grave. People have been hiding their dirty laundry out in dose swamps for hundreds a years. If they're diggin' holes in the ground, sure as shit is brown, somebody got sumpin' dey wanna dump in it.'

'That's what they're planning for Emilia.' Tess was stating the obvious, but they all needed reminding. Her greatest fear wasn't that Emilia was in the back of the van, but that it was her corpse. Maybe they were already too late to save her, and her dead body was being delivered to its final resting place.

Approaching the turn-off at speed, Tess began applying the brakes in anticipation. The Toyota was still traveling too fast, but she fought the back-end skid, fishtailed briefly, and wind-blown forest litter was kicked up in its wake as she eased on the gas once more. Pinky jostled, but continued to hold out the phone. The Dodge Ram was now only a hundred yards or so ahead, following a narrow track into the swamp.

'We need to back off a little,' she cautioned the Chatards, 'and drop your lights or they'll know they've got a tail.'

'Where they gonna go if dey do spot us?' Darius demanded. 'I'm betting dis is the only road in or out.'

'They didn't bring heavy excavation equipment down this track. There must be other ways in.'

Darius shut up.

The lights of the Dodge went dark. Following their lead, she shut off the Toyota's headlamps. Immediately the night engulfed them, but she could see enough of the Dodge's dim shape to stay on the track. The foliage grew close to the trail, and here and there had fallen astride it. The tips of twigs and branches rattled on the paintwork, and others were crushed to mulch under this the fourth vehicle to grind over them in the space of a minute.

The cellphone still had an open line, but all had fallen silent in the Dodge. Tess took the moment of calm to make a suggestion. 'Let's see exactly where they're going first. We wait until we get eyes on Emilia, and then take things from there. Agreed?'

The cellphone went dead.

'Buttheads,' Pinky said, but Tess thought the lack of argument meant the family had realized she was speaking sense. They'd lost the opportunity of catching the van on the open road, and now that another pickup had gotten in place between them, they had to take things more careful. If they moved on the pickup, those in the van might be alerted and make their getaway, and now they were on this narrow track, hemmed in by bog on both sides, there'd be no continuing the chase.

The track led into the heart of the swamp. As it progressed the going got tougher for the saloon car. But Tess remained dogged, and got them through the worst of it. Finally, she had to pull over, and she clambered out alongside Pinky, but it was OK, as the Dodge had also slowed, with Francis reversing it onto a grassy knoll alongside a stagnant stretch of water. The sky was overcast, and yet Tess's vision had adjusted to the dimness. Through the shroud of the forest she could spot a break in the canopy ahead. A trio of figures moved around the Dodge, the Chatards disembarking for a better look.

Tess and Pinky hurried to join them as they crouched in the undergrowth at the edge of the forest. Darius glowered at Pinky, and Pinky tsk'd under his breath, but largely their disagreement of minutes ago had been put aside now they'd other enemies to contend with. She ignored their rancour as she peered out across a broad strip of land recently terraformed to support the pipeline: it was an ugly wound in the landscape. The grey earth shone dully beneath the lowering clouds, glistening with patches of seeping moisture, but a huge embankment had been built at its centre and stretched away into the distance, and along it a number of concrete plinths had already been erected, and culverts set in place to divert the swamp waters. Huge excavation equipment stood idle, awaiting the return of the workforce at dawn – bulldozers, excavators, backhoe loaders, and dumper trucks were immediately recognizable, other pieces of heavy machinery took a little more figuring out, but she guessed some were used to clear the trees before digging could commence, others to compact the earth afterwards. She wondered which was the tool of choice when it came to burying the dead.

But she spent no more time on consideration. Beyond the fleet of excavators was a collection of buildings, and unlike those at the compound these were permanent structures. They were tall and blocky, and from them extended large industrial machines. Her guess was that it was a pumping station, situated at the point where the pipeline changed direction. The van and the pickup truck had drawn up abreast a fence that surrounded it.

Having no need to go without lights, those of both vehicles lent ambience to the scene, and Tess took an involuntary step forward as she spotted someone being unloaded from the side of the panel van. She halted, grabbing at Darius's sleeve, because he too had taken a lunge forward when spotting his daughter being manhandled by a stocky guy with close-cropped hair; thankfully Emilia was still on her own two feet. Tess urged him to wait and take stock before acting. Reluctantly he agreed, but he gripped the butt of a revolver tightly, counting the numbers of those he wished to punish. Three other figures stood guard, none of them recognizable as either Menon brother, but Tess thought the fattest guy was Rory, the man Pinky had tripped and held under his gun while Po extracted information from his friend. She took a closer look at the others, and yes, decided that one of them was the driver dragged by his lip from his pickup outside Emilia's apartment. She didn't know who the bearded guy was, but he exhibited the mannerisms of one who believed himself in charge. Even as he directed the activity, he held up a hand, calling for quiet, and then delved in his pocket and fished out a cellphone. The blue glow from its screen picked out his features like a photographic negative.

The bearded man spoke briefly into it, then turned to peer into the distance, further along a wider service trail that ran parallel to the pipeline-levee. Following his gaze, Tess spotted distant headlights dipping and flaring as a vehicle approached. It struck her that the service trail must originate adjacent to the compound headquarters, to allow access back and forth to the dual sites, but that the panel van wasn't equipped to handle the boggy terrain and had therefore taken the longer route they'd followed, as well as gone to rendezvous with Rory and his friend in the pickup. The vehicle now approaching had come via the shorter route so would most likely be an off-roader. As it got closer, she made out the shape behind the headlights, and it was one of the 4x4 pickups employed by Al Keane's construction workers. It was the same type of vehicle Zeke Menon had driven away from the hospital.

'I think it's them,' she wheezed. 'Zeke and Cleary.'

'They don't trust those other assholes to finish off Emilia by themselves,' Darius growled.

'No. They don't want to miss the fun,' Tess corrected. 'They want to do it themselves.'

'Sick motherfuckers . . .' Francis began to move and Tess was afraid he was going to run directly into the fray. But he didn't, he began marshalling his father and cousin into motion. 'We have to do this before we're outnumbered. Papa, you're not very mobile on that lame foot. I think you should stay up here with the truck, and just come on down if it gets too much for us. Jean, you with me?'

Jean hefted a sawn-off shotgun. It was the only answer necessary. But Darius wasn't for staying behind.

'I'm coming.'

'You'll slow us down.' Francis aimed a finger at the Dodge. 'Better if you bring down the truck once we have Emilia, and you can get her out the way.'

'I'm not leaving 'til Zeke's paid up in full.'

Tess butted in. 'Francis is right, Darius. We need someone to bring down the truck to transport your daughter to safety. You're the best man for the job.'

'While a skinny-assed girl like you gets in on d' action. Do I look fuckin' useless to you?'

'I'd do it, but our car can't make the trip,' she said. 'Besides, there's no more time to argue about this. We have to move now before the Menons get here. We can have Emilia safely out of the way before the real fighting starts. Isn't that what's most important?'

'Do you have a gun?' he demanded.

'No. But . . .' She was about to say she'd take his.

'Francis. Give her d' keys to the truck. She can bring it on down, but I'll be damned if I'm gonna be sidelined while my kin are in danger.'

Tess bit down on her response. He did have a valid right, after all. She glanced once at Pinky, caught his nod of agreement with the menfolk, and turned to face Francis. 'OK. Give me the damn keys.'

As soon as he handed them over, Francis searched along the

road at the approaching vehicle. 'We've got two minutes at most. Let's do this.'

The four immediately moved out, Pinky moving away to the right as the Chatards headed in a clump towards the pumping station. Darius lurched along on his injured foot, but his kin stuck closely to him. Tess shook her head. Bunched together like that they invited gunfire, she was glad that Pinky had used savvy and gone alone. She was confident he'd do his bit though to help free the prisoner, as would she. Because she was damned if she was going to sit idle while a rescue was underway.

THIRTY-EIGHT

Held hostage in the back of the panel van for the second time in hours, Emilia couldn't help feel that she was stuck in a continuous loop of torment, and she had begun to wonder if she would again be secured in a chair in a tiny, airless room, to be threatened by Zeke Menon and his knife. It was wishful thinking, because she knew she hadn't been spared his blade earlier just so he could repeat the process. Wherever she was to be delivered this time it wouldn't be a holding cell. The first time she was loaded into the van, her jailer was Cleary Menon, and he'd been very attentive of her, not giving her more than a few inches of freedom at any time. He'd practically laid over her, fondling her hair and stroking his hands up and down her outer thighs as he exhaled deeply in her face, his breath coppery and foul. This time her captor kept his distance, only threatening to strike her if she as much as moved. There was no doubt that he'd follow his warning, because she could tell by his jittery mannerisms and the cold sweat flooding his features that he was out of his depth here, and totally uncomfortable with what he'd become embroiled in. He'd strike out in reaction to his own disquiet. She had heard the stocky man referred to as 'Croft' by his bearded pal, Tyson. Croft wasn't a murderer, or perhaps he'd never imagined he could be, because he'd looked almost as fearful as she about reaching their destination. She thought that perhaps she could have reasoned with his better senses, convinced him to let her go before he got in worse trouble, but for the gag that was still firmly in place. Then again, no amount of reasoning with him would work, because she could tell he was terrified of betraying the Menons: if he allowed her to escape, then he knew full well who'd end up their next victim.

Croft bickered with Tyson who drove the van. Tyson sounded only marginally more assured about their orders, but Emilia could sense that he too wished he were elsewhere. They were victims of consequence almost as much as she, but she felt no pity for them. As long as they remained cowards, they were to be reviled. Instead of trying to earn their sympathy she stayed silent, thinking and plotting her escape. Her hands and legs were free. When Zeke had handed her off to Croft back at that construction site, she'd been too stunned from being hurled against a doorframe to struggle, and she'd easily been delivered to the side door of the van. But since then she'd determined she wouldn't go as easily to her grave. There were only the two men. Her hope was that when they arrived at their destination, she could break free of them and flee. She was confident she could give them a run for their money, and perhaps their lack of enthusiasm for the task wouldn't match her need to get away. She'd first thought about waiting until they opened the sliding door, feigning weakness and forcing Croft to help her step down, when she'd kick him where it hurt and run for it. But that plan had been dashed when she heard Tyson announce that their friends were in place, and she heard the names Harry and Rory. What hope did she have of giving four men the slip?

She felt the van decelerate, and take a sharp left turn. From what she could make out, Harry and Rory were following in another vehicle. It didn't matter, she had made up her mind, she was going to go for broke, whatever that meant. If she was going to die, she was going to make it less than pleasurable for any of her abusers.

Her mom's face flashed into her mind.

Hours earlier she'd been desperate to reach Clara's bedside, horrified that she'd be too late to say goodbye. Was her mother still alive, or would Emilia be first to pass over? Absurdly, she wondered who of the two of them would be waiting to greet the other when they reached the afterlife. As a child she had been under the illusion that there was an order to mortality, that parents always went ahead of their offspring, but she had come to learn different. She bet Clara would be surprised if Emilia was the first to take her hand when she arrived at the Pearly Gates. Then again perhaps not. She had to consider that it was her mom who'd sent that mystery woman to the construction site to look for her, perhaps Clara feared more for her welfare than she'd ever been given credit for. Who else would have engaged the woman's services: not her father. Darius had raised her, but had never exhibited any genuine affection for her, and the overriding emotion she'd experienced growing up when it came to him was aloofness. He probably had no clue that she had never reached the hospital or that she was even missing, and if he did wouldn't bother to come looking. When she'd spoken to him from the convenience store in Lafayette he'd offered to send one of the boys to come collect her . . . if he was any kind of father he'd have jumped in his car and collected her himself, without the threat of dragging her back by her hair. But as usual he had proved more pre-occupied with himself – she'd sensed there was somebody else with him and she'd disturbed an important business deal – and the only emotion he'd exhibited was anger at what he'd perceived as her wrongdoing.

She couldn't rely on dear old Papa. She doubted that even her older siblings Francis and Leon could be relied on to seek her out, because Darius wouldn't permit her to get in the way of business. The mystery woman was an unknown quantity, but she had been chased off, and if she had any sense would have kept on running. So whom did that leave? Nobody. If she was going to get out of her predicament, it was down solely to her.

The van was driven down a rugged trail. Jostling and bouncing, Emilia rode the bumps in the road, flexing her fingers and her calf muscles, readying herself. It wouldn't be long before they reached their final destination. Croft barely gave her much notice now as he leaned over the front seats, in rapid conversation with Tyson – it sounded as if he were trying to convince his friend that as soon as things were done out here they should disappear. They knew the Menons were out of control, and anyone associated with them would crash and burn alongside them. Croft suggested that Mr Corbin – the big shot who Zeke served – wouldn't put up with their activities for much longer and would most likely order a hit on the Menons and anyone involved in the mess they'd caused of what should have been an easy task. If Tyson agreed with his pal he didn't let on, but his reflection in the rear-view mirror showed he was equally worried by the prospect.

The interior of the van was flooded with spectral light. She hoped a police helicopter was hovering overhead, aiming its searchlights on it, but it was false hope. The light was because they'd come out from under the forest canopy into a clearing. Beneath her the tires picked their way across the scarred earth, and she watched as Croft turned to observe her, biting his bottom lip.

'Don't give us any trouble,' he warned, as the van came to a halt, 'or else.'

Emilia couldn't answer if she tried. She remained meek, subdued, frightened into compliance, all false manifestations of her true intention. She waited for Croft to reach for the interior handle and slide open the door – then she'd be up and barging him out of her way. Sadly he didn't. Tyson got out first and opened the door, sliding it wide. Even as Croft turned and urged her up, Tyson blocked her escape route, and two other figures moved into view. One of them was a fat redneck she didn't know, the other a scrawny asshole she dimly recognized from their high-school days: Harry Theriault. Harry was a low-level punk back then, and had sunk lower in the pond muck since, but he'd never struck her as a person to get involved in abduction and murder. He was another reluctant party in all this, and as fearful as Croft. As she clambered down from the van, aided by the tug on her elbow by Croft, she caught a glimpse of Harry's face as he blinked at her in astonishment. His lips were swollen and bruised, and there was a nick in one nostril that had leaked blood, now black and scabrous. She wondered if he'd been forced into helping, but again he was another she felt no pity for. Given the chance she'd make both his nostrils bleed.

First she must hurt Croft.

She angled herself so that she could ram a knee into his groin.

Before the opportunity came, Tyson's cellphone rang. 'Hold her!' he snapped at Croft, and her captor pulled her tightly in against his side, one hand now on her collar, the other cupping her elbow as before. The moment for kneeing him where it hurt had been missed.

'Yeah, Zeke, we're here.' Tyson said. He glanced at his

confederates, lifted his eyebrows and then nodded at the near distance to the north, conveying a silent message.

Emilia followed the gesture, and spotted distant headlights. A knot formed in her gut and she was on the verge of vomiting.

Tyson listened to his phone, and this time looked up at the nearest towering structure of some kind of oil-pumping plant. The structure was clad in sheet metal, not yet painted with any identifying decal, only bearing a dull grey undercoat. It was the same colour as the lowest of the threatening clouds.

'If you do her in there, it'll mean more clean-up,' Tyson said. 'We don't want to leave evidence like we did at the Thibodaux place.'

Emilia heard a bark from Zeke that made Tyson hold the phone away from him, and though she couldn't make out the words knew that Zeke didn't expect his commands to be questioned. Tyson was quick to respond. 'I'm sorry, Zeke. Yeah, sorry, man. You're the boss. I'll have her taken inside.'

'This is nuts,' Croft said, but he ensured his voice didn't carry to Zeke, waiting until Tyson had hung up before speaking.

Emilia couldn't agree with him more. She looked up at him, gave him her most beseeching look in the distant hope he'd come to his senses and allow her to run. Croft purposefully ignored her. Instead he beckoned the fat man over. 'Rory, take her inside.'

'Fuck you, man,' said the big redneck.

'Harry,' Croft said.

Harry made out he hadn't heard, pretending to be watching the approaching vehicle.

'If we take her in there we become complicit in her murder,' Croft told Tyson.

Even Emilia was stunned by his naivety. All four of them were already complicit; it made no difference which one of them dragged her to her doom. What did he expect, that if he handed her over, he could wipe the dust from his hands, and with it any involvement? A sudden spurt of anger shot through her, and again it was as if her stomach was about to purge itself. If she were sick while gagged, she'd choke to death. Her anger at his ignorance manifested in a more violent manner. She was held, but not fully immobilized. She swung round and before

Croft could react she had a grip on his face. Her fingernails dug into his forehead, her thumb deep in the socket of his right eye. Her hand made a tight fist, but it wasn't in an effort to pluck out an eye, to blind him. She wrenched away, ripping out the metal piercing from his brow and a chunk of flesh with it.

Croft's reaction outweighed any pain he suffered. It was shock at the sudden and dramatic attack that made him rear back, throwing his hands over his abused face, while letting out a strangled cry. Emilia drove a kick between his legs and got him square with her shin. Croft now buckled and his torn eyebrow was forgotten as both hands transferred to his groin. Emilia took no pleasure in his punishment; she raced away, no direction or destination in mind other than away from the approaching headlights.

Behind her the trio of standing men hollered at her, and at each other. Croft only moaned in agony as he rolled on the floor. Emilia ignored them, instead rushing across the open ground for the road they'd entered by. She knew she'd never escape them on foot, not while running up the trail, but that wasn't a consideration, she hoped to lose herself in the forest on the far side of it.

Another trio of silhouetted figures shambled towards her.

She had no idea who they were, only that they were bad news and that they blocked her escape route. She almost went down on her side in the mud as she skidded to make a turn and flee again, this time to where the fleet of excavators and bulldozers was lined up in rows like a herd of colossal alien creatures, part-biological part-mechanical monsters.

More voices joined those of her original captors, but her pulse was hammering inside her skull, and her breathing – confined by the balled socks and gag – roared in and out like a steam train climbing a mountainside. She bent at the waist, stamping through mud, and again her feet almost skidded out from beneath her. Fighting for balance, she grabbed at the heavy caterpillar tracks of the nearest machine. She slapped her way along, using the track for stability, and rounded the front of the huge excavator, and ducked to avoid the lowered backhoe boom. She fled into the shadows between the mechanical behemoths.

As she ran she tugged at the gag, but couldn't free it, and was in danger of losing her balance. She let it be, concentrating instead on putting as much distance between her and the – how many now? – *seven men* trying to catch her. In her haste she clipped an ankle on a piece of machinery and went down. She barely felt the pain that flared up her leg, and swarmed up, but as she ran on it was with a noticeable limp. She swerved, cutting between large trucks and diggers, and swerved again, so there was no direct path for anyone to chase her down. From behind her there came a sharp *crack!*. The noise echoed off the silent machines that surrounded her. Before it had stopped reverberating a second *crack!* followed and a third shot, this one a *boom!*. Gunfire. They were shooting at her, trying to bring her down. A vehicle roared to life, she could hear it distantly, but had no idea where the noise came from. She ran harder, cutting left, and then took shelter in the huge bucket of a bulldozer. She smelled wet iron and turned earth. She wasn't sure if the smell was from the bulldozer or her. Gasping for breath, she tugged and twisted at the duct tape around her mouth, got it yanked down beneath her chin, and wrenched free the sodden socks. As the soaked material was finally extricated her relief was huge, but it was as if the unblocking of her throat also encouraged the purging of her stomach contents she'd been fighting so hard to contain. She was sick between her feet, her stomach convulsing painfully. Dizziness assailed her and she staggered to one side, a shoulder the only thing supporting her against the steel wall of the huge bucket. Bleary-eyed, and spitting a string of foul-tasting saliva, she knew she must get moving again. She scrabbled through her own vomit, without a care, and started a wobbling run for a brighter spot between the towering machines. Beyond the row of diggers she saw wet ground, and beyond that the rearing bulwark of the recently erected levee. It blocked her passage, but not entirely. From experience, she expected that culverts would have been inserted at regular intervals to allow for the rising and falling water table, and for the native wildlife to pass from one ancient stomping ground to another. She'd happily slither like a snake through any pipe wide enough to lead to freedom.

She bounded forward, her equilibrium back, eyesight clear

of tears now that there was a hope of sanctuary beyond the levee . . .

And ran full tilt into the arms of one of her hunters, who grappled her close, and fell with her in the dirt.

THIRTY-NINE

Tess was no sooner seated in the immense Dodge Ram pickup than she was almost compelled to leap out again and run into the fray. The pickup sat just within the perimeter of the forest above the still stretch of water, but from the cab she could see all the way across the barren ground to the pumping station. The panel van and truck blocked most of her view of what was going on but the sudden jerky movements of the small group of figures told her something was happening. The smallest figure abruptly pelted around the back of the van, heading directly for her. Unfortunately, because of the undulations of the landscape, she couldn't spot the Chatards, but they were somewhere between the Dodge and the running figure. Hope swelled in her that Emilia would rush into the arms of her family within seconds, but alas it was fleeting. Emilia could have no way of recognizing her kin in the dark as they broached the small incline between them, and she made the mistake of thinking them more enemies. She dodged so sharply she almost went down on her side, but regained balance and sprinted away, this time towards the rows of excavation equipment.

Hoping that the young woman would recognize one of the voices calling out to her, Tess pushed open the door, about to jump out and join the chase, but Emilia kept running. The Chatards' voices were mingled with those of Emilia's hunters, three of whom were rushing laterally to cut her off.

Emilia disappeared among the massive machines, and then Tess was unsure which of the running figures was friend or foe. Except for one. She could make out the stockier figure of Darius, who had been left behind by his fleeter-footed son and nephew. He had turned to limp towards the panel van. One of the bad guys still remained behind it, hidden from view, and a quick check showed her that the approaching truck was now barely a minute out. Darius had decided to forgo chasing after his daughter in favour of settling a score with one of her abusers.

'What the hell are you doing?' The question could have been aimed at any of them, not to mention her.

This was insane. She was an investigator, not a member of a FBI Hostage Rescue Team. This was a job for specially trained law-enforcement officers, not a bunch of gun-happy Cajuns on a revenge trip. Beating herself up about it wasn't helping, but she experienced a moment of panic concerning the future. They could all go to prison for their actions. She should call the police and try to salvage what was left of all their lives. Prior to this there was no proof that Emilia had been taken, let alone by Zeke Menon, but now the confirmation was right there in front of her. Call the police. Get backup.

Instead she started the engine and the pickup roared to life.

This wasn't her case. Never had been. It was all about Po finding resolution for past mistakes and misfortunes. When she said she was coming with him to Louisiana she knew what she was buying into. She'd made her decision to accompany him, so just had to suck it up and take the consequences. It would have been better if Po were actually here, but somehow he was going to miss the end game. So if there was ever a chance of a happy ending to any of this, she must get moving and do something about it. Back home she drove a tiny Prius, but when she was with the Cumberland County Sheriff's Office she had gained experience with various departmental vehicles, so the huge pickup didn't intimidate her. She sent it rolling down the slope, picking up speed, still without lights. She had a suspicion where Emilia's flight might take her, and she hoped to be in position to grab her and get her out of there before everything went south.

Muzzle flash signified the abrupt deadly turn to the proceedings. She had no idea who was first to shoot, but then bullets were traded, the flashes coming from different points. A deep-throated boom told her that Jean had joined in with the sawn-off. Tess hauled down on the steering wheel, taking a sharp right turn, and the chunky tires of the Dodge tore through a soft mound of dirt, then lost traction as it bounded down the decline of a dip in the earth. Swamp water curtained either side of the truck, momentarily blinding her as the deluge washed over the windshield. She didn't bother with the wipers, in the next second the truck was powering out of the low point and up the other side. The truck ramped off the crest of the next mound, and then it was downhill from there.

She intended driving around the fleet of immobile excavators, ready to assist Emilia if she made a mad dash for freedom. Emilia couldn't continue to evade her pursuers by playing cat and mouse among the bulldozers and dumper trucks and would have to traverse open ground at some point. She snapped a glance to the left. The lights from the pickup were now sharp flares against the dimness as it powered towards the pumping station. The Menons, inside it, would have to be blind to miss the muzzle flashes. They hadn't stopped, or tried to make off. They were coming faster, eager to join the fight. She swung the Dodge to the left, and clods of mud rained from the sharp grooves her tires dug from the ground. Gearing down, she hit the gas and the Dodge lurched forward again, this time not for the bare ground between the site and the levee but back towards the service road. She didn't have a gun but somebody had to slow down the Menon brothers.

FORTY

Kicking and flailing in the dirt, Emilia fought against her assailant. Since losing the gag she had found her voice again, and she screamed like a demon released fresh from hell as she punched, kicked, and clawed. She was like a small child in the big man's embrace, and if anything, all of her efforts were wasted and only served to tire her out. If she could bust loose, she wouldn't have the energy left to run to the levee, let alone squirm through one of the culvert pipes to freedom. Finally she arched back, crying out in futility, her palms pressing at the man's chest for leverage, as she begged him to release her. But he wasn't letting go. In desperation she tried to headbutt him. The move was sloppy, and her forehead bounced uselessly off the soft flesh of his shoulder. One of his arms was around her lower back. It surprised her when his other cupped her head, pulling her tighter into his embrace as he stood and lifted her with him.

'It's OK, little Emilia, I'm here to help, me.'

In her panic, the dark, the roiling wash of despair that had filled her mind in those few frantic seconds, she had never gotten a look at the man she'd run into. It was difficult seeing him clearly now, and her only impression was of skin darker than the night, and the white flash of sclera and teeth as he smiled to reassure her of his good intentions. He was a stranger. He hadn't hurt her, hadn't even tried to fend off her blows as she'd tried to battle free, but how could she trust him? For all she knew he was another one of her abusers, and was trying to win her trust, so it would add to her torment when his true nature was revealed when he slung her down at the feet of the Menons.

'Get the hell off me!'

'Ain't gonna happen. I let you go you'll run again, an' I ain't built for speed, me. Now hush, you, or them peckerheads is goin' hear you.' The big black man transferred his arm from behind her back to under her knees, so he could carry her better.

'Put me down.'

'Told you. I ain't lettin' go, me.' He began to walk with her into the lee of one of the huge excavators.

'I can walk. I don't need carrying like a baby.'

'So stop squalling like one. An' keep still, or we'll both end up rollin' in the mud like a coupla hogs again.'

'Who are you?'

'You can call me Pinky, little Emilia. I'm a friend of your brother.'

Emilia suddenly looked at him with more interest, but also a little doubt. Perhaps he wouldn't be surprised to find her kin weren't usually friendly to folks of his persuasion. She wasn't exactly thinking about his skin colour either. The big man's tone was effete enough to tell her he wasn't the type of drinkin' buddy any of her siblings usually hung with. 'Which brother?'

The big man neglected to answer, and it was because she thought she'd caught him in a lie, but there was more to his avoidance than that.

'Are my brothers here?'

'Francis is here,' said Pinky. 'Your father Darius too. Plus . . .' he pondered for the correct words '. . . a couple more of your kin.'

Emilia was struck by how close she'd come to safety. The newcomers she'd spotted approaching from the forest had been members of her family on a rescue mission: misconstruing their intention, she'd run from them. Now it sounded as if they were in a gun battle with those who'd held her prisoner.

'Goin' to put you down now, so's I can take out my gun, me. You needn't fear, it's not for you.'

'Who are you?' she asked again.

'I told you. Call me Pinky.'

'No . . . I mean who exactly are you? Why are you here?'

'To get you safely to your momma's bedside.' He set her down on her feet. She slumped against the sidewall of a tire that dwarfed her, rubbing at the ankle she'd hurt earlier. As she caught her breath she studied her supposed saviour.

'I've never heard any of my brothers mention you before,' she said, still mistrustful. She was surprised by the fact that she had no intention of trying to escape him, though.

'I'm not from roun' these parts, me,' he answered enigmatically.

She had to admit she'd never seen his like. He was an oddly shaped person, his face almost jovial, and looked totally at odds with the gun he held: he was reminiscent of a child's favorite cuddly toy rather than a rescuer. But somehow she felt safer in his presence than at any time since before that night of Jason's fatal weed run.

'I won't run away, I promise,' she said.

'You can run, just not away from me. Come on, and stay close, you. I've another friend out there looking for us.'

Emilia followed his gesture, and saw a Dodge Ram pickup churning through the loose dirt a couple of hundred yards away. It had no lights, but stood out against the grey earth and grey sky. Even as she spotted it, the driver yanked down on the steering and wheeled off in a tight arch towards the other end of the site. It disappeared beyond the fleet of excavators, heading towards the panel van she'd arrived in.

'OK, so our lift has been diverted. Doesn't matter,' said Pinky and held out a palm for her. 'Let's go, little Emilia. Stay close.'

She offered no argument. She didn't take the proffered hand, but fell into step behind him, obscured from her hunters by his bulky figure. Pinky surprised her: he was spritely for a big man, exhibiting the natural grace that some heftier guys occasionally displayed on the dance floor. He led her through an aisle formed between two rows of the massive diggers, listening constantly for a hint that any of her pursuers was closing in. The gunfire was sporadic, and not close by. But he advanced with his finger poised alongside the trigger guard, ready for instant action. Emilia pressed her left palm flat against his lower back, comforted by the contact. He glanced back and gave her an encouraging wink.

FORTY-ONE

Everything had gone into meltdown in the space of less than two minutes since Zeke instructed his lackeys to deliver their prisoner to a vacant office in the administration block of the sub-station. Zeke had promised Cleary his prize, and he'd earmarked the office as the place where Cleary could have his fun, rather than have them all rolling around in the dirt. Earlier he'd made preparations, sending Tyson off to cover the floor with tarpaulins to catch the blood. He'd learned his lesson from leaving forensic evidence where they'd slain Hal and Jamie Thibodaux, and wasn't going to make the same mistake again. It would be weeks until the pumping station went live, so any trace evidence on the walls could be scrubbed clean before the decorators got to work with their paint and brushes. From the office to the dumpsite was only a few hundred yards, so their workload of disposing of Emilia's remains afterwards would have been simple. It should have been simple, he corrected himself. Four guys he had on Emilia and they couldn't hang onto one damn girl!

Though uneven and potholed in places the service trail was thoroughly compacted by the passage of far heavier machines than his pickup, so the going was safe enough to put his foot down. The sporadic flashes of gunfire lighting up the pumping station spurred his urgency. If any of those limp-dicked idiots shot Emilia dead, they'd be sorry. Cleary could have them instead, but he wouldn't be appeased. A quick glance over at his brother showed he was having similar thoughts. He sat, hunched forward, fingertips digging into the dashboard as he glared through the windshield, eyelids flinching with each corresponding muzzle flash. His lips had flared wide, and his tusky incisors stood proud amid his hirsute features.

The muzzle flashes came from different points.

It wasn't his guys shooting at Emilia; they were trading rounds with somebody else.

There was a distinct lack of emergency lights, so Zeke was confident the interlopers on the site weren't of the official variety. But if not the cops, then who?

As he screeched the pickup to a halt ten yards short of Tyson's panel van, he got his answer.

'Son of a bitch,' he snarled. 'What's Darius Chatard doing here?'

As he watched for the briefest of moments, the old man pounded Jim Croft's face against the side of the van. When the young thug collapsed in semi-consciousness to the dirt, Darius braced his left palm against the van, supporting his weight while he drove a kick into Croft's liver. The kick gave Darius some satisfaction, but as he turned to observe the arrival of the Menons, his features also appeared pained. He limped round on an obviously injured foot, and brought up a revolver. Darius barked angrily and pulled the trigger.

Zeke felt the impact of the bullet striking the truck, and steam billowed from the punctured radiator. A bullet caromed off the cab, and another struck the windshield. The glass starred but held, the bullet only glancing off. But Zeke was certain the integrity of the glass was threatened. 'Get out, Cleary. Out now!'

There was no view of Darius because of the pluming steam, which was turned almost opaque by the reflection of the truck's headlights. But another bullet striking the engine confirmed he was still shooting. Cleary pushed his door wide and went out at a loping run, heading for the concealment of the nearby forest. Zeke threw open his door, and immediately it was punctured by a bullet. Good job he'd anticipated Darius's intent, and gone the other direction. He clambered over the passenger seat and out the same way as his brother then backed alongside the pickup, using the steam to shield him from Darius's view. As he retreated he drew his knife from its sheath. It wasn't much of a weapon against a loaded gun, but Darius was spitting bullets like pistachio shells. Unless he had a handy speed-loader, the revolver would take time reloading. Some took more or less, but most revolvers that Zeke had come across held six shells, and Darius had already expended four. Two bullets were still enough to kill him twice over, but he wasn't sticking around like a sitting duck. Darius fired again. There was an explosion of glass as a bullet cut through the cab. Zeke went round the back of the truck. Once he was clear, he abandoned his barricade and sprinted for the oil plant.

'Cowardly sumbitch,' Darius hollered after him. 'Think you can run after tryin' to fuck me over for a dollar?'

Darius's revolver cracked a final time.

The bullet came so close to his head, Zeke was certain he felt the sonic wave following its flight. He wondered if once again his lucky ball cap had saved his life, and if it held another scorch mark where the bullet had missed by a hair. But there was no time for whimsy. He immediately pivoted, his boots digging in the dirt for traction, and charged directly at Darius.

If he'd miscalculated the load capacity of Darius's revolver he was supremely fucked, because he charged directly at the older man, his right arm raised to stab, offering his chest as a wide-open target.

Darius fired.

But the hammer clacked down on an empty chamber.

The old man had advanced from his original position adjacent to the van. He stood in open space, wreathed by gun smoke as he flipped open the cylinder and emptied tinkling brass around his feet. He dug for his pocket, seeking spare ammo, but wasn't going to be quick enough to reload and shoot. Zeke sprang at him, spearing towards the old man's throat with his blade. Darius's mouth split wide, but it wasn't in a shout of terror. He bellowed a challenge, even as he swept his gun across his body, and slammed Zeke's wrist. The knife stabbed empty air to the side of Darius's head.

Yet the moment was fleeting.

Zeke crashed into Darius, and the old Cajun's injured foot couldn't support both their weight. He went down on his back, and Zeke stumbled over him before falling to his knees. Zeke had more alacrity than his opponent. He used the momentum to scramble up again, and immediately slashed in a backhand swipe at Darius to keep him down. Foolishly, because it was never going to find his face, Darius tried to cover his head with his arms and took the blade in the meat of his left forearm. He cursed vilely, and Zeke's retort was equally colourful.

Zeke ran forward, stabbing down.

Miraculously, Darius again fended off the blade with the barrel of his gun, then clubbed at Zeke with it. Zeke dodged back, danced a few steps in place as he sought an opening to finish off his enemy. Darius rolled over, ungainly and in pain, and got his knees under him. When he tried to stand his injured foot rebelled, and he ended up turning sideways, hoping to find support to help him rise. Zeke grinned maliciously at the pathetic creature before him. He briefly put off serving the coup de grâce: he was enjoying Darius's discomfort too much.

'You had d' gall to offer your services to me, when all along you was holdin' my daughter prisoner,' Darius snarled up at Zeke. 'You're a piece of work, you sumbitch.'

'I didn't have her then,' Zeke responded, 'but as luck would have it I overheard where she was goin' when she called you. Damned if I was gonna pass up the opportunity to kill two birds with one stone.'

'What d'you want with her?'

'Don't be stupid, you know fine well. Would you let a witness to a murder run free?'

'I'd kill who needs killing,' Darius admitted. 'Dat's why you're gonna die, Zeke. You and dat crazy brother a yours.'

Zeke ran in, kicked Darius in the midriff, and spilled the old man on his side. Darius's only weapon flew from his outstretched fingers. He gasped for breath, his face contorting with the effort.

Zeke danced around him, and his face was rigid, eyes almost extending from their sockets. 'Cleary isn't the crazy one. I'm the fuckin' crazy man. And I'm not going to die, you stupid old fool. You are!'

To punctuate his point, Zeke lunged in, crowing in victory.

The roar of an approaching vehicle drowned out his shout. A split-second from burying his knife in Darius's body, his attention was snatched away by the sound, and it was fortunate for him that it was. A huge Dodge Ram pickup slammed the back corner of Tyson's van with such force that it was shunted around, its tires scoring deep ruts in the earth before the combined forces of impact and velocity threw it on its side. The Dodge didn't stop, and the van roof lifted Zeke off his feet and threw him in a tumble over Darius. The old man wasn't spared the impact, he was knocked back a few feet too, but not with maiming force.

Disorientated by the last few seconds, Darius lay huddled in a ball, awaiting his doom be it by blade or the crushing force of a ton of mangled wreckage pressing him into the dirt.

It was moments before he recognized the voice coaxing him up, or felt the hands assisting him to sit.

He blinked into the face of Nicolas Villere's girlfriend as she asked him if he could walk.

'Between you and dat man of yours I'd swear you was both tryin' to cripple me for good.'

'Can you walk, Darius?' Tess Grey demanded again.

'Think so. Help me up.'

He struggled to stand, but his stabbed foot had endured enough traumas for one day. He had to lean on the woman as she led him back to the cab of the Dodge. He stared at his pickup in dismay. The front end was crumpled, but the pickup was a workhorse, and a few bumps and scrapes wouldn't harm its mechanical integrity. Tess helped him slide up into the driver's position.

'Can you drive with that sore foot?'

'Better than I can walk,' he growled.

'Where's your gun?'

'Back there . . . uh, where'd dat sumbitch get to?'

There was no sign of Zeke Menon.

'He must have crawled away,' Tess said. 'The gun, Darius?'

'Dropped it over dere someplace.'

Tess turned to retrieve it.

'Hey, girl!'

She turned and frowned at his disparaging tone. But he had the grace to look abashed. 'Thanks,' he said. 'You're a tough girl. An' you just saved my life. I owe you.'

'I might just call you on it,' Tess said.

Darius nodded in understanding. 'Here,' he said, and dug in his pocket for his spare ammunition. He handed over an opened box of .44 S&W Special rounds. 'You're gonna need those. Hopefully you won't use dem on me.'

'As long as you don't give me a reason.' She gave him the briefest of smiles before she rushed off to find his dropped gun.

FORTY-TWO

While Darius and Zeke were engaged in combat, Po lay in the back of the pickup truck he'd travelled to the pumping station on. Neither of the Menon brothers had been the slightest bit suspicious that they'd picked up a stowaway. Back at the compound, they'd been too engrossed in their urgency to rendezvous with their pals they'd sent ahead with Emilia to check their mirrors, so had missed spotting the figure running after them. As Zeke had picked a route across the compound, then stalled briefly at the gate before crossing the road and finding the entrance to the wide service trail used to move the excavation equipment to and fro, Po had slid belly first onto the pickup's flatbed, and concealed himself in the tight angle where the body met the cab.

During the journey from one work site to the next, he had contemplated reaching through Zeke's open window and jamming his blade to its hilt under the punk's ear. Zeke's death would have been instantaneous, and the likelihood that the pickup would have crashed and burned was high too, thus ending the life of Cleary. The downside was Po saw no way of saving his own hide before the truck went out of control. His anger had been piqued the instant he overheard Zeke tell his demented brother what he should do with their prisoner. It didn't come as a surprise to what depravation the Menons could sink – he had guessed that Emilia's fate was going to be horrific at their hands – it was when Zeke mentioned catching up with Nicolas Villere's bitch that he truly contemplated murder. After briefly capturing her earlier, Zeke must have identified Tess as Po's partner. He'd learned already that Zeke wanted to claim double the bounty Darius Chatard had placed on his head, and fair enough. Zeke had a boner for him, his hatred originating way back to their tussle in Angola. He'd happily give Zeke a shot at revenge if that were what he longed for, but Tess was strictly out of bounds. Simply planning what they'd do to 'Blondie' was enough for Po to decide that dying with them was preferable to allowing one of them to live and carry out their plan. The thing that stopped him sheathing his blade in Zeke's neck was the off-chance Cleary would survive the ensuing crash, and that he'd be unfit to stop the monster.

Instead, he remained calm, and under the radar.

Po planned to wait for an opportunity to slip undetected off the pickup when the Menons slowed on the approach to their destination, yet the opposite occurred. Instead of decelerating, Zeke hit the gas and the pickup tore down the track. A few times Po was thrown up from the bed of the truck, and was concerned they'd hear him as he bumped down again, but the pickup creaked and rattled, the suspension squeaking and knocking wildly as the rough terrain abused it, and the sporadic sounds of gunfire were enough to cover any dull bangs he made.

The pickup slewed to a halt, Zeke exclaiming something about Darius Chatard.

Po went to his hands and knees, preparing to act, when bullets began drilling the pickup. Steam billowed from a punctured cooling system. Bullets caromed off the hood, the roof, and windshield glass, even as Cleary Menon ran for the forest. Zeke threw open his door, and Po heard the solid impact of a bullet striking it. Through the small window in the rear of the cab, he caught sight of Zeke lunging out of the passenger door, and he began to rise up, his blade in hand, within easy stabbing reach of the bastard as Zeke backed up, using the blanketing steam as cover.

Po went down, not hard, more a slow deflation of his pent-up frame, as his world grew dark. Darius, shooting blindly, had sent a bullet directly through the windshield, and the small window in the rear of the cab. He'd sworn for years he'd kill Nicolas Villere, and his prophecy had come true . . .

Po jolted back to lucidity.

He had no idea how long he'd lain unconscious on the bed of the truck, but it couldn't have been long. Steam still gouted overhead from the ruptured radiator, and from a distance he caught the popping of handguns: the gunfight was yet underway. As he rose up, he reached for his dropped knife, and clutched it, before he probed the wound on his forehead. Blood poured

down his features, but all he discovered was a ragged cut in
his skin: beneath it the bone hadn't been compromised, and his
brains weren't leaking out. He'd been hit not by the ricocheting
bullet, but a piece of shrapnel torn from the cab on its way
through. The sudden impact had been enough to briefly turn
out his lights, but he wasn't dead yet.

He pulled himself upright, leaning on the edge of the cab
while he found his bearings. The blood in his eyes, the billowing
steam, thwarted him for seconds. He dashed his sleeve across
his face, smearing the blood, but getting enough off his eyelids
that the world was no longer tinged red. Through the cloud of
steam he spotted the panel van lying on its side, and to its left
another abandoned truck. A huge Dodge Ram pickup was
backing away, sans lights, and he pictured the collision it would
have made on the van moments ago to knock it off its wheels.
It must have been the terrific impact between the Dodge and
van that had snapped him out of dreamland. The Dodge was
the one belonging to Francis Chatard, but it wasn't the tall
figure of a man that skirted round the rear of the van and began
kicking around in the dirt.

What the hell was Tess doing?

He lowered himself over the side of the pickup, and had to
hold onto it as his knees threatened to buckle. His thighs were
leaden from his earlier beating, and his ribs felt two sizes too
small for his lungs. One eye was swollen almost shut. When
he called to Tess his voice was barely a wheeze. Yet she froze,
knees bent, hands flexing, as if she was preparing to leap aside.

'Po . . . is that you?' she finally said.

He slapped his way to the front of the pickup, inhaling deeply,
and by the time he emerged from the swirling steam cloud,
could walk without assistance. The more he moved, the easier
it got. He went towards Tess, and she rushed to meet him. She
got to within a couple of feet and stopped, her face stricken at
the state of him.

He touched the wound in his forehead. 'Looks worse than it is.'

'My God! What happened to you?'

'It's only a nick. Bit of shrapnel got me. But don't worry,
I'm hard-headed.'

'Hard-headed and wooden-headed are two different things,'

she chastised him. 'How is it every time you go off on your own you turn up bloodied?'

'All I was doing was hitching a ride,' he told her.

She hugged him briefly. And in a few short sentences told him what had happened in the last few minutes.

'Where's Pinky?'

'I don't know,' she admitted.

'The Menons?'

She shrugged.

'Emilia?'

She shook her head, but held up a hand at his sudden alarm. 'She broke free from her captors and ran. From the sound of things she's still on the loose.'

'Good. C'mon. Let's go kick the pig.'

The Louisianan term was a new one to Tess, but she got the gist.

'Hold up a second,' she said, 'Darius's gun's around here someplace.'

'No time to find it. Take mine instead.' Po pulled the Glock he'd been given by Pinky, and handed it over.

'You'll need it,' she said.

He held up his knife. Flicked a mirthless grin. 'I always bring the wrong weapon to a gunfight.'

'That's because you're such a wooden-head,' she reminded him, but accepted the Glock 20. It came fully loaded with fifteen x 10mm rounds, and knowing Po he wouldn't have used any of them yet. It was a more formidable weapon than the one she was hunting in the muck for. 'Let's go find those Menon pigs,' she said, 'I want to kick them fifteen times.'

FORTY-THREE

Voices called for Emilia, but her new-found protector wouldn't let her go towards them, even though she assured him they were the voices of her brother and cousin. To approach them would mean re-entering the warren of aisles formed by the fleet of trucks and excavators, and the chance of running into some of the bad guys was too high. Every now and then a brief gunfight broke out between the Chatards and those assisting the Menon brothers. Pinky wasn't going to allow her to catch a stray bullet when their safest option was to keep to the edge of the action where nobody could sneak up on them from behind. He had a car waiting for them, hidden up among the trees beyond the service trail.

'I can't leave them out there fighting for me when I'm already safe from harm,' she told him.

'Worry not, little Emilia, we won't be running off and leaving them. I've friends out there fighting for you too. I've no intention of abandoning them, me. Soon as you're out of harm's way, I'll make sure they get the message.'

Reluctant, but seeing his logic, Emilia stuck closely to Pinky's side. He kept between her and the action, and once they were parallel with the pumping station, he led her at a run across the barren earth towards where he'd left the car. As they ran, they could both see that much had happened since Emilia had first broken free. For a start the panel van she'd twice been imprisoned inside was now lying on its side, and another truck was belching steam. The Dodge Ram was in motion, and Pinky assumed that Tess was at the wheel, but he'd no easy way to hail her without relying on a phone, which he had no time for yet. The Dodge drove off towards the fleet of excavators. Pinky caught Emilia by an elbow. 'There's still a car up there, a Toyota. We'll head for it, us. Soon as we're there we'll call my friends and get them back there, your kin too.'

A crackle of gunfire sounded, but it was distant, on the far edge of the pumping station. It galvanized Emilia, who ran alongside Pinky over the rough terrain, through a boggy trough that bore the deep tire tracks of the Dodge, and up and towards the trees. Emilia could barely breathe by the time Pinky escorted her through waist-high underbrush and into the forest. Just beyond the first rows of trees a glade opened up, alongside the narrow road she'd recently been brought down and hemmed in on the other side by stagnant water. The silver Toyota Camry was familiar, and she realized that it belonged to her cousin Jean. Its familiarity gave her hope that everything from there on would be fine. It also earned Pinky some trust, because she finally accepted that he was working with her family to rescue her.

Pinky pulled open a rear door, and indicated she clamber inside. She refused, but not out of stubbornness. She leaned over, bracing her palms on her thighs as she sucked in oxygen. She still trailed duct tape from her wrists, and a heavy necklace of twisted tape below her chin. She began tugging at the remnants of her gag.

'Forget that for now,' Pinky counselled, 'and get out of sight, you.'

The bits of duct tape were symbols to her, and until she was free of them she'd never feel safe. She stood, resting her backside against the body of the Toyota while she clawed at each wrist. 'I will but . . .'

'Emilia. You can do that inside.'

'Just give me a second . . .' Emilia, throughout her abduction, the time she'd been held hostage, escaping and subsequently being chased almost to ground again, had never felt the panic so acutely. It overwhelmed her. Crying with frustration she tore at the offending duct tape, and even resorted to using her teeth to rip chunks free.

Pinky stood alongside her, allowing her to vent. He held his gun in both hands, staring towards the construction site, alert to approaching danger. The howl that broke loose came from behind him.

Pinky whirled around, his gun tracking for the source of the noise, but he hadn't completed his turn before a massive weight slammed into him and knocked him backwards. His gun went off. The muzzle flash lit up glaring eyes and clenched teeth. He tried to bring around the muzzle, to aim at those targets, but huge fingers were squeezing his hands. He fought Cleary Menon for control, but the gun was remorselessly shoved aside. He was also being pushed further away from the getaway car, and Emilia.

Pinky was no slouch in a fight, and his physical appearance belied his strength. But he was overwhelmed by the man-mountain who scooped him off the ground and flung him bodily down. The breath blasted from his lungs, and his head smacked on the earth. It was as if a bell tolled, his ears ringing loudly, and a scarlet flash of agony forced cognizance from his brain. His discombobulation was acute, but thankfully brief. He brought around his weapon, which throughout his brutal manhandling he'd never relinquished. He fired. But at that instant Cleary kicked at his hands, and the Glock 20 tumbled into the undergrowth. Cleary stamped on Pinky's abdomen. The giant howled again, the ear-splitting call of a triumphant beast on its prey. But that wasn't it: Pinky wasn't his prey; he was only interested in Emilia. Cleary immediately turned, seeking his prize.

'Run!' Pinky croaked. 'Run, Emilia!'

Since Cleary's arrival and Pinky's defeat mere seconds had passed. Emilia was stricken by shock, and hadn't yet as much as reacted. She was still before the open door of the Toyota, a single lunge away from Cleary's grasping hands. She stepped forward, knew she had no way of avoiding his clutches, so threw herself backwards inside the car, pulling the door shut with her. Cleary almost caught the door before it could slam, but his forward momentum was his foil. He crashed against the door, his weight slamming it shut. Emilia slapped blindly at the central locking, and all four doors made a satisfying clunk as the mechanism did its work. Emilia backed away across the seat as Cleary pressed his face against the glass and growled at her. He slammed his palms on the glass. Then backed up a step, but only to gain leverage as he threw his shoulder against the car. The Toyota was shunted a full yard in the air, before Cleary again backed off. The car slammed down again, rocking on its suspension. Emilia was thrown around.

Cleary kicked at the window, but his muddy boot squealed off the glass. The window wouldn't thwart him long, though. He charged in again, throwing his weight against the car. This time the Toyota skidded in the wet earth, the back end sweeping in a tight arch. Cleary hammered down on the roof with both meaty forearms. The ceiling buckled a couple of inches towards Emilia.

Emilia had once been fearful of attracting the rougarou's wrath: an illogical fear because she didn't give the Louisiana werewolf legend much credence, but now, under the enraged assault of Cleary Menon, she was fully engaged in the dark fantasy. What else was he but for a monstrous beast intent on rending her limb from limb? She could believe the shaggy-haired brute was some kind of mythological or cryptozoological creature, or indeed a supernatural *thing* loosed from the bowels of hell to bring terror to its victims. She screamed.

Momentarily defeated by the shell of the car, Cleary cast around, looking for a boulder he could use as a hammer. There was nothing in reaching distance, so he changed tack. He rammed the point of his left elbow repeatedly against the windshield until the glass shattered. With his bare hands, Cleary tore chunks of broken windshield aside, opening a gap large enough to lean through. He lunged in, mindless of the crystals of glass catching in his hair and beard, and clawed for Emilia. She scrunched down in the back seat. Cleary grasped the headrest on the front passenger seat, yanked it wildly, and the entire seat broke clear of its moorings. Enraged that his prey continued to defy him, Cleary slammed the seat back and forward, hoping to force Emilia from her hidey-hole.

He was still in that position, wedged in the opening in the broken windshield, when Pinky charged in and similarly employed an elbow to the giant's liver. He struck the giant twice more in the lower spine. But Cleary reared from the broken screen, trailing nuggets of broken safety glass that tinkled on the car's hood. He rounded on Pinky with a vicious swat of his left arm. This time Pinky dodged, but Cleary was after him in a second, charging like a grizzly bear with a taste for human flesh.

Backpedalling rapidly, Pinky swung his fists in a flurry, and clipped the giant's forehead. Cleary brushed off the punch as if it were a gnat's bite. His right fist hammered Pinky's chest. Pinky snagged his fingers in Cleary's shaggy beard. He used the leverage to pull his own weight forward, and he slammed his forehead into the bigger man's nose. As huge and powerful as Cleary was, the cartilage in his nose was no match for Pinky's skull. The nose was deformed and spraying blood when Pinky reared back to butt him a second time. Before he could strike again, Cleary grabbed him around his middle, the giant's arms equal to Pinky's girth. He hauled him off the ground, and began to squeeze. With his fingers entangled in hair, Pinky couldn't immediately let go. Cleary roared as he wrenched on Pinky's spine, attempting to shatter it. Cleary's blood sprayed Pinky's face, and he emitted a roar of his own; sadly his was tinged with agony. In desperation, he wormed his fingers upwards and sank his thumbs in Cleary's eyes but Cleary had anticipated the attack and screwed his lids shut. When he couldn't blind him, Pinky transferred his thumbs to the flaring nostrils and forced up on the already broken nose.

This time Cleary's vocalization was of pain as he hurled Pinky away. Pinky hit the dirt, rolled through undergrowth. He felt as if his spine had been separated, but when he came to his knees he could push up on his palms and his back worked fine. He searched for his opponent, couldn't immediately see him, but the giant was making enough noise to alert somebody a mile away. Pinky spotted his silhouette as he reared back and howled at the sky in premature victory.

'Is that all you've got, you Bigfoot-looking fool?' Pinky snapped as he pushed up to his feet. 'C'mon, I haven't finished with you yet!'

Cleary snapped off his howl and stared back at Pinky. His shoulders dropped a few inches, a sign of his disappointment. But his reaction was momentary. He began to lumber forward, picking up speed with each step. Pinky braced himself for impact, his bare hands flexing, as he wondered why the hell he didn't just stay down and keep his big mouth shut. Hopefully Emilia would put his sacrifice to good use and make her escape.

The sounds of Cleary's footfalls and the swish of his legs through the undergrowth were disconcerting. There was a discernible rumble. Pinky felt as if he faced a charging bull. He was nimble, but he was no toreador. He chose to meet force with force.

Lights flashed to life, as bright as a magnesium flare.

They bathed Cleary's charging figure from directly behind and his shadow loomed tall over Pinky. Cleary halted in realization, and turned to peer over his shoulder.

His decision to meet force head on was wrong. Pinky hurled himself out of the way as the rocketing Toyota Camry battered into Cleary from behind. He didn't pinwheel up and over the hood. The car had caught him square behind his thighs, buckling him, his feet dragged beneath the chassis, bearing him forward like the ugliest hood ornament in existence. The Toyota had shuddered at the impact, but it ploughed on, to smash into the trees at the edge of the glade a few seconds later.

Stunned by the turn of events, Pinky sat up and peered at the wreckage. The front end of the Toyota had folded around the trunk of an ancient oak tree. The engine had died. Steam billowed in the glare of the one working headlight. It writhed around Cleary's form, mingling with the wet heat released from his body. Emilia had certainly taken advantage of Pinky's sacrifice. He only hoped that by coming to his rescue she hadn't paid the ultimate price. He staggered up and went to the wreck. Emilia was sitting behind the wheel, the deflated airbag now drooping in her lap. She turned and blinked at Pinky, her face slack, eyes not quite focused.

'Is he dead?' Her voice was barely audible.

Cleary was wedged between the buckled hood and the tree. His upper body had flopped backwards at an unnatural angle towards the shattered windshield. A vestige of life remained in him: he groped his fingers across the warped dash, his neck craning, his gaze zeroing in on Emilia. 'Prize,' he wheezed. But then his features slackened and he sunk low on the hood, blood pouring from between his lips.

'He is now,' said Pinky.

Shuddering, Emilia placed her face in her hands and was wracked by a chest-deep sob.

'Don't blame yourself for this, Little Emilia,' Pinky said.

'I'm not: that monster needed killing.'

FORTY-FOUR

Searching for their main quarry, Tess and Po instead came upon Rory and Harry where they'd taken cover under a dumper truck, crawling in the darkness beneath it. Out of ammunition, and nerve, they actually hailed the two as they approached, and surrendered. They tossed out their empty guns and crawled out from hiding. Po's expression was thunderous, and his features were painted with dried blood from his head wound, as if he'd donned war paint. When Harry spotted Po, his face collapsed around his swollen lips and he wept, expecting a similar beating he'd suffered last time they met.

'You punk-ass,' Po called him. 'Quit blubbering like a child and get on your goddamn knees.'

'Please don't shoot me,' Harry bleated. 'I wanted no part of this! Jesus, man, it was those Menons. They made me do it. Rory! Rory, tell him, man! Zeke threatened to bury us if we didn't do as he said.'

Rory squinted sideways at his pal, disgusted by his cowardice, but he didn't offer any resistance. He kneeled and interlocked his fingers at the back of his neck. Still weeping, expecting his execution to be swift and resolute, Harry dropped to his knees in the dirt, but he clasped his hands in front of his chest and prayed.

'Hypocritical son of a bitch,' Po snarled. 'Where in the Bible does it say it's OK to kidnap and murder women?'

'Po. Don't torture him.' Tess held the two men under guard with her Glock. She had no sympathy for them, except Harry was probably telling the truth. 'These guys are just flunkies. It's Zeke and Cleary we really want.'

Po looked keen to torture Emilia's location out of them, but Tess's point was valid. They'd been drafted in by Zeke at the last minute and probably didn't have a clue to what ends he intended using them when they'd answered his summons, but were too scared to defy him. They had once professed to being terrified of Cleary's retribution, and things probably hadn't changed in the few hours since last they'd spoken.

'Jean Chatard?' Po called out. 'You can come out now. We've got these two under control.'

Twenty feet away, Jean's head rose tentatively over the top of a backhoe. He had taken shelter inside the steel bucket after his shotgun ammunition had run out. Unbeknown to both parties they'd pinned each other down with the threat of useless weapons. He came forward still cradling the sawn-off: if nothing else it was useful as a club. 'Where are the others?' The young man's face was grazed; he'd caught a ricochet or piece of flying shrapnel during the gunfight but was otherwise unharmed.

'Hoped you could tell us,' Po admitted.

'I've got this puke-ball,' a voice announced. Francis Chatard led Tyson from between the machinery. Tyson was abject in his failure, face down, eyes hooded. Blood dripped from both nostrils and his usually immaculately combed hair stuck out in tufts. A bald patch in his beard glistened redly. Apparently when Francis took him prisoner, he hadn't been as lenient as Po and Tess with their prisoners. He forced Tyson to kneel alongside the other two. His gun was enough to ensure they behaved them-selves. He searched Po's damaged face.

'Where's my father?'

'Last we saw him he was cruising around in the Dodge still looking for Emilia.'

'She hasn't turned up yet?'

Po shook his head, and Francis cursed. But Tess held up a hand, stalling them. Her cellphone was ringing in an inside pocket. She dug it out. The others watched her expectantly as she answered.

'Pinky? Thank God you're OK. You have her?' She looked at her companions and exhaled as hard as they did at the news. 'Emilia's safe. Pinky has her.' Pinky was speaking again. 'Oh, and we needn't worry about chasing down Cleary . . . Pinky says he's roadkill.'

'He's dead?' Po was conflicted. He wanted to pay back Cleary for everything the man was responsible for, no less his physical abuse of Tess earlier.

Tess continued to relate Pinky's rushed words. 'Emilia

rammed him with the Toyota. She's OK, Pinky's looking after her.'

Francis and Jean wanted to go to Emilia immediately, But Po halted them. He gestured at their prisoners. 'Take these punks back up to the entrance with you. Don't let them out of your sight. Tess?'

Tess hung up her call with Pinky, and looked at him expectantly.

'Call the cops. Get them out here. If any of us is going to stay out of jail we need to hand these idiots over.'

'There are still two of them out there.' She meant Zeke and Jim Croft, whose name they were yet to learn. Croft wasn't a priority to Po, but if the guy was still out there, and armed, he might try something stupid like try to free his captured friends.

'Give Jean your gun,' said Po.

'Like hell,' Tess said. 'We still have to capture Zeke and I'm not doing it unarmed.'

'Zeke's mine,' Po told her. 'I can't have you shooting him dead before I square things away with him.'

'I'm not leaving your side.'

'Didn't ask you to. But give Jean the gun in case the other asshole tries something.'

'Zeke could be armed,' Tess argued.

'If he had a gun, he'd have shot Darius. He has a blade. He's in my arena now.'

Tess stared at him in disbelief. Po only looked back: he wasn't for changing his mind.

'We've got this.' Francis was still armed, and his gun was threat enough to get their three prisoners off their knees and moving. 'My bet is the other sumbitch has run off and hid someplace.'

As the Chatard cousins led the trio of prisoners away, Jean used the stock of his shotgun to prod them to greater speed, while Francis kept an eye out for Croft. Tess called the police. She described the situation as briefly, but concisely, as possible, and gave directions to the responding officers to rendezvous with Pinky at the end of the service trail. She iterated that they were the good guys.

Once she was done, she turned to Po. 'You're on the clock

now, lover boy. If you're going to do this before the cops arrive, you'd best get moving.'

He moved. She fell in step a few yards behind him, guarding his back, the Glock held in a two-hand grip as she swept it from side to side. All trace of Po's limp had disappeared. Actually, her pain had left her too, because she was still riding the wave of nervous energy, but she suspected that soon she would crash and burn. It had been the longest of days, and the night promised to stretch eternal before her. The sooner they found Zeke and handed him over to the police the better.

Except it was Zeke who'd found them, and he'd been hiding close enough to overhear their discussion and the fate of his brother.

He dropped ten feet from the boom of the crane he'd scaled, landing heavily behind Tess. Alerted by the impact in the dirt, she whirled, her gun sweeping round, but as fast as she was, Zeke was faster. He lunged deep inside her arch of fire, looped his left arm over both of hers, jamming them under his armpit. Her Glock was ineffective against him, as he sent his blade towards the hollow of her throat.

FORTY-FIVE

'**D**on't do it, Zeke. It's not her you want . . . it's me.'
Hearing the impact of boots on the ground, Po had also pivoted to face the ambush. But Tess was between him and their assailant, and she'd made the mistake of swinging her gun around at arm's length. Zeke had her arms locked, the barrel of the gun aiming beyond him and his knife at Tess's neck before he could snatch her out of harm's way. If he were to rush in and engage, Zeke need only jab the point into the soft flesh, slash open her windpipe and Tess would die. He stepped back instead, holding up his hands, but didn't drop his knife. Zeke was practically face to face with Tess, though he loomed tall enough to glare over her head at the person he really wanted dead. He ignored Po's words, in favour of his own.

'Drop the gun, bitch, or I swear to God I'll cut you wide and long.'

Tess wasn't the type to give in easily, and the rule of any law-enforcement officer was to never relinquish her weapon. But she wasn't a law-enforcement officer any more, and her throat could be slashed long before she managed to juggle the Glock into a position where she could shoot. She didn't want Zeke to lay his hands on the gun either: she chucked it away, and it landed alongside the caterpillar tracks of the crane Zeke had just jumped from.

'I've done it,' she told him. 'I've dropped the gun like you said.'

Zeke was loath to take his attention off Po, but he glanced quickly at her empty hands. Confident that she was unarmed, he wrenched her around so she faced Po, his left arm tight around her chest, knife hand under her chin. The blade he held flat against her skin, sharpened edge uppermost. It would take a tilt of only a few degrees for it to slice her open. He growled directly into her ear. 'I should cut off your damn head for the trouble you've caused me. That stunt with the fucking truck, you almost crushed me to death.'

Tess could have appealed to him, explained she was desperate only to save a man's life when she rammed the panel van, but it would never appease him. Besides, she'd felt him stiffen as he spoke those last words; as though he'd sensed an echo of the fate his brother Cleary had suffered. She said nothing, just stayed as calm as she could with a knife at her jugular, and played a suitably cowed hostage.

'It's me you want,' Po said again. 'Let her go.'

'I do want you. But once I've killed you, I won't stop until all of you bastards are in a hole in the ground. I'm going to cut off the head of your faggot nigger buddy, and those Chatard fuckers one after the other for what they did to Cleary. Then I'm going to kill Emilia nice and slowly, the way Cleary would have, then . . .' he grunted in disgust at the weakling in his arms, 'I'll do this bitch. Even slower.'

Surprisingly to Tess, Po threw aside his knife. What the hell was he doing? His knife was his only defence if Zeke killed her and then went after him. She tried to import how insane his action was through the fixed expression she wore, but Po wouldn't look at her. He kept his gaze on Zeke, latched on with laser intensity.

'Everything's gone to shit for you, Zeke. You must see that. Your brother is dead, your pals are rounded up like dogs, and Emilia's safely out of your way. The cops are coming. You were listening; you know I'm not bluffing. They'll be here soon. Time's short. You think you're going to be able to kill anyone before a sniper puts a round through your stupid-looking head?'

'I heard. Thing is, if the cops get here before I'm done, I can still kill this skank. Whaddaya say, Villere? Should I kill your girl and then you?'

'Harm her,' Po said, his voice barely above a whisper, 'and it's the last thing you'll ever do.'

'Tough words coming from an unarmed man.'

'I don't need a weapon to kill you.'

Zeke's laughter was full of scorn. He had taken in Po's swollen eye, the dried blood, and older bruises, and decided he wasn't as tough as he once was. 'I was a boy last time we met and you broke my collarbone; things'll be different this time.'

'You can bet your ass they will. This time I won't spare you.'

Again Zeke laughed bitterly. 'I know what you're trying to do, Villere. You're trying to goad me into a fight . . . so I'll release your little whore and she can escape.' He shook his head. 'Where's the fun in that? When I can goad *you* into an even tougher fight by slitting her throat in front of you.'

Tess wasn't prepared to stand idle while Zeke cut her open. She would fight, and go down fighting if she must, if it gave Po an opportunity to avenge her. She tensed slightly, began raising her hands beneath Zeke's line of vision, about to snatch down on his forearm to yank the knife from her flesh. She poised her other elbow to ram it into his solar plexus: her strategy was a long shot, but better than nothing. Yet before she did either, she sensed Zeke stiffen again, and this time it was in disappointment.

'Yes, dat's a gun to your head, you sumbitch,' Darius Chatard announced. 'Now let the girl go free or I'll blow your brains out.'

Before Darius could pull the trigger, Zeke could easily cut Tess's throat as a parting shot. Before he was executed he could still win a small victory over his enemies. But at heart he was controlled by the survival trait intrinsic to all living things: he lowered his arms, held them out to his sides. He didn't let go of his knife.

Immediately Tess ducked out of the way, going left so she was beyond a last-second stab and she backed up against the huge tracks of the crane. From her position she had a good view. Darius stood with his feet planted one in front of the other, his right arm extended, the Glock 20 she had recently thrown down pressed tight to the back of Zeke's skull in the hollow between the dome of his scabrous baseball cap and the size-adjustment strap. Darius glanced over at her, and nodded. She'd saved him, now he'd returned the favour. Po still faced Zeke.

'Don't shoot him, Darius,' Po said.

'Whaddaya mean? Of course I'm gonna shoot dis fucker. I'm gonna put one right through his skull for fuckin' wid my family.' Darius jabbed the barrel harder against Zeke's head, prodding his point home. 'You hear me, butt-wipe? You fucked wid my girl, you fucked wid me, now I'm gonna fuck wid you!'

'Don't worry, he won't be walking away without punishment.' Po egged Zeke forward, directing his next words at him. 'You have an old score to settle. Well I've more than one. You just threatened my girl's life, and I'm not gonna let that go.' He briefly glanced at Tess, and she knew the unavoidable had arrived. 'What you don't know is that Emilia is my baby sister. For what you planned to do to her, I'm going to hurt you bad. Your choice, Zeke: a bullet from Emilia's father, or you can try your luck with me.'

A smile squeezed its way onto Zeke's mouth. 'What's to stop the old man shooting me after I fuck you up?'

'What's to stop me shooting you now?' Darius snapped and seemed a fraction away from doing so. 'But where's d' fun in dat when I can watch you fight for your life first? Trust me, though, asshole, I swear I'm gonna put a bullet through dat stinkin' cap before I'm done.'

Zeke rolled his neck, flexed his shoulders. The gun had risen to a point higher up his cap. Zeke looked unconcerned, as if his grungy old cap were made of Kevlar. He purposefully took a step forward, confident in its impregnability.

Darius chewed his lips in frustration. Tess suspected what was going through his mind: right there before him were the two men he hated most and he had a full clip he could empty into them. He looked tempted, but then he caught her eye, and the sternness of her visage – her unspoken promise – and the indecision slipped from him, and he lowered the gun.

Zeke glanced back at him, made a subtle adjustment of the brim of his hat. But then he all but dismissed the old man, centring his attention on Po.

'Pick up your blade, Villere.'

But Po didn't move to retrieve his knife. He waved Zeke forward. 'Like I said: I don't need a knife for a punk like you.'

Zeke barked in laughter.

He lunged, going for Po's throat.

Po had predicted the attack.

He pivoted and brought down another blade; this one was the stiffened edge of his hand. His move was akin to a karate chop, short and sharp and directed to Zeke's wrist. The impact sent an electric shock to the ends of Zeke's fingertips, and he could only gape as his deadly weapon flew from his grasp, neutralized.

'What now?' Po asked.

Zeke screeched in fury and swung at Po with his other fist. Po bobbed aside, struck again with the blade of his hand, this time across Zeke's cheekbone. The sound of his face breaking was sickening to Tess, but also strangely satisfying. Po struck again, blindingly fast, both hands slashing and chopping with such rapidity the individual blows were hard to follow. Zeke was overwhelmed, but not out of the fight entirely. He grappled Po, but while he was holding on he wasn't delivering any counter-strikes, and he left parts of his anatomy vulnerable to further attack. Po's elbows and knees pounded him, and Zeke cried out and staggered backwards. Po slashed downward, and the edge of his hand smashed through the same clavicle he'd broken years earlier in prison.

Crying out, Zeke went to his knees in the dirt. His arm hung limp, cupped across his abdomen. He blinked up at Po through tears of agony. 'You bastard!' he croaked. 'You broke it again!'

'I'm not finished yet.'

Po's hand scythed down, and the resulting *crack!* signalled the breaking of Zeke's opposite collarbone. Zeke screamed, and both his arms flopped in his lap.

'You won't be hurting anyone else from now on,' Po told him.

Zeke howled. Unlike when he'd joined in with Cleary on a hunt, this was a cry of frustration and torment.

Po had heard enough. He powered a knee into Zeke's chin, and Zeke collapsed backwards, his feet trapped beneath his backside, floppy arms flung wide. His hat had fallen off. Even from where she spectated, Tess could see why he always covered his head. His pate was bald but for a few tufts of greyish hair, laced among dozens of interlocking scars and a raw wound on his right temple. One older scar was dominant on his forehead: a ragged Nazi swastika. It wasn't a case of self-mutilation; the scar had been cut into his head years earlier by the same Aryan Nation heavies who he'd failed to serve to their satisfaction. Little wonder he hated Po with a passion, because it was he who'd thwarted Zeke and his friends' orders to gang-rape Pinky Leclerc. For years Zeke had concealed his shame beneath his hat, and carried it in his heart. His hatred wouldn't have been curtailed by this latest punishment.

Po stared down at the defeated man. Then he stepped closer, head cocked to one side as air bubbled wetly between Zeke's flaccid lips. His hands flexed.

'Po. That's enough,' Tess said. 'Let it go.'

Po was a second from ending Zeke Menon's life. Yet he listened to her words of reason, though not through any sense of compassion. If he slew Zeke, he would not escape justice. When the cops arrived he'd struggle to explain the man's grievous injuries as it were.

Darius wasn't as concerned with the consequences of breaking the law. He limped in, planted a foot either side of Zeke's head, and aimed the gun directly at the swastika.

'Darius, don't be stupid,' Po warned.

The gun barrel came up, and now it was aimed directly at Po's chest. 'When I swear an oath, I keep it.'

For a long drawn out second their eyes locked. Then Darius snatched the gun down, and pulled the trigger.

Po's eyelids pinched at the muzzle flash, and he exhaled slowly.

A hole was punched cleanly through Zeke's hat, the expended round lost deep in the dirt beneath.

'Told you I'd put a bullet through dat stinkin' cap.'

Darius turned the gun around and offered the butt to Tess. She took it.

The sounds of the approaching couple drew their attention from the unconscious murderer. Now the fighting was over, Pinky allowed Emilia to run forward. She threw herself into her father's arms, and he pulled her close, allowing an uncharacteristic shout of joy that she was safe.

Tess watched Po.

He stood stoically, watching the family reunion without comment. He couldn't tear his gaze away from his sister; it was understandable, being the first time he'd laid eyes on his blood kin. To Tess, Emilia's parentage could never be in question again, Emilia only had to look at him and she'd see her male counterpart staring back.

FORTY-SIX

I t was hours later before any of them made it back to Clara's bedside. Without exception all had been rounded up by the responding police officers and taken to the New Iberia Police Department on Main Street, where they were questioned individually. Zeke, and Jim Croft, arrested but whisked off to hospital rooms of their own, were exempt from questioning while they underwent surgery. Croft, it transpired, hadn't been clear of the panel van when Tess rammed it in order to save Darius Chatard's life, and had been found soon after the police arrived at the scene, having only managed to crawl a short distance with his legs broken. Both patients were under armed guard, while Tyson, Rory, and Harry were all jailed at the Iberia Parish Sheriff's Office facility off Broken Arrow Road. The Chatards faced possible charges, but there wasn't a district attorney who would seriously consider sending them to prison for acting in self-defence or for assisting in the rescue of Emilia, who was to be the latest in a string of murder victims of the Menon brothers. Emilia had killed Cleary; but again, to save her life and another's. The police also viewed the brave actions of Pinky Leclerc, Po, and Tess favorably, and they wouldn't be facing charges either, if all went to plan. As a special dispensation, in light of Clara's failing mortality, further questioning was suspended in order to allow the closest family members to attend her bedside. They were all under instruction to return to the police station later in the day.

Tess stood outside the private room, with Pinky seated in the same chair as yesterday when first spotting Zeke Menon. But instead of vigilantly watching the halls for anyone who might disturb Po and his mother, Tess peeked through the narrow slots between the window blinds at the gathering of people inside the room. The sombre family members were huddled around Clara's bed. She was a tiny figure, with a white sheet pulled up to her armpits. As Tess watched, she saw the old woman's head tilt to one side, and her lips move fractionally. Tess followed the direction and saw Emilia seated alongside her mom, holding the woman's left hand. Emilia wept openly. Darius stood over her, Francis next to him. Leon – the brother Tess hadn't met – stood on the other side of the bed, one arm in a sling, his other hand bandaged. Jean Chatard was also there, and a couple of women that Tess took to be the wives or girlfriends of some of the Chatard males. A doctor and a nurse attended to their duties in respectful silence, but on hand for the unavoidable. Po stood apart from the others at the foot of the bed. Tess wanted to enter the room, to hold his hand, but he had asked her to wait outside. She didn't feel embittered by the exclusion, and knew it was for the best.

Clara had said what she wanted to impart to Emilia. Her daughter turned and stared at Po, her face blanched of all colour. She didn't rise from her seat, nor go to him and hug her long lost brother. But then, Tess suspected that Emilia had an inkling of her true parentage all along, and the instant she'd laid eyes on Po she'd *known* who he was. Under other circumstances, the young woman's response might have exhibited as anger. Po was the man who'd killed two half-brothers she'd never met. But there wasn't a shred of accusation in her turquoise gaze as she peered at him. He'd also fought to save her life and stop the men hunting her, and the evidence was in his battered appearance. She mouthed two small words: thank you.

Her job done, Clara died.

There was no sense of the miraculous to Tess as the old woman passed over, no melodrama, nor hysteria from her loved ones.

Clara simply closed her eyes, and those in the room only stirred momentarily as the ECG monitor fell silent. Then the doctor and nurse moved in, and Emilia bowed her head, and clutched Clara's hand to her face. Darius rested a comforting palm on his daughter's shoulder – despite Clara's final message Emilia would always be his child. The old man's face was clouded as he peered down at his dead wife. When he regarded Po it was with wet eyes.

Po left the room and respectfully closed the door to allow Clara's nearest and dearest to grieve in peace.

Tess hugged him. He hugged her as well, but as he did, he moved with her to leave. Pinky stood, but before he could follow, the door opened again.

'Nicolas.'

It wasn't his friend. Tess turned around with him, and faced Darius Chatard.

'You're leaving?'

'Soon as we get clearance from the police,' said Po.

'You aren't staying for your mom's funeral?'

'It's probably best that I don't.'

Darius nodded – he understood – but it wasn't what he had hoped for. His accent wasn't affected by anger when next he spoke. 'Things weren't good between you and your mom for a long time. I get that. But you know, everything's different now.'

'It is?'

'It is to me.'

'Does that mean we're friends now?'

'I wouldn't go that far.' Darius smiled sadly. 'But we needn't be enemies.'

'It was never by my choosing.'

'I know that was on me.' Darius limped over to face Po from a mere couple of feet. Emotion reddened his eyes. 'I just didn't know when to let things go. But I was an idiot back then. You might say I'm still prone to episodes of idiocy these days, too. But I'm not a fool, and I'm not ungrateful. If it weren't for you' – Darius took in Tess and Pinky with his assertion as well as Po – 'Emilia would have died. You took away two of my boys, but you've given back to me my girl and to your mom some peace of heart before she died. I can't give you back your father. Back then, if I'd manned up and took a beating from Jacques, nobody else needed to die, lives needn't have been ruined. I wish I could turn back the clock, because I swear I would do that. It was all on me, Nicolas, and I do see that now. All I can give you is an apology and my hand. I'm sorry.'

Tess didn't offer a word of guidance to Po. Their family feud had run and run, an unhealed, scabrous wound that occasionally festered into an open sore. It had affected Po's life negatively for decades, made of him an ex-con and an exile from his own homeland. Forgiveness of Darius Chatard might prove a bitter pill to swallow, though it was the only thing that might heal the raw wounds still afflicting him. After everything he'd endured she wouldn't blame her man if he spat on the offer of reconciliation. But the decision was his to make. She'd stand by him whatever he chose to do.

With that resolution in mind, she was still relieved when he accepted Darius's hand and shook it.

FORTY-SEVEN

One aspect of Louisianan culture that had always raised Tess's eyebrows was the practice of playing jazz music at funerals, usually a dirge beforehand and an upbeat ragtime tune after. But apparently the tradition was unique to New Orleans and hadn't yet found its way to New Iberia. There were no jazz bands playing in Memorial Park Cemetery when Clara Chatard was laid to rest, the proceedings sombre, almost subdued, as her family and friends observed her coffin lowered into the grave. Darius and his children, Emilia included, stood closest to the edge, waiting until the coffin settled at the bottom before scattering handfuls of consecrated dirt and tokens of affection – flowers and favourite baubles – on the casket. They didn't linger. The day was clear, the skies a pale blue, but the cold spell had yet to lift and the promised warmth of their cars was welcome.

Of her children, only Po waited a little longer, and Tess and Pinky didn't rush him. He was deep in thought as he watched the funeral directors arrange boards covered in fake turf over the open grave, then set upon them the floral memorials brought there by the other mourners. Clara's grave would be filled in once the members of the funeral party had left the cemetery. There was no permanent marker – it would be erected after the backfilled earth settled – but even then would be a headstone unlike those Tess was familiar with in the north. Those she'd noticed nearby were more akin to inscribed paving stones, set into the lawn, unobtrusive monuments. Over many years the grounds had been developed to include a wide variety of trees and shrubs, and the inclusion of upright stones would have spoiled the natural look. If she didn't know otherwise Tess would swear she was standing in a recreational park, a place for family picnics and leisure and not where the bodies of the deceased resided underfoot.

Despite his words to Darius at the hospital Po had decided

to attend – they couldn't leave New Iberia parish until lawful process had been completed anyway – and Tess was glad that he had. It was necessary if he were going to truly put the past to rest. She wondered what was going on behind his stoic features as he observed the funeral directors at work. In the end he gave no clue, only turned and walked away. Tess and Pinky glanced at each other, and then fell into step in his wake. He didn't return to their car.

Jacques Villere, Po's father, was also buried at Memorial Park. She remembered the time on their first case together when she'd believed that he had abandoned her in Baton Rouge, and later discovered that he'd snuck off to visit his dad's grave, right here. Jacques had a headstone, a flat polished granite slab set deep in the turf. Po knelt and touched the stone, speaking too low for her to hear. But when he stood, his features weren't as stony as before, and his gaze clearer. He offered the flicker of a smile, but then his gaze settled on a point beyond his friends, and he grew an inch in height as he straightened up. Tess followed his gaze.

Walking towards them was Emilia, bearing a single rose. Beyond her, Darius Chatard waited at the open door of a black limousine that had carried him and his closest family to the cemetery.

'I wanted to see where our dad was buried,' Emilia said as she came to a halt directly in front of them. Po's eyelids pinched as he spied Darius, noting the man's slow nod of approval. He'd obviously given Emilia his blessing to visit the grave: proving he was a better man than any of them had initially thought.

Po turned and indicated Jacques's resting place.

Emilia stood alongside him. She peered down at the grave of her biological father, and Tess was struck again by her likeness to the man she loved. Both Villeres stood in silent contemplation, before Emilia finally knelt and laid the flower on their father's memorial stone. She stood, and her right hand found Po's left. It was the first time the siblings had touched, and for the briefest moment Tess expected Po to draw away. Yet he didn't. He folded Emilia's smaller hand in his and held on.

'I hated him,' Emilia whispered, then looked up at Po, tears glistening in the cold light.

'Understandable,' Po said.

Emilia shook her head.

'I don't now that I've learned the truth. I used to hate you too.'

'Also understandable.'

This time she didn't immediately answer. She turned and gazed at Tess and then Pinky, whose lips quivered between a smile and a grimace: he wasn't good at hiding his emotions the way Po was. 'But that was . . . before,' Emilia finally said. 'Everything I was told was based on lies. Nicolas . . . I don't hate you now.'

Po nodded marginally, and Tess wished he would give his sister a hug, but knew he wouldn't. But his nod told her that he was of a similar opinion to Emilia, without having to display a range of raw emotions. Again Emilia took in Tess and Pinky. 'I'd like to get to know you all better, but I know that isn't really possible.'

'There's no reason why not,' Tess offered.

But Emilia shook her head softly. 'Y'all are leaving today, right?'

Pinky was driving them back for their return flight to Portland from Baton Rouge immediately after they left the cemetery.

'I'll be back this way soon,' Po said, which came as a surprise to Tess until she considered that they would probably all have to return to give evidence at the trials of Zeke, Alistair Keane, Nathaniel Corbin, and the others. 'Maybe we could spend some time together then?'

'I'd like that,' Emilia said, but she still wasn't satisfied.

'Or you could come visit us,' Tess improvised on the spot. 'Have you ever been to Maine?'

'I've never even been out of Louisiana,' Emilia replied.

'Then you'll need a guide in the north,' Pinky interjected, 'and I know the very man for the job, me. I've been threatening to go back to Portland after my last vacation there was cut short.' He didn't mention that his last trip to visit Po and Tess had ended with him getting shot. 'How's about we travel to Maine together, little Emilia, keep each other company, us?'

Emilia looked expectantly at Po.

'I've got the room at my place,' he said, 'if you've got the inclination.'

Pinky clapped his hands together. The deal was sealed and he wasn't about to allow any second thoughts to creep in. 'So we'll exchange contact numbers, and get our heads together, see what we can come up with, us. Now, Nicolas, give the girl a hug, so I can get you on that plane home. Sooner you're gone, the sooner we can come avail ourselves of your hospitality.' He turned to Tess. 'Don't worry; you won't be left out, pretty Tess. Come here and give me a hug, why don't you? Just in case we don't get the opportunity for a proper goodbye at the airport.'

'You'll use any excuse to get your paws on me,' Tess grinned, but loved it when his warmth engulfed her and she was hauled off her feet. As Pinky spun her in one of his patented embraces, she watched over his shoulder as Po and Emilia held each other briefly. Theirs wasn't as exuberant a display of affection, but she believed it was every bit as heartfelt. She didn't feel at odds feeling as overjoyed for Po even in the surroundings of a grave-yard: and even hoped that if Jacques and Clara could do so they'd observe the coming together of their children and be as happy for them.

FORTY-EIGHT

After . . .

'So . . . Ron Bowen wasn't murdered,' said Po, wearing the faintest of smiles. He was sitting in the office of Charley's Autoshop in Portland, Maine. Although it wasn't his name above the door, Po owned the business, while Charley managed the day-to-day workload. Po had adopted his usual position at his desk, feet propped up on it, crossed at the ankles, with his arms behind his head. His cuts and bruises had all but disappeared, but then it was a week since Clara's funeral.

'He wasn't strangled,' Tess confirmed, before shaking her head at the inanity of her next words, 'the ME report states he choked to death on a bolus of food that got wedged in his throat.'

'OK, so I'm no Sherlock Holmes, but I was right about him choking to death. Maybe I'm not the worst detective in the world?'

'Doesn't say much for me,' Tess said, leaning in the open doorway. There was little room in the cramped office and most of it was taken up with discolored paperwork, old spare parts brochures, and an archaic computer that was as grimy as the desk it sat upon. Everything was covered with oily fingerprints. Po looked perfectly at home. By trade he was a mechanic, but since teaming up with Tess found that tinkering with engines wasn't an occupation that played to his greatest strengths. These days he rarely visited the autoshop, or the public bar he owned, content to be by her side on a case.

'You're an excellent detective,' he reassured her.

Since their return from Louisiana she'd raised the subject a few times, of how they had been very fortunate to solve the case and save Emilia. Most of their success was down to being in the right – or wrong – place at the opportune time. But Po had reminded her that much of what she was working from was off the back foot, and having to react to messes he caused. Left to her own devices she'd have conducted a more pointed and resolute investigation, and gotten the same result, but she'd allowed him to have his way, for which he'd be eternally grateful.

'If only I'd dug a little deeper at Bowen's house I'd have spotted the half-eaten sandwich in the kitchen and come to the correct conclusion about his death.'

'It sure looked as if there'd been a struggle to me.'

'The consensus is he was eating lunch, and went to the door – perhaps to gather his mail from the mailbox – and began to choke. In his panic he left the door ajar while trying to rush to the kitchen to sick up the food in the sink. But before he got there he grew woozy, knocked into the furniture, and collapsed. The other part of the sandwich he was eating was found squashed underneath him when his body was moved. And wouldn't you just know it, his sandwich was a shrimp po'boy?'

Po's smile grew wider at the dig about his nickname. 'Did you get any stick from your old colleagues for crying wolf?'

She snorted. 'Poor choice of words.'

'Perfect choice of words.'

Down in the Deep South the 'Rougarou Case' was still making headlines. Alistair Keane and Nathaniel James Corbin had swiftly been arrested and charged alongside Zeke Menon and his lackeys. Their parts in the various kidnappings and murders were subject to further, and prolonged, investigation, but all the conspirators were facing long jail terms on serious federal charges. The bodies of Hal and Jamie Thibodaux, Jason Lombard, and an environmental activist identified as Christina Swan had all been exhumed from the foundations of a soon-to-be-erected concrete stanchion on the route of the pipeline. Nate Corbin had engaged the services of a very expensive law firm to fight his case, and had been awarded bail set at seven figures. Corbin was good for the money, but he left the others to fend for themselves in the county lock-up. If all went to his plan, Keane and the bunch of rednecks he'd hired to do the dirty work would take the blame, while he was confident he would be exonerated. He swore he was ignorant to what the subcontractor was doing to meet deadlines and ensure his productivity bonuses.

It had later come to light that Corbin – through his legal intermediaries – offered Al Keane certain incentives should he accept all responsibility and exculpate Corbin from any involvement in, or knowledge of, any wrong doing; the incentives came with a caveat that if the promise of reward didn't win Keane's loyalty, then Keane could expect a visit from an 'associate', one not as crazy as Cleary Menon but every bit as terrifying. Fearing for his life Keane had accepted the terms. Corbin believed himself untouchable, a Teflon man. He should have kept his fearsome 'associate' close by.

Three days after making bail he was found dead in his office in New Orleans.

Corbin had been stabbed in the heart with a knife. The assassin was never discovered, and nobody but Corbin knew what he'd whispered in his ear as he plunged the blade between his ribs. 'Darius Chatard sends his regards.'

When hearing the news of Corbin's manner of death they'd shared a wry look. 'Good job we'd already returned to Maine by then or some people might have thought you were responsible,' Tess said.

'It was indirectly through his greed that my sister became a victim of the Menon's. Corbin got his just deserts, Tess.' Po shrugged the man's death off. He wouldn't be missed. 'I've killed, and would kill for my loved ones, but I'm no murderer.'

'Hopefully now you won't have to kill again. Not since Clara brought you and Emilia together and healed the rift in your families.'

'I'm confident there'll be no more trouble from the Chatards,' he'd agreed. In the coming months they would have to return to New Iberia to attend the court cases of the various conspirators in Emilia's kidnapping and the murders of the other four victims. They would be in close proximity to the Chatards throughout, and happily to Emilia in particular, until the legal system was done with them. Though their anticipated court appearances were quickly diminishing in number.

Two days after Corbin perished, Zeke Menon also died. With his upper body held together with surgical pins, and encased in tight dressings, he couldn't defend himself when a fellow prisoner stole into his sick room and hammered a makeshift shiv through the swastika scar on his forehead. There was no whispered message this time, but there were rumours about who had put the prisoner up to the job. A pot of money once set aside as a bounty on Po's head had been freed up and put to good use elsewhere.

Now, in the autoshop office, Tess clucked her tongue, deep in thought. 'There's a bit of me that regrets that the Menons were killed. They've escaped proper justice.'

'That depends on who you're talking to. Justice isn't always found through legal process. They got what was coming to them.'

'Cleary Menon too?'

'Especially Cleary.'

'He was mentally ill.'

'So are all murderous psychopaths,' Po said. 'It doesn't exonerate them from their actions.' He chuckled to himself. 'I spoke with Pinky earlier about him and Emilia visiting soon. Apparently they've been in touch quite a lot and are becoming bosom buddies. He's had a few heart-to-heart conversations with her about what happened that night, and has put her mind at rest. You ask me he had it right about how Emilia killed that lunatic with the Toyota. Cleary believed he was a werewolf; he got put down like one when she hit him like a silver bullet. End of story.'

ACKNOWLEDGEMENTS

Thanks to all the team at Severn House Publishers and also to my agent Luigi Bonomi and his team at Luigi Bonomi Associates for making this book happen. Thanks are also due to my wife, Denise, who keeps everything in order around me as I sink into the fictional worlds I create.

Speaking of fiction, I should make it clear that the events depicted in Raw Wounds are figments of my imagination. The oil pipeline mentioned in the narrative does not exist, and has no relation to any business or company in the region (or elsewhere for that matter). Being a fiction author I have taken a liberty with the terrain and actual locales mentioned in the story for the purposes of creating drama and action. No actual rougarou was hurt during the writing of this book.